CONVERGENCE

First published in Australia by Harbour Publishing House 2017
This edition published in Australia by Marita Smith 2022

Text Copyright © Marita Smith

www.maritasmithauthor.com

The moral rights of the writer have been asserted.

This is a work of fiction.

Graphic Design by Design For Days

Cataloguing-in-Publication entry is available from the National Library of Australia
catalogue.nla.gov.au

Book Title: Convergence
Series: Kindred Ties
Number: Book One
ISBN: 978-0-6456821-0-6 (Paperback)
Subject: Science Fiction

KINDRED TIES
BOOK ONE

CONVERGENCE

MARITA SMITH

The cure for anything is salt water: sweat, tears or the sea.

– Isak Dinesen

To my one-of-a-kind family.

1

Sheet Dreams

"*The program has come under scrutiny. Some of the directors think it is unnecessary now we've found the boy.*"

"*You mean Vulcan wants to axe it.*"

"*It's not about Vulcan. It's about the objectives of the Institute. It's been eighteen months, Brock. They've found nothing.*"

"*There's something about her, something I can't explain.*"

"*We need results, Brock, and the program hasn't delivered them. You are blinded by your sentimentality for the girl.*"

"*I could say the same for you. If any of them are going to crack this, it will be Robyn.*"

"*We'll see.*"

"That is bullshit, and you know it. You need this more than anyone." Kara's Doc Martens flattened against the wooden floor with a thump and Robyn flinched at the sound. A wave of startled glances washed over them as Robyn swirled the dregs of her coffee and tried to disappear further into the chair. She really did want to finish processing her samples. She didn't have the insatiable social appetite of her best friend. Loud music and alcohol weren't really her thing, but Kara was probably right. She needed to get out more. She spent more time with chromatographs than real people.

Kara tipped her head back and let out a low, irritated growl. The cafe was full; it was one of those ten-minute, prime-time windows between lecture end and beginning. Another set of heads turned and Robyn felt her ears grow pink.

"Are you even listening to me?" Kara drummed her fingers on the table, her own mug long empty. Double shot, three sugars. Diabetes in a mug.

Someone cleared their throat a few tables down. A guy in a scarf, even though it was barely autumn. Plaid.

"Yeah, okay," Robyn had reluctantly resigned herself to her fate. Toga Party, the highlight of Orientation Week.

"I'll help you at Toga."

Kara almost chirruped. "Good," she beamed. "You done? We've got heaps to do."

Robyn chugged the now-bitter coffee and grimaced. "Ready."

Campus was quiet as she followed Kara over to the law building, students having once again scattered to lecture halls or hunkered down in libraries. She didn't miss the gruelling undergraduate timetable – early lectures, late labs, rushed sandwiches in between. Kara was glued to her phone, tapping away. For a law student, she spent a lot of time writing code.

"You're going to have a great time, trust me." Kara hopped across the stepping stones set into Sullivan's Creek. Robyn followed more warily, envying her friend's natural grace.

"What are you doing, anyway?" Robyn asked as she navigated the mossy rocks.

Kara shrugged. "Just working on a couple of projects. You know, the usual."

She didn't know. Kara always had her secret projects. They shared clothes and the occasional toothbrush, but Kara's projects were taboo.

A wedge of a shopping trolley moved with the sluggish current like a rusty iceberg. Robyn grimaced. There was no way she was falling into this particular microbiological soup. She wondered how many drunk, sheet-clad undergrads the creek would claim at sundown when the punch started flowing. Kara seemed to read her mind.

"I'm staying at the law building. Someone else can fish the college kids out of here."

Robyn nodded. "Ditto."

"So you're staying, then?" Kara didn't give up.

"Haven't made up my mind. I said I'd help you set up, I didn't say I'd be here until midnight."

"Whatever, Cinderella." Kara pocketed her phone and jogged up the slope.

The sandstone building was up above the creek, a temple wedged between the weird arty buildings placed in the seventies that someone had probably long been fired over. A group of guys in dress shirts hovered in the soaring entrance hall. *Probably single-handedly keeping Abercrombie and Fitch in business*, Robyn mused.

The mannequins turned as one. Robyn couldn't help

staring, but in the same way an anthropologist might observe an exotic tribe. No-one wore proper shirts in the evolutionary genetics wing. Yellow guy wore a variation on the same yellow tracksuit every single day and smelled of grilled cheese. A haze of cologne choked the air as one of the mannequins waved.

"Hey, Kara."

Robyn took a shallow breath through her mouth. She didn't think it was necessarily an improvement over Jarlsberg.

Kara nodded and Robyn kept her head down. Her definition of micro and macro didn't fly here. The squat evolutionary genetics wing where she spent her time couldn't be more different to this place. The law courtyard was peppered with bronze plaques donated by old money. Her building was blighted by mould instead. Who knew, maybe the next penicillin was crusted outside her office window.

Kara clipped across the central courtyard toward the sound of scraping tables, and Robyn hurried behind her. A throng of potential yacht owners straightened collars and stepped back to admire the long impromptu service counter. A girl in a red dress waved at Kara. Robyn froze, mentally searching for her name. She'd met her maybe four times, on the myriad different committees Kara insisted on being part of, and which Robyn invariably got dragged into.

"Robyn, thanks for helping out," the girl said. She was just showing off now, remembering her name. Robyn chewed her lip. Lily? Or was it Lexi?

"Kara was quite persuasive," she managed.

The girl grinned. "That'd be Kara. Okay." L-something looked around. "I'm going to put you guys on punch duty. We need someone responsible monitoring what goes in the vat." She jerked her head toward what looked like an enormous copper silo that had been hacked in half.

"Jesus," Robyn muttered.

"Thanks, Lisa," said Kara, dragging Robyn over to the gleaming cauldron. Robyn desperately tried to commit the name to memory. She'd been so close. *Lisa*. She played through images in her mind. Saxophone. Lisa Simpson. *Lisa*. She could remember complex compounds at the drop of a hat, but apparently two-syllable names were beyond her.

"Looks like you're staying, Ms Responsible," Kara said, counting spirits and mixers with a hovering finger.

"Just for a few hours." Robyn ran an eye over the liquor on the table. There were at least a dozen bottles of high-end vodka, champagne, and vibrant green and blue spirits she didn't know the name of. If she were a typical 24-year-old, she would probably have memories of nights punctuated by blue-tinged vomit by now.

"Got enough alcohol?"

Kara's hand stopped mid-count. "You're right, I'll tell Lisa to get more. Less of this mixer crap." She gestured at the lemonade and cola with a frown.

"I was kidding."

Kara put her hands on her hips and chewed her lip. "I'm not." She clapped her hands together, her mouth forming a little 'o'. "I've got an outfit for you, too. I almost forgot."

Robyn blanched. "What's wrong with what I'm wearing?"

Kara looked her up and down. "This," she waggled a finger, "is daytime PhD student. You need after-hours toga babe."

Robyn looked down at her Converse, then her faded jeans and t-shirt. "I thought I was Ms Responsible," she muttered.

That was how she found herself wound in a sheet, ladling punch into a steady stream of paper cups. The fabric itched where it rode up under her armpit, and she wondered if Kara had bothered to wash it after snagging it from Vinnies. Probably not. Robyn tried not to dwell on it as she scanned the crowd. She thought she recognised the Abercrombie and Fitch crew, but she couldn't be sure. The writhing amorphous, slutty mass in front of her was a far cry from the Acropolis in Athens. She ladled on autopilot, missing wavering cups as the undergrads clutching them swayed. She wasn't sure if it was in time to the music or just gradual loss of motor skills. Maybe both. The dull bass beat had penetrated her skull hours ago, and the burnt veggie patty sat uneasily in her stomach. Her favourite Converse reeked of liquor. She wanted to be home an hour ago. Toga Party, just as fun as she remembered it.

"Robyn? Is that you?" The voice was slurred but familiar.

Robyn turned to the next person in line. She cringed. "Travis."

She felt Travis' eyes sidle up her body. It was different than when Kara did it, throwing a dress at her before a party, or blocking the door until she switched her solvent-stained t-shirt for a blouse. Predatory.

She hated it.

Robyn slopped punch into his cup, deliberately overflowing it. Liquid spattered across his chest. "Sorry." Her heart was pounding as she willed her face into a placid mask. Travis swayed, and Robyn noticed the girl by his side. Her grip on Travis' arm was as firm as a sailor's knot. Travis slopped more punch onto his date's arm, but she didn't budge despite the deluge. Weatherproof.

Robyn watched him disappear into the crowd.

"Having fun?" Kara yelled in her ear.

Robyn shook her head, nauseated by the memory and the alcohol fumes. "I'm going to head home," she said.

Kara bopped to the beat. "What?"

Robyn thrust the ladle into her hand. "Home," she yelled.

Kara nodded. "Meet anyone interesting?"

"Saw Travis."

Kara stilled. "That bastard? Where?"

Robyn pointed vaguely at the surging mass before them. So Travis still liked them thin. Robyn shuddered. Maybe she should have pulled the girl off him. *Go home,* she would have said. *You don't need him.*

"I know it was last year, but what he said to you was totally out of line. Just because you didn't want to sleep with him …"

Robyn shook her head. "It's fine. Honestly." Her backpack was calling her name. Her dry responsible clothes.

Kara grabbed her arm. "Hey, I'll come with you. Let's grab pizza or something."

"No, it's cool, I …" Robyn felt her throat swell. "I'm good. Just tired."

Kara released her arm. "I'm sorry. I didn't mean to bring up all of that." Kara pulled her phone out of her bra and waved it in Robyn's face. "Call me the moment you get back."

"Will do." Robyn grabbed her backpack and headed for the toilets to change.

The acetone-laced air of the lab hit her like a comforting embrace. Shucking her backpack, Robyn leaned against the cool benchtop and surveyed her dominion. The shoebox lab wasn't much, but it was hers. The gas chromatograph hummed in greeting from the bench by the window, the sound more than welcome after her immersion in the discordant DJ set. The dull throb in her skull had levelled into a persistent ringing, pre-empting the headache she'd have tomorrow. Probably shaved a few hertz off her hearing range in the process. The glamour of university life.

The chromatograph screeched as it switched vials. Robyn kicked her backpack under the desk and was rewarded with a rancid whiff of liquor. *Ew.* She'd have to dump the toga sheet or it would make the whole bag reek. Plopping onto the stool, she skimmed through the data output. Another forty-five purified samples idled in the loading rack. Almost two months of analytical work neatly contained right there in front of her. She should have been thrumming with anticipation, but instead she just felt drained. The effects of the afternoon's coffee had well and truly faded.

Travis. It was funny how a chance encounter could dredge the bed of memories and bring them rising to the surface in a muddy cloud. Maybe everyone had their dating epochs.

Sean in seventh grade didn't really count. She held his sweaty hand at recess, as mandated by the unwritten rules of the playground. She still had the silver necklace with the letter 'R' he'd given her, somewhere in the back of a drawer.

First had been Levi. The cute boy in calculus. Dinner and a movie. He had two mums – one used to be his Dad. That wasn't the problem. The problem was that Levi took a different girl to dinner each week. The post-Levi era had been a terrible one of self-assessment where Robyn came up wanting in every algorithm. Then Travis, the geology student who surfaced in chemistry class to whisper a joke in her ear and stayed late at lab sessions to walk her to her bike. It had been easy, convincing herself he cared. Until he didn't.

It wasn't a great track record.

Maybe she was cursed or something. Everyone else seemed to have cracked the code, seemed to be one half of someone else. Except her. Robyn sighed and ran a finger across the ridge of skin that bisected her right eye – a thin line above with a mirror reflection underneath. Like a scarecrow. The birthmark had been removed with laser surgery when she was seven, but she could still feel the puckered skin. Marked, cursed. Were the two so different? Logically, she knew they weren't related, but the thought lingered.

The mechanical arm stilled, the silence loud in the wake of the party. The heating procedure kicked in and Robyn watched the temperature climb for a moment before cupping her hands against the window to peer out at the winding paths, the maze of poorly-lit buildings. At least she could control what happened in the lab, cursed or not.

Too many nights were spent in the camp bed under her desk, but she liked the confined space, and the early starts it afforded her. Tonight, she couldn't face the cycle home to her apartment.

She pulled her sleeping bag out and called Kara. Her friend picked up on the third ring.

"I'm all good. Have a fun night, and I'll see you tomorrow."

"Uh, hey, Robyn." Kara sounded distant. "Great, cool. Night."

Robyn brushed her teeth, locked the door behind her and settled into her sleeping bag.

It wasn't until she was drifting to sleep that she realised she had heard Kara perfectly. No crescendoing screech or bottomless bass drop. There was no way she was still at the party.

2

Discovery

"She's sleeping in her office, at least three nights a week. I'm worried about her."

"Dedication? That's hardly troubling. I would have thought you'd be pleased."

"She's running herself into the ground."

"For all you know, she could be close to the breakthrough that will change everything."

"Ow." Robyn grimaced as she banged her head on the underside of her desk. She reached out for the phone and cut off the shrill blasts.

"What?" It was still early, too early for anyone to be calling her.

"Breakfast?" Robyn groaned at Kara's chipper voice.

Robyn scooted out from under the desk feeling

groggy, even with the rising egg on her head. "Sure. Usual place?"

"Yeah. Kate's coming, you mind? She's got a craving for pancakes."

"Cool. Give me five minutes." Robyn sniffed at her t-shirt, then pulled open the desk drawer to investigate her clothing options.

Kara sighed. "Did you sleep in your office again?"

Robyn pulled a blue shirt from the pile. "Maybe." She could almost imagine Kara rolling her eyes. "It's not a big deal, honestly."

Robyn heard someone else mumble in the background.

"Kate says that if you're there, she could use another Erlenmeyer flask. Apparently there was an accident involving her last one."

"Let me guess. It involved gravity and a hard surface." Robyn wrinkled her nose as she tossed the toga sheet into the bin and shimmied out of the sleeping bag.

"Something like that. She says her morning OJ just isn't the same without that tapered, illicit glassware."

"On it. Order the muesli for me, okay?"

Kate muttered something in the background that sounded distinctly like "health nut".

Kara cleared her throat. "I'm the one on the phone, okay?"

Robyn hung up and pulled yesterday's shirt over her head, adding it to the hamper by the window. Maybe she *was* getting too comfortable here.

The pink-tipped mohawk was easy to spot. She waved, but the twins were hunched over Kara's laptop. Kate's neon hair bobbed as she nodded at something Kara said. Different disciplines, different haircuts, still twins.

"Whatcha working on?"

Kara slammed the laptop lid down. "Robyn. You scared me."

A waif-like waiter interrupted them, balancing two enormous stacks of pancakes and Robyn's muesli. Kara used the distraction to slip the laptop into her bag. Robyn reached out for the bowl and the girl looked ready to cry with relief. Her wrist shook as she deposited the other two meals.

"She could use a pancake or two," said Kara, watching the waiter rub her wrist in retreat.

Robyn made a noncommittal noise, wondering if the

girl was just busy, or if she scrawled lists in the back of her notebooks like Robyn used to, post-Levi and pre-Travis. *Monday: Oatmeal, green tea. Salad. Salmon and green beans.*

Kate ignored them both. "Hot damn." She forked a huge, buttery slice into her mouth.

Robyn stared into her bowl. *Half-serve muesli, soy milk.* No, that was behind her now.

Robyn couldn't shake the feeling that her best friend was keeping something from her. "How's the thesis going?"

Kara tipped her hand in a so-so motion. "Getting there."

"She's already bound it," said Kate around a huge mouthful.

Kara elbowed her sister in the ribs. "Kate."

"What?" Robyn glanced between them, then settled on Kara. "You're done?"

"It's different to science, honestly Robyn. It's all regurgitation and discussion, not hard data like your research."

Robyn separated pumpkin seeds to one side of her bowl. "I'm not even halfway." An understatement.

"Plus, it's just a Master's, not a PhD like your project," Kate interjected. "Not even comparable."

Kara's phone vibrated, sending her fork clattering.

"I've got to go." Kara shovelled in a massive hunk of pancake. "See you later, okay?"

Kate reached over and added Kara's last pancake to her stack. "I told her to bind it in snakeskin, but I think she's going to get leather."

"Snakeskin?" Robyn couldn't believe it. "Great ecological choice." She waved as Kara jogged away, wondering where Kara had to be in such a hurry.

"Hey, can I come work in your office this morning? I'm sick to death of the Econ crowd." Kate crammed six chunks of pancake onto her fork.

"The more the merrier." Robyn smiled into her bowl as Kate tipped her head back to enjoy the sun. A thin trickle of syrup was all that remained of the pancake mountain. Jesus. Robyn loaded up her spoon with muesli.

It was always weird having someone else in her office, especially now that it was starting to feel like a mini-apartment. As Kate wandered around, Robyn kicked the clothes hamper under her desk and cracked open the window. Robyn hadn't realised how stuffy it was without an outdoor reference point. She hoped Kate didn't notice. Her effortless coolness made Robyn's office seem cramped and dated.

Kate tapped on the poster Blu-tacked to her wall, one of those terrible 3D renderings of a mitochondrion labelled ninth grade science class style. The adenosine triphosphate molecules had little happy, smiling faces. It hid the gash where she'd hurled a textbook, though.

"This is what you study, right?" Kate's leather jacket creaked as she crossed her arms.

"Yeah." Robyn switched on her monitor as Kate peered closer to read the labels. A queue of last night's chromatograms began popping up. So much data to work through. Each sample would have dozens of individual compounds to identify and quantify.

"These are the energy guys, right?" Kate pointed to the poster, pink hair catching the sunlight. Robyn didn't need to look.

"Mmmm." Robyn wondered if she could get out of her shift at the wholefoods co-op tonight. These samples weren't going to analyse themselves.

"So, you look at blood samples hoping to find weird

mutations?" Kate turned to face her.

"Kind of. I'm looking for unusual compounds. My theory is a little left field."

Pulling out her laptop, Kate settled at the desk wedged against the window. "Remind me again."

"Well, you know about symbiosis, right? Different animals co-operating in nature? Algae in coral and all that. You can also see symbiosis on a cellular level. The mitochondria in each and every human cell are the product of an unintentional, long-ago symbiosis between two bacterial cells. Over time, these two cells became one cell, indistinguishable from their original parts and instrumental for sustaining complex life."

Kate nodded, somewhat blankly. "So …"

"So, I think it's possible that mutations in mitochondrial genes might enable humans to form symbiotic connections with animals. Maybe even direct communication."

Kate snorted. "Holy shit. What does your supervisor think about all this?"

Robyn frowned. "He's been really encouraging, actually." Brock had always been excited about her work, even when she was deep in a data slump, hurling textbooks at walls and feeling like giving up.

Kate turned to face the window, but Robyn saw her shoulders shaking as she tried to contain her laughter. Flushing, Robyn turned to her computer. Well, they couldn't all be law or economics prodigies.

Sunlight angled across her desk, and Robyn found her right leg cramping. A faint thread of music over Kate's headphones reached her as the pain came into focus. The morning had zipped past as she hunched over her computer. She uncrossed her legs and switched them over, pins and needles erupting in protest.

Robyn ignored the pain. This sample was different. Several tall peaks preceded a big hump of unresolved compounds.

She tapped her fingers on the desk, picking up a rhythm. It's hard to tell what a mutation will do. Some mutations disrupt existing pathways in the cell. That's generally bad. There's a whole spectrum of bad — it might slow down the system, or it could terminate it altogether. It's rare for a mutation to be advantageous. But that's the basis of evolution. Some of them are.

A mutation can result in the synthesis of a new

compound. She cross-checked the sample ID. The blood bank samples included a mix of age, race and gender. This particular sample came from a sixteen-year-old Native American boy.

Kate sighed at the window and Robyn blinked in surprise. Kate was working so quietly she'd almost forgotten she was there.

"What's up? I'm assuming you're not practising for a highland dance recital, so what is it?" Kate yanked her headphones out.

Robyn gaped at her for a moment, then stilled her bouncing leg. "I have something," she managed. "But I don't know what to do next."

The chair groaned as Kate got to her feet. "What have you got?"

"I have a hit. The first hit in over two years, actually." Robyn tried to tamp down her giddiness. A result, a real result. She didn't know whether to dance around her office or throw up.

"So what's the problem?" Kate leaned over her shoulder, squinting at the squiggles on the chromatogram.

"There's no way I can get access to information about a blood donor." Robyn rubbed her eyes with both hands, working out the crusted sleep she found there. She needed more samples. But to do that, she needed a name, an address.

Kate pulled out her phone, snapping a photo of the sample ID. "Leave it with me. I have a friend who could maybe help you out."

Robyn's hands dropped to the desk. "Seriously?"

"Look, I still think your theory is batshit crazy, but it's the least I can do." Kate looked up from her phone. "Seriously."

Attempting to distract herself, Robyn half-heartedly began organising her desk. A real-life result, finally. And so young – sixteen. Robyn tried to imagine what the boy looked like, just walking around, going to school, completely oblivious of the mutation in his mitochondria. She stacked textbooks next to her computer. Or maybe it was nothing.

Robyn spun in her chair. She felt sick to her stomach. Two years she'd been screening blood samples. There was just something there in the back of her mind, urging her onward. Some strange conviction that this ability existed. Maybe she was a freak; a cursed, marked freak.

She flicked a glance at Kate, tapping away at full speed by the window. Kate certainly seemed to think so.

God, it wasn't fair. The don't-mess-with-me attitude, genius IQ *and* she could touch type. Robyn envied her. The best she could do was a weird half-type where her right hand skittered across the keyboard and the left hand had dominion over three or four keys.

"The kid's name is Fletcher. Fletcher Lowman." Kate turned around.

Robyn snapped upright. "What? You got a name?"

"My *friend* got a name. Durham, North Carolina. Goes to the state school there."

Robyn felt Kate's eyes boring into her.

"So, what are you going to do about it?"

Robyn scooted backward in her chair. North Carolina, half a world away. An *expensive* half a world away.

Robyn ran a hand through her hair and tried to still the rising nausea in her gut. Was there still alcohol on her skin? The room seemed closed in, too warm.

The boy in her mind had a name now. Fletcher.

"I'm sorry I laughed at you, before." Kate watched her from the window. "That was rude."

Robyn studied the faint mould patches on the ceiling,

taking shallow breaths to calm her stomach. Penicillin. "It's fine. It is a stupid idea." Everyone else thought so. Everyone except Brock. Robyn closed her eyes. Even her parents stepped carefully around her work. Tears threatened at the corners of her eyes. She'd show them. She'd show all of them. Robyn stared at the mould until the tears receded.

Kate's chair whirled and keys clattered. "Yeah, it is. But you should girl the hell up and follow it through."

Girl the hell up? Robyn got to her feet and shuffled over to Kate's desk.

"What are you doing?" Robyn had a bad feeling about this.

Kate grinned. "Booking your flights."

"No way in hell."

"Too late. You leave in three hours. Better get packed."

The ancient printer stirred to life, hacking out an itinerary with a sound like a cat regurgitating a hairball. Robyn held the paper at arm's length. "I'm going to America?"

"Yeah. You owe me like, six hundred dollars."

"I think I'm going to be sick." Robyn clutched the edge of her desk.

Kate grabbed her laptop and satchel. "Have fun." The door clicked shut behind her.

Robyn rested her head on the desk. Brock. She needed to talk to her supervisor.

"Come in." Usually Robyn loved her supervisor's cosy office, its teetering shelves filled with books that seemed to tilt toward you. She was sure one day she would find Brock buried beneath a hardcover avalanche, all unforgiving corners. Today she barely noticed. She was busy concentrating on not vomiting on his rug, like she was trying to convince her fourth-grade teacher she had only said "sheesh" instead of "shit".

"Robyn." *Silver fox*, she'd heard some of the other students call him that when she managed to drag herself to postgrad barbecues. Frozen bubble and squeak patties, no-name sausages, white bread. A gastronomic nightmare. Brock rolled up his shirtsleeves as he turned in his chair, the wheels grating. Nothing in this department was new, or brand-name.

"What can I do for you?" He gestured to the faded

armchair next to him. It was a well-rehearsed dance, and she knew her lines. *A bit of everything*, she would say, and he would smile and throw his hands in the air as if she'd asked for ten new gas chromatographs.

"I may have done something rash," she said, deviating from the script.

Brock exhaled sharply, not quite a laugh but close. "Rash?"

"I found some unusual compounds in one of my samples and tracked down the donor, a boy in North Carolina."

Brock jumped as if someone had struck him. A flash of excitement crossed his face but disappeared so quickly Robyn convinced herself she'd imagined it.

"And the rash part?"

"I'm flying there to meet him, get more samples. Tonight."

Brock didn't say anything for a long moment. Robyn fidgeted in the armchair.

I swear, I just said "sheesh".

You swear, Robyn? Is that a confession? I'm taking away your gold star. I'm very disappointed in you.

"Let me know how much the ticket cost you. I'll

reimburse you."

Robyn jerked her head up. "Thank you, sir."

"Let me know how it goes." Brock's hands were clasped tight in his lap. She could see the whites of his knuckles.

Robyn nodded. "Of course."

3

Fletcher

"Robyn's found something. Maybe another candidate. She's en route to North Carolina."

"Excellent. I'll send the reactionary team. This couldn't have come at a better time. The first is proving ... difficult to examine."

"Intercept only; I don't want Robyn to get hurt."

"I can't make any promises, Brock. You know that."

"The Mystic Paw?" The cashier twisted a dreadlock between thumb and index finger, examining the book.

"Yeah." Fletcher shrugged. "School project."

"Cool, man." Dreadlocks peered at the barcode. "Twelve dollars."

Fletcher pushed a handful of bills across the counter

and tucked the book under his arm. Pressing open the door to the tinkle of wind chimes, he left the oppressive aroma of incense. The alternative bookstore always freaked him out. He crossed the street head down in case he bumped into anyone he knew.

Flipping the book over in the relative safety of the bus shelter, he read the blurb: *From ancient times, the bear has stood alone among animals. Gifted with senses beyond man's reach, yet still close to the crucible of life, his paw is mystic beyond all comprehension.*

Fletcher stifled a snigger. Spiritual mumbo jumbo, but he was desperate enough to be looking for answers. He shoved the book into his backpack and caught sight of his watch. "Shit," Fletcher muttered, dragging the zipper closed and tossing it onto his shoulders. He ran back toward the school.

Jake threw a basketball at him from across the court as the whistle blew sharp, persistent blasts. Fletcher caught it against his chest and slowed to a stop. Late.

"Where'd you go?"

"Dentist." Fletcher bared his teeth in a huge grin. "Only a dozen cavities, so she says I'm on the mend.

Sugar rehab is working." The lie came easily.

"Yeah, sure. Coach is annoyed." Jake jogged to the stands, where a group of boys clustered around a broad-shouldered man. Coach Dustin.

Fletcher ran over, stifling a yawn. These weird dreams were doing his head in. Just this morning, he could have sworn he'd seen something off the roadside on the school bus ride – an enormous shadow following him. He had been freaked out enough to go to the hippy bookstore, but not stupid enough to tell his parents or visit the school psychologist. It made him dread sleep, knowing the bear would be there.

"Fletcher, you got a problem?"

Fletcher started, shaking his head. "No, sir." He had no idea what Dustin had just said. Damn it.

"Then you won't mind running ten laps."

Fletcher gritted his teeth. "No, sir." He dropped his backpack and headed for the track field. Great, his layups would never improve at this rate.

Each silent lap was interrupted by reverberating impacts for twenty seconds or so as he passed the basketball court. Sweat dribbled onto his eyelashes. He flicked his head to clear the droplets without breaking stride. It felt good just to run. On the court, you had to be hyper-aware of everything, but here his mind could drift. *An ancient, sacred presence.* The book looked readable, despite his misgivings about the bookstore. He wondered if he'd sleep easier tonight. Maybe. He ran faster, outpacing the patches of darkness between stadium lights.

Pulling up in front of the stands, Fletcher rested his hands on his knees as he caught his breath. Practice was over. Chugging water, Fletcher reached the knot of players as Dustin read out names for next week's game. Fist pumps accompanied each one. Fletcher dropped onto the bench, his likely starting position. Sure enough, his name wasn't called.

"Be on time," Dustin muttered as he passed Fletcher, collecting the bright orange cones arranged in a logarithm curve before the hoop. Fletcher sighed. He couldn't exactly explain why he had been late, not even to himself.

Headlights flashed through the wire, and Fletcher blinked against the glare. His Mom always came to pick him up. Someone sniggered by the cluster of bikes and

Fletcher felt his neck grow hot.

He dropped into the passenger seat and the antiseptic smell of the clinic hit him instantly. He dumped his backpack next to the bundled bag of scrubs on the floor. Mom went out of her way to pick him up from practice. He shouldn't be so ungrateful.

Turning out of the carpark, she glanced at him. "Why didn't I see you on the court?"

"I was there, Mom. We took turns running laps, and I was last." Another lie.

"No need to get defensive." Her arms tensed around the wheel as they turned onto the main street. Scattered bike lights appeared behind them, bobbing in the rear-view mirror. Fletcher wondered what it would be like to ride home with them, to be part of the pack.

"Your father's making dinner."

"Oh," said Fletcher, trying not to sound disappointed. His Dad could deconstruct classic literature but couldn't wield a spatula to save himself.

"Don't worry. I've got some backup taco mince defrosting." She grinned.

The sharp edges of *The Mystic Paw* poked through his bag. Fletcher shifted in his seat. He couldn't tell her about the dreams.

"Mom?"

"Yes, honey?"

"Thanks for picking me up."

The taco bowls were delicious, even eaten in the haze of smoke that left a sour, burnt odour hanging in the kitchen.

"It was supposed to be beef bourguignon," Dad sighed, reaching for more guacamole. "Sorry, cupcake."

Fletcher made a face. Cupcake, sugarplum, honey pie. Gross. He scraped up the last few skerricks of brown rice and dumped his bowl in the sink.

"I'm going to bed."

Mom straightened from her slumped position on the couch. Fletcher noticed the bags under her eyes. "Remember, I'm at the clinic tomorrow until after lunch, and your father has tutorials."

"Copy that," Fletcher yelled down the stairs.

"Do your homework before you go down to the lake."

He read until he fell asleep, dreaming of the bear again.

Saturday. The note on the kitchen counter pointed him in the direction of taco leftovers and reminded him to do his homework.

"Thanks, Mom," Fletcher said aloud. "I don't remember where the fridge is." He chucked leftovers into a container, grabbed his fishing rod and a thermos of hot chocolate, and pronounced himself ready.

From the back of the house, the path to the lake was only a few miles along a narrow trail. Fletcher breathed in the heavy scent of pine, relishing this one precious moment of the week he truly had to himself. No teachers, no essays. Even the air smelled crisper when you didn't have to be anywhere in particular. The lake opened up a wide horizon of shimmering, reflected sky when he reached the end of the trail. Fletcher dropped his backpack and stared for a long moment before casting his line.

The flick and dance of the lure on the water calmed his mind. Fletcher propped *The Mystic Paw* on his lap and sipped hot chocolate. Every few pages he flicked his attention back to the river, gave the line a jerk. It beat the calculus textbook he usually hauled down here, though at least mathematics is a predictable language.

Tugs on the line grew infrequent and the book absorbed more of his attention. Eventually, he anchored the rod in the ground by his feet, nudging it when he remembered.

A splash caught his attention. His inner angler perked right up, scanning the water. He rarely caught anything. Today might be his lucky day. He squinted against the glare on the water, searching for the source of the sound.

Holy shit.

Fletcher stared at the dark shadow on the rocks. His nightmare made flesh stood on the opposite bank. The bear. His throat tightened. Alone in the woods, no-one for miles.

Heart pounding, Fletcher leapt to his feet, the book falling onto wet stones. Some part of his mind winced, knowing it would be soggy in minutes, but he didn't dare look down. Didn't dare let the animal out of his sight. The drawings didn't do it justice – the brown bear sniffing the air was enormous. Shaggy cinnamon fur hung on thick limbs ending in massive claws, claws designed to rip and cleave.

One word echoed in his skull. *Predator.*

Fletcher licked his lips. All that separated them was 25 feet. Screwing his eyes shut, he counted to three, willing the apparition to disappear. When he opened them, the bear hadn't moved. *It wasn't a dream, then.*

Again there was a splash in the water, this time on the other side of the lake. The line strained and his reel spun in a tight circle. Unable to move, Fletcher watched as the rod jerked free and sailed into the water, heading downstream.

Another splash. He didn't see the actual movement, just caught the ghost of it in his peripheral vision. He only had eyes for the bear.

The animal tensed, launching itself from the rocks and flying through the air for a graceful, long second before hitting the water. A cascade erupted as the bear went under.

Fletcher backed up, tripped and fell on his butt.

Get back, his mind screamed.

A wet snout appeared above the waterline, holding a flailing, shiny fish.

Shit. The bear doggy-paddled, not back to its side of

the lake but *toward* him.

Fletcher scrabbled backward, felt the mushy leaves beneath his fingers as he left the bank. The bear closed the gap, faster in the water than Fletcher could have imagined.

Go go go. Scrambling to his feet, he ran, battering at branches, stumbling along the track he thought he knew inside out. It was an age before he clattered up the porch stairs. Slamming the door behind him, Fletcher brought the dining table screeching across the floor. Blood pounded in his ears, and his legs felt jerky. The floor was cool under his bare feet. He hoped the table would be enough.

His heart kept hammering as he slid down the fridge and cradled his head on his knees. Safe, he was safe here. Jesus, it had been so *big*, so bloody *close*.

The door lurched, hit the table, retracted. He screamed, couldn't help it.

"Fletcher?"

Dad. Fletcher pushed upright onto shaky legs and peered out the window above the sink. Just his Dad.

Fletcher dragged the dining table back to the middle of the room.

"What the hell?" The professor shrugged off his jacket and tie as he stepped around the puddle near the fridge. He was transformed instantly back into Dad – tired, hungry, TV sports lover.

"The lake. Bear. Fishing." It was hard to get the words out. Spots appeared on the inside of his retinas, they wouldn't budge.

"Huh. Where's the taco mince?" Dad poked around in the fridge, not listening.

Fletcher hit the floor, unconscious.

He woke up swaddled in dry clothes under a blanket on the couch. He worried a loose edge.

"Fletcher, honey." His Mom's voice. She shifted into focus, waved a finger between his eyes.

"He's tracking well enough," she said to his father before turning back. "We were both worried about you."

Fletcher coughed. A glass of water appeared at his lips.

"What happened?"

Fletcher drained the glass, thinking. "Something down at the lake. I guess I freaked out." *An appropriate response to seeing a bear*, Fletcher thought.

"A bear." Dad sank into the couch opposite, holding a sandwich.

Fletcher backtracked. "I'm not sure. I – I didn't get a good look. Whatever it was looked big, so I just ran for it."

"Darling?" It was the voice Mom used when she expected something. *Darling, could you change the taps. Darling, I thought I asked you to fix the lawnmower.*

Taking the hint, Dad put the sandwich down. "I'll check it out. You'd better show me where you were, son."

They walked in single file. Fletcher focused on the glinting shotgun bouncing against his father's shoulder. He felt silly now, wrapped in a big coat and traipsing behind his father like he was twelve, needing reassurance that the monsters under his bed weren't real.

Except the shotgun only came out for real things.

The lake was still, misting over as the temperature dropped. On top of his backpack sat his book, his rod resting against its spine.

"Ho, you didn't mention your haul," Dad exclaimed.

Frowning, Fletcher looked to where his father had pointed. On the rocks lay an enormous, gleaming fish.

There was no sign of the bear.

4

Contact

"The boy's blood is difficult to analyse; they assure me it has something to do with the mutations."

"Why isn't Fang working on it?"

"She's busy with the main experimental subjects. We will crack this, Brock. Can you imagine breaking through the barrier that divides life itself? It will prove the legends are true. All of them."

"We're not gods, Miranda. Something that has lain dormant for millennia ..."

"... Deserves to be freed."

Robyn couldn't remember ever feeling so grimy or on edge. Long-distance travel sucked. The packed arrivals hall hemmed her in on all sides. Clutching her backpack strap with one hand, she edged through the crowd, holding the phone to her ear with the other.

"We're having gin and tonics on the deck. I thought you'd call, dear."

Robyn cursed under her breath. She'd completely forgotten that her parents had left on their cruise today. Robyn glanced at her watch, trying to reconcile the time difference and failing. God, she was *tired*.

"What was that?"

"Nothing, Mum, just traffic noise. Reception is terrible." Not to mention costing her mother a fortune.

"I thought I gave you the dates?"

"You did, Mum. I'm so sorry. Uni has been hectic the last few weeks." *China? Or was it Canada?* Robyn couldn't remember. She picked her way through arrivals. *There it was. Bus terminal.*

Robyn tried to decipher the faded runes on the timetable. Greasy film covered the plastic surface. Static rippled in her ear as her mother jostled the phone on the other side of the Pacific. Her father's gruff voice made her smile.

"Ro. Can you check on the farm while we're gone?"

"Of course. Remind me, how long is that?" Robyn said.

Her father guffawed at the other end. "Three months. It's a big world, apparently."

Robyn cringed. *Right.* "Sorry, Dad, I've just got a lot on my mind. Have a lovely time."

"We love you, honey, make sure you take care of yourself —" The phone cut out as Robyn entered the terminal. *Great.* Pulling her backpack closer, she got on the bus.

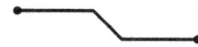

Fletcher woke up unsure of his surroundings for a heartbeat, the smell of humus and decay in his nostrils. He bunched the blanket in his hand. He was in bed, his bed, still wearing the jeans and t-shirt he'd had on yesterday.

The evening came back to him. Grilled fish and salad for dinner. Exclamations at his prowess while his parents had finished a bottle of red wine. He'd collapsed into bed early, slipping into sleep as their giggles from the couch rose up the stairs.

He sat bolt upright, the gentlest tug on his mind. His whole head jerked and he found himself on his feet, moving toward the window. Bright sun tumbled in when he shifted the curtains.

Fletcher wasn't sure what he'd expected, but it wasn't this. The bear sat in the backyard, a dappled statue. His mouth went dry. A dream, another dream.

When he cracked open the window, cold air coiled into the room. The bear seemed to shift without moving, like a mirage. Flickering.

The tug again, more insistent this time.

What do you want from me? He screamed in his head at the animal. *Leave me alone.*

Curling fingers bore into his skull. Nausea rose in the back of his throat.

I found you.

Fletcher gagged as pain ricocheted through his head. He vomited on the floor in a thick stream. Gasping, he rested his elbows on his knees. Now he heard voices? A female voice. Maybe it was food poisoning. Or schizophrenia.

None of these.

Fletcher wheeled back to the window. The bear was on the roof. He'd broken a dozen slate tiles one summer when he tried to climb the downpipe to watch the stars.

No way in hell could they hold the bear's weight. He was having a psychotic breakdown. Chest heaving, he started to hyperventilate as he backed toward the bed.

The bear poked a wet snout through the open window and tilted its head.

My name is Eva.

Jesus. The bear has a name now. Fletcher searched the room for a weapon. Anything. Even if this were some self-inflicted delusion, he'd feel better with something in his hand. His right hand itched toward the heavy book under the raggedy quilt.

You are Fletcher.

His hand caught the edge of the hardcover book.

You know my name? He chided himself. Of course a delusion staged and directed by his subconscious would know his name.

Yes. You are a walker, able to see the spirits. The bear's voice. The fictional bear his mind had created. The animal that shimmered and appeared on rooftops.

He faltered. The fish had been real enough.

The bear nudged the window. Fletcher blinked and it was now crouched on the floorboards, stepping around the pool of vomit. Frozen in place, he could only watch in horror as it advanced. The bear reached forward with a muscled forearm and curled thick claws. To his surprise, he found himself reaching for her.

Their knuckles grazed and something raced through his arm, zinged into his chest. Images flashed before his eyes. A green orb of light, a rush of voices, dozens of flickering pairs of eyes.

You see?

It was too much. He fell back on the quilt as the spots appeared in his line of vision, a mixture of humus and floral perfume in the air. His last thought was one of mild outrage – again?

5

First Meeting

A deep humming enveloped him, brought him swimming back to consciousness. It was a beautiful sound. The quilt wrapped around him was a snug cocoon. He wondered if the bear – Eva – had done it.

Of course. You are my spirit partner.

Fletcher blanched, spinning on the bed. Eva curled against the headboard, her muddy paws on his pillow.

Oh my God, I can't have a bear in my room. The absurdity of his reaction brought a giggle to his lips.

Your den is homely. Eva's smooth voice reminded him of molasses. He felt his eyes close again, the humming building in volume.

He snapped them open. *What are you doing?*

The bear blinked, long, dark lashes fluttering. *It's not me. It's the spirit energy.*

Spirits? Fletcher felt the remnants of the strange, zinging sensation in his system, as if he'd drunk two of those terrible energy drinks before finals. His skin itched with it. Fletcher scratched his forearm as the sound went up an octave. His skin began to thrum with a faint green colour. When he looked up, Eva's fur rippled with light as well. The green of a forest canopy.

The green aura faded as quickly as it had appeared.

What was that?

Eva answered him. It began to twig that she wasn't talking, but speaking in his mind. Somehow it wasn't as terrifying as he knew it probably should be.

You are the spirit walker of the earth, and I am your guide. We have both been called.

We are both called what?

A dull thud carried up from the open window. *There's someone at the door*, Fletcher thought. The old clock on his nightstand read 9:24 am.

Eva yawned. *A girl. She can be trusted.*

Fletcher peered out the window. A woman in jeans with a navy backpack stood on the porch, fiddling with her sleeve. When he looked back, Eva's butt was hanging out of the doorway.

Where are you going? Fletcher's heart hammered. He heard a thump as Eva hit the stairs and followed at a jog.

There was a note on the stair rail. *Gone out for flour and eggs, pancakes at 11 am. Love, Mom and Dad.*

Good. His parents weren't here. It was a small miracle, all things considered. Eva pawed at the doorframe, shaking the entire door on its hinges. Fletcher elbowed her in the gut, at least what he guessed was her gut.

What do you think you're doing? She'll freak out if she sees you.

"Hello?" A tentative female voice.

I'll get it. Fletcher cleared his throat. "Just a minute."

Fletcher turned to Eva. *You have to hide. Right now.*

Eva pivoted heavily on the spot, knocking the hall table over. Loose change and keys bounced off the floor. Eva wailed in apology, rearing up on her hind legs. A real-life Wookiee in his hallway.

"Is everything all right?"

Fletcher assessed the big open space. Without siblings, he'd never catalogued hide-and-seek spots.

The kitchen. Get into the kitchen, and don't make a sound. Fletcher wiped sweaty palms on his jeans and opened the front door.

"Hello," he said, trying for a winning smile. The woman was pretty, with dark hair that fell to her shoulders. She stared at him as if he were a different species, mouth agape for a long moment.

She coughed and collected herself. "Hi, my name's Robyn Greene. Are you Fletcher?"

Fletcher nodded, eyes wide. "I'm sorry, I don't know you." He shifted his weight and crossed his arms. Robyn looked slightly manic. He'd already had enough excitement for one day.

We can trust her. Let her in. Eva spoke in his mind again.

Fletcher sighed. "Come on in." He felt Eva hum in approval.

Robyn crossed the threshold, tugging on both shoulder straps.

He existed. A real-life research subject. It made Robyn's head spin as she let her backpack fall to the floor and perched herself on a worn couch. *Fletcher Lowman. I've found you.*

Robyn rotated her aching shoulders. "Sorry for dropping by so early," she called out to Fletcher, who was in the kitchen pulling mugs from the draining rack.

"Tea?" he queried.

"Yes, please." She'd rather have coffee directly injected into her veins, but tea would suffice. The pine-clad house was deceptively large inside, with a fireplace smack bang in the middle of the open plan kitchen/living area. Now that she was here, Robyn didn't have a clue how to broach the subject. *Hey, you're a mutant, and you should let me take some blood samples?* Yeah, right.

Fletcher shuffled around the kitchen and eventually thrust a warm mug into Robyn's hands. It was a godsend.

"Thank you." His shirt looked crumpled, as if he'd slept in it. Not that she could talk.

Fletcher sipped his tea. "So, I assume there's a reason for your visit?"

"I'm a researcher. Evolutionary genetics." *He looks so normal*, Robyn thought.

"Okay." Fletcher put his mug down on the coffee table. "My parents aren't here, if you're looking for Rob or Denise. They'll be back soon."

"I'm not here to talk to your parents. I'm here to talk to you."

"Me?" There was real fear in Fletcher's eyes. He sent

a glance back toward the kitchen.

Crap. Coming on too strong. Less psycho killer, more likeable scientist.

"Do you know about prokaryotes and eukaryotes?"

Confusion clouded Fletcher's face. "Yeah, I guess. Different DNA. You and I are eukaryotes, bacteria and stuff are prokaryotes."

"And eukaryotes have mitochondria. Organelles that produce our cellular energy," Robyn continued.

"Look, I'm sorry. It's Sunday, and I don't feel like a science lesson." Fletcher rubbed his eyes as a wet, heavy sneeze issued from somewhere behind him.

Robyn started. "What was that?"

The draining rack clattered onto the floor, pans bouncing. Robyn jumped to her feet as Fletcher crossed the room and glared at something behind the counter.

"Nothing, just a breeze."

Robyn frowned. "That was a sneeze."

Fletcher shrugged. "The neighbour's cat, maybe."

Pans skidded across the floor, the sound brash and jolting, followed by a heavy thump.

Robyn's throat went dry. Not a cat. "Fletcher?"

Fletcher stepped backward, his arms wide. "She says

she wants to meet you."

Robyn backed into the coffee table, sending her tea sloshing out. "Who? *What* wants to meet me?" Her heart pounded in her chest. "I thought no-one else was here?"

Robyn heard loud breathing and something heavy scraping across the floorboards. "Fletcher?"

"Robyn, meet Eva."

A bear stumbled out from behind the counter. *A goddamn bear.*

Robyn felt the coffee table connect with her skull, then darkness.

Something damp snuffled her ear, tickling the hair plastered to her scalp. Coming to with a gasp, Robyn shrieked at the mass of brown fur looming in front of her. The fur shifted, revealing a huge green eye with a dark pupil like a black hole. It hovered for a second then disappeared. Robyn blinked at the empty space before it filled with Fletcher. He scrutinised her.

"A … a bear," she managed. There was a bear in this boy's living room.

Fletcher flicked a wary glance over his shoulder. "Eva. I'm still getting used to the whole thing myself."

The bear loitered near the dining table, snuffling into the rug. Robyn stared as Fletcher propped an arm under Robyn's armpit and half-dragged her to her feet. Robyn had been upright for all of two seconds before she collapsed into the embrace of a faded recliner. The bear shuffled toward Fletcher and stopped a few paces away, as if sensing her unease. Robyn blinked, assessing the green haze surrounding them. It was how she'd imagined the northern lights would look, a swirling spectrum of light. It wasn't a colour you could find at a paint store; it was almost … ethereal.

Fletcher and Eva shared a glance. Fletcher seemed uneasy, staring at the bear with almost the same intensity as Robyn.

It's real. They're communicating. Robyn dug her fingers into the sides of the couch. "How long have you been joined? Connected?"

"I've been dreaming about her for weeks, but this –" Fletcher waved a hand between himself and the bear, "just happened." He shuffled his feet.

Robyn ran an eye over the enormous animal. A

brown bear, the largest terrestrial carnivore in the world. Robyn inhaled at the intelligence she saw behind those forest green eyes. Green. The green light, she couldn't explain. A mutation couldn't explain that. What the hell was going on?

"Eva says we can trust you, that you're going to help us." Fletcher sighed. "I don't know what to believe anymore."

Robyn licked her lips. *I can't just take blood samples and leave.* Eva's silent stare was starting to unnerve her. This bond was beyond anything she'd imagined.

"My research looks at mitochondrial mutations, mutations that might enable humans and animals to communicate."

Fletcher brightened. "So you know all about this."

Robyn dug her nails further into the couch. *Not exactly.* "I can help. I –"

Eva wailed, a long otherworldly screeching sound. Robyn shivered. The bear tensed, bobbing her head and huffing into the air. *This is a wild animal*, Robyn reminded herself, sinking further into the couch, *an unpredictable wild animal.*

"She can smell people outside." Fletcher grabbed

Robyn's hand, his face pale. "We have to go. Right now."

Robyn struggled to her feet, feeling woozy as if drugged. People? It didn't make any sense. The edge of her backpack peeked around the couch. Robyn hooked an arm under the strap and followed Fletcher across the room.

Fletcher froze, his bare feet twisting in the rug, and Robyn slammed into his back.

Robyn heard the screech of tyres. Yelling voices. A popping sound.

And again.

The door banged closed as Fletcher disappeared outside, Eva on his heels. Gunfire erupted in earnest.

In the driveway, his Mom's car idled, two figures slumped over the dashboard. Fletcher didn't want to look at the car, but his gaze fell on the familiar blue sedan as if it were magnetised. The shattered windows didn't hide anything. His Mom's blonde hair covered her face, but his Dad stared forward, unseeing. Fletcher smelled the iron wafting from the dark stains. Blood. So much blood.

No! Everything shuddered to a stop. Fletcher

closed his eyes as a weird pressure built behind his eyelids. When he opened them, bright light bathed the surroundings, illuminating the forest. Picking their way through the long grass were dark-clad men with rifles at their shoulders. They seemed to move in slow motion. *This isn't happening.* The air hung heavy, sweat mingling with the harsh, acrid, metallic scent of gunpowder.

Eva materialised by his side, green energy fizzling around her.

Twenty men. Eva's voice, somehow calm, anchored him.

Fletcher heard the swing of the rifles then bullets biting into the gravel. He ducked, hands over his head. His skin crawled with green light.

His mind flooded with the multitude of information pouring in via his senses.

Eva?

Ceasing fire, the line of men advanced. Fletcher curled his fists by his side, heart beating erratically in his chest. They only had the one car, so driving out of here wasn't an option. If they ran, they wouldn't stand a chance of outrunning guns. *Think. There must be something.* His phone was back in the house by his bed, useless. Anyway, the police would never make it in time.

Eva began humming, the song forming a veil around them both. The green light from his skin arced to hers, enveloping them in a green sphere of light. It slowed the mass of input into his brain.

Fletcher extended an arm. The sphere moved with him. The humming intensified as if hundreds of voices had erupted in his head. Swaying, he nearly fell, but Eva nudged him, and the voices quietened as if waiting for him.

Good. You learn quickly. You must be aware of the others, but not let them overwhelm you. Eva watched the line of men.

Others? Fletcher frowned. The voices jumped up a notch in volume.

Who dares threaten the earth walker? said a foreign voice, sharp as flint.

Who dares? hissing voices chorused.

Fletcher swallowed, the green light holding as Eva hummed.

Stop them, he projected, feeling the call reach hundreds of minds.

Stop them. Stop them. Stop them.

The scene in the clearing accelerated back to full speed in a rush. A howl cleaved the air, then another. A sickening, terrified sound. Men disappeared in the long grass one by one. There one second, gone the next. One of the men pivoted like a ballerina, sending a circular burst of gunfire into the field.

Fletcher closed his eyes but could still see everything. Saliva filled the back of his throat as he leapt out of the grass, raking his claws across the man's throat, slashing at his chest. Thick warm blood coated his jaws. Three bobcats darted in and out of his vision, felling the line of men.

Stop them.

Fletcher blinked and returned to his body. His claws were now fists, yet the metallic taste of blood lingered in his throat. He ached to conquer, destroy, reclaim. He was hungry for it.

The cracks echoed across the clearing. His mind flitted back to the field, and he drew long, ragged last breaths with the bobcats as their hearts stilled. A small knot of men stood in a bewildered huddle. Fletcher heard their screaming, but it was as if he no longer understood English. As the men turned toward the house, the voices clamoured again for space inside his head. Fletcher couldn't stop them, felt his head droop. Eva bowed before him, scooping him onto her broad back.

He clung to her as the humming faded.

6

Rogue

Robyn shook for a long time, legs drawn up to her chest on the sandy floor of the cave. She'd seen the bodies in the car as she ran, holding Fletcher on Eva's back. They had to be Fletcher's parents. A fresh wave of nausea rose in her stomach.

Eva had disappeared over an hour ago, and Fletcher hadn't moved at all. She'd remembered enough first aid to check his pulse and prop him in the recovery position. *Wake up, damn it.*

At least his green aura had faded. She thought she'd imagined it back at the house. Fletcher and the bear had been wreathed in it, bloody glowing. Somehow they'd slowed the men down, though she didn't know how. The screams, she'd never forget the screams.

Robyn rubbed her eyes. God, she was so tired. Her

legs ached from the long run beside the bear, but her mind would not rest. She couldn't shake the feeling that she had somehow led the men to Fletcher. That the death of Fletcher's parents was somehow all her fault.

Kara. She would know what to do.

Her thoughts were interrupted by the return of Eva. The bear dumped two fish at her feet, their mouths puckering open and closed.

"What am I supposed to do with these?"

Eva flared her nostrils, kicking a pile of rough wood in the corner.

"Oh." Comprehension dawned. Robyn stacked wood and kindling and found a sharp stone. Her mind needed a task, any task, even one she was rubbish at.

Fletcher's moan sent the rocks tumbling from her grasp after twenty minutes of useless striking. A spark skittered onto the dry wood. Robyn nearly screeched in triumph as a tentative flame rose then caught.

"Fletcher, are you all right?" Robyn sent him a glance, afraid to look away from the pile of wood. The boy sat upright, rubbing his left temple.

"Yeah, I think so." He looked around the now-lit cave. Robyn preened inwardly at her success. *Take that, Duke of Edinburgh.*

Eva filled the cave entrance, dropping to her knees before Fletcher to nuzzle his chest. Robyn turned away, feeling like an outsider. Kara. She rummaged through her backpack and found her phone.

"Hey, Robyn! Kate told me she dropped you in the deep end."

"It's a bit deeper than I expected," Robyn said. "Listen, I need your help. Or rather, Kate's hacker friend's help. Someone else knows about Fletcher." Robyn took a deep breath as the fear rose again. *I could have died today. Would have died a virgin with a shitty half-completed PhD project and only two real friends.* "I don't know what to do," Robyn whispered, glancing up at Fletcher and Eva. "Fletcher thinks I've got this all worked out." The boy was nodding at the bear, his face calm. Robyn swallowed the bile at the back of her throat.

"Okay, take it down a notch." Kara's voice cut through the rising terror in Robyn's gut. "So you found Fletcher."

"And his bear, Eva."

"Wait, what?"

"My crazy theory was right, but other people know about Fletcher too. Men with guns, Kara. They shot

Fletcher's parents. Nearly killed us too."

"Holy crap. Okay. Leave it with us, Robyn. Stay put; I'll call you back in a couple of hours. Don't go anywhere."

Robyn stared at the phone for a long moment. It didn't seem possible that Kara's voice could sound the same when Robyn's entire world had been upended.

The smell of roasting fish made her stomach rumble.

"Thanks," Robyn mumbled as Fletcher passed her a skewer. Cracking noises reverberated against the walls as Eva munched on the second fish, raw and bloody. Robyn winced. No intact cartoon skeletons here. Fletcher seemed okay, not quite leaning against the bear's flank, but close. She swallowed her mouthful and added to the pile of fine bones by her feet. His parents were dead. Robyn closed her eyes. The bloody clearing filled with the scattered bodies of men and bobcats was already permanently seared into her consciousness. She put the skewer down. Would she be able to help him when all she'd brought so far was death? She had to try.

"What exactly happened back there?" she asked after the knot in her stomach eased.

Fletcher looked over at Eva.

"The green light, the men. How did you stop them?"

"I– I channelled the voices. Eva showed me how." Fletcher waved his fish skewer.

"The voices? Which voices?"

"The animals in the forest. I could hear them; they listened to me."

Robyn swallowed. Had Fletcher controlled the bobcats? "How?"

"I don't know."

"What about now?" Robyn asked. Eva curled up and snorted, sending Robyn's pile of bones skittering across the floor of the cave.

Fletcher twisted his skewer and closed his eyes. "There's a buzzing in the back of my mind. You know, when you turn the volume down during the ads but yank it back up for the show? It feels like that."

"How?" Robyn's mind whirred with possibilities. Not a single animal, but many? A connection like that was way beyond the scope of her hypothesis.

"I have no idea. It's all her." Fletcher pointed to Eva with his fish skewer. The bear's fur fuzzed with green light for a moment, then shifted back to caramel. "Look, I'm not saying it isn't freaking me out." He finished his fish and began drawing patterns with his stick in the sand. "But I know what I saw, what I felt. I … I killed people. Animals sacrificed themselves so that we could get away."

"I'm … I'm sorry about your parents." Robyn hated how useless the words sounded. "I didn't know …" She didn't know anything, wouldn't have believed any of this if she hadn't been there, hadn't seen Fletcher and Eva. Robyn didn't finish her sentence, just wrapped her arms around her knees.

Fletcher hunched over the sand. Droplets splattered onto the lines he'd drawn, a circle with a line through it.

"There was nothing you could have done. Absolutely nothing." Robyn hoped she was getting through. She hated funerals, never knew what to say. Life just seemed to get snatched away when you weren't expecting it. It was a shitty game with shitty rules.

"I know," Fletcher said, his voice small.

Robyn desperately wished she could offer Fletcher some answers. "You're special, unique." The words slipped out as Robyn rummaged for her folder. She spread out the chromatograms on the sand and jabbed the peaks she'd circled in red pen. "I've studied over five hundred blood samples, and yours is the only one with these compounds."

Fletcher stared at the two peaks, eyes red-rimmed. "What are they?"

Robyn chewed the inside of her lip. "I have absolutely no idea."

7

MRI

"Kate. Robyn's in trouble." Kara put her head down as she spoke into the phone, powering across the bridge. Morning classes be damned. Students strode past her in loose groups. She picked out a mob of first-year college students, huddled together like wary sheep.

"What, she get lost?" Kate said. "She's a big girl. Robyn can handle herself."

Kara hit the tree-lined central avenue, striding past the fancy new chemistry and biology buildings, a mess of hexagons that would make bees cry.

"Nuh uh. She's got herself in the middle of something big. Where are you?"

"Economics common room. There's cake."

Kara shook her head. *Of course there was.* "Meet me at the ops room in ten minutes."

Kate spluttered. "It's bigger than free mud cake?"

"It's big, Kate. What *hacker* friend did you invent the other day?"

Kate was silent for a moment. "I had to tell her something. I thought I was helping her."

"Ops room. Now."

The dorm basement had been sealed off for over a decade, hidden behind rogue bamboo that no-one could be assed to tame. Kara stepped under the heavy chain and padlock and the CCTV camera poised on the door frame whirred, tracking her. She waved, feeling for the panel inset into the metal door with her other hand. The screen backlit her face in neon blue as she plugged in the eight numbers. The phone number for Fat Tony's. They did a great thin crust.

The door had barely sealed behind her when Kate accosted her. "What the hell is going on?"

Kara shoved past her sister and dumped her bag by the glowing central wall of monitors.

"You practically shoved her out the door!" Kara said. "Robyn's not crazy, Kate. These children do exist. She freaking found one."

"You're shitting me."

Kara sank into her chair and wheeled to her station. Screens flickered to life. "She just got caught in the middle of a shoot-out in suburban Durham because of a kid with a bear."

"That Fletcher kid?" Kate crossed her arms. "A bear," she repeated lamely.

"There." Kara tapped at the keyboard to bring up the article.

Double murder in Durham. Local professor Rob Lowman and wife Denise found dead, son Fletcher missing and feared dead. A photo of a wooden house, the clearing covered in police unspooling crime scene tape. *Police are asking anyone with information to please come forward.*

"Shit," said Kate.

"Robyn's out in these woods somewhere." Kara pulled up a topographical map of North Carolina. "We need to figure out who's hunting her."

Kate nodded. "And why. *Jesus*, Robyn." Kate rolled her shoulders and pulled up her chair. "Who else knows about Robyn's research? I didn't even know her crackpot theory until the other day."

"She doesn't talk to her family about her research." Kara's fingers sped over the keyboard. "So that leaves –"

"Yeah, her supervisor," finished Kate. "I'm on it."

The heady cheesy scent of pizza made her head swim, and Kara almost regretted the midnight dash to Fat Tony's. The box lay open on the table where the congealed mozzarella caught the glare of the harsh fluorescent tubes. The basement was their space. The ops room. She and her sister built the bank of computers from scratch. Programming was easy money; the real challenge was intel. People paid a king's ransom for the right information, and Kara and her sister were experts at finding it. For the right price.

Kara sighed. She'd spent hours working out the feasibility of routes through the Great Smoky Mountains National Park, but the bear posed a problem. A big hairy one.

"Okay, I think I'm ready," said Kate, waving with a drooping slice of salami. "Shit, you're not going to believe this."

Kara rested her hands on the back of Kate's computer chair. "The supervisor?"

"Yeah, Brock. His email is encrypted, but I chipped my way in. He's been sending off weekly reports about

Robyn for nearly two years."

"Two years?" *The length of Robyn's PhD so far.* Kara's grip on the chair tightened. "What sort of stuff?"

"Lab results: pages and pages of data. Robyn's mood, the compounds she's doodling in her notebook. Everything. He keeps mentioning some program."

Kara shivered. "Brock?" This was the guy with a rota of knit cardigans. Robyn looked after his cats when he went away. "Brock is *spying* on Robyn?"

Kate pulled up a company website crowded with lab-coated scientists in spacious laboratories. "Introducing the Mitochondrial Research Institute, or MRI, located in Washington DC."

Kara stared at the screen as her sister continued. The idea that some man was watching Robyn made her sick to her stomach. Now she did regret the pizza; she didn't want to taste it again on the way back up.

"Ostensibly, the MRI is a non-profit organisation funding research into genetic diseases. Registered six years ago, it provides nominal quarterly returns, and just quietly exists." Kate guided her slice into her mouth and Kara swallowed past the bile in the back of her throat.

"What has this got to do with Robyn?" Kara said.

Robyn was just one student, plodding away in a shoebox lab on the edge of campus. In Australia.

Kate clicked on a page entitled *Current Research Students*. Five faces appeared. "Recognise anyone?"

There was a tight-lipped African-American guy, a tall blonde woman, a bespectacled, mussy-haired guy and a stern-looking Asian woman. Kara stared at the last photo.

Robyn smiled up at them, lab coat and all, with an accompanying bio about her research.

"Holy shit," breathed Kara. "What the hell have you got yourself mixed up in?"

"We need to find out as much as we can about the others," said Kate.

Kara looked more closely at the other four scientists, all of them strangers. "Yeah, we do."

8

Wild

Robyn's phone vibrated in her jeans pocket and she jerked awake. Even wearing every piece of warm clothing she'd stuffed in her backpack, she was still freezing. Fletcher was curled against Eva, a slack expression on his face. He looked toasty warm.

It was early morning, a crimson glow stealing around the edges of the cave, curls of moisture condensing in the air. Robyn dug her phone out with difficulty, the three jumpers making her movements stiff and wooden. *Like a proper scarecrow*, she thought with a grimace. She hated the childhood nickname.

A message from Kara listed four names:

Terence Jones, University of Edinburgh.
Catherine Heather, McGill University.
Derek Smith, Duke University.

Xiaofang Fisher, University of Beijing.

They meant absolutely nothing to Robyn. She scrolled down.

Brock is a plant – he's monitoring your research. Head for Derek, he's closest. Talk soon.

Robyn downloaded the military-grade map Kara had sent through, trying to commit the key points to memory while hoping her battery would last. Wishful thinking. It had a conniption at the huge file and went dark. Robyn jabbed at buttons but couldn't coerce it to restart.

"Damn it," she groaned.

Eva yawned, dislodging Fletcher completely. He sat up and stretched.

"Hey, I know where we're going," Robyn told him by way of a good morning. She so wanted Kara to be mistaken. Brock couldn't be mixed up in all of this. For one thing, he was all the way back in Canberra. Plus, his cats would never be so trusting. The Bombay and Persian were excellent judges of character.

Fletcher watched her. His eyes were puffy. Robyn wondered if he knew, or cared. "So?"

"Duke. There's another researcher there, like me." At

least, she hoped so. Was that what Kara meant? Robyn screwed her eyes shut, willing the map to surface. "I think we head northwest."

"Do you know them?"

"No," Robyn admitted. "I don't. But my friend thinks he's our best bet, and I trust her."

"Those men are probably still after us, and you want to pin our safety on some stranger." Fletcher's level voice made Robyn's stomach plummet.

"No, that's not what I want. But I don't think we have a choice. Either we stay here and get picked off eventually, or we hedge our bets with Derek."

Fletcher turned to Eva. Robyn found their silent exchanges unnerving. "Fine," Fletcher spat. "Eva can get us there. I've been there before, on a school trip."

Stuffing clothes into her backpack, Robyn got to her feet. "How long, do you think?"

"Four days."

"*Four days?*" Robyn repeated. Fletcher just nodded.

It turned out that cycling fitness didn't equate to hiking fitness. It must have been pure adrenaline that had carried her to the cave with Eva. Robyn's legs ached, and the straps of her backpack had worn angry red creases into her shoulders. Fletcher seemed to bounce beside Eva, the duo always ten paces ahead of her. She'd start running again, she decided. Just as soon as this was all over and she was back home. Though Canberra winters were bitter. Spring, definitely in the spring.

Fletcher turned and pointed. "There's a stream this way," he said in the clipped tone she'd become accustomed to over the last couple of days. Robyn nodded, picking her way down the slope behind Fletcher and Eva, keeping her distance.

It's my fault, she wanted to say, though she didn't understand why and doubted it would help him. *My plan sucks, and I don't have a clue what's going on*, wasn't much better.

The water was cool and clear, and she drank until her stomach felt bloated. Exhausted, Robyn lay on the grass and watched the trees dance in the breeze.

"Hey, Robyn."

Robyn tipped her head back, narrowing her eyes against the glare. Fletcher sat wedged on a high branch holding an orange frisbee. Blinking, she sat up.

"What are you doing?" she asked. Fletcher waved the

frisbee above his head. A stack of orange discs protruded from the trunk above him.

"Chicken of the woods. Can I throw them down to you?"

Robyn pulled the bottom of her shirt out, a makeshift net. "Sure. I can't make any promises, but I'll try."

Only one disc was obliterated, shattering into angry, soggy pieces by Robyn's feet. The mushrooms she'd managed to catch wafted butterscotch into the air and left orange fuzz on her shirt. Fletcher shimmied down the tree, stopping to kneel at the base before returning with a handful of greenery.

"Dandelion greens," he said, holding them aloft. "Eva says they're good to eat."

Taraxacum officinale. Robyn recognised the indented leaves, even though it had been a while since she'd rooted around in the garden with her mother. Too long.

Eva huffed by the stream, splashing a paw now and then.

"No fish," Fletcher said. "But we'll still eat well."

The mushrooms did taste like chicken. Robyn's mouth was watering by the time the rough skewers had cooked. The firm, pink flesh seared with charcoal filled her belly, and the bitter green leaves left a familiar tang on her tongue.

Robyn shivered in the cool night air despite her multiple layers. Fletcher and Eva shared another one of their silent glances.

"What?" Robyn sighed, tired of being the third wheel. "I wish you'd just talk to me."

"Eva says you should sleep with us tonight." Fletcher met her eyes, a trace of softness in his voice.

Robyn nodded, not sure if she could handle another night of cold seeping into her bones. She'd take any truce measure that involved warmth.

Eva's thick fur against her back felt better than any sleeping bag. They slept head-to-toe against Eva's belly, and Robyn drifted off to sleep dreaming of four other people in her laboratory, poking around and making a general nuisance of themselves. *Derek. Terence. Catherine. Xiaofang.*

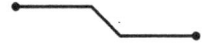

Fletcher twitched in his sleep as the now-familiar dream overtook him. Their faces changed in a collage of time and place. Icy plains, misty forests, dark city alleyways. Fletcher blitzed through them like an old-fashioned slide projector. *Click click click*. Strange clothing of times long past, a cacophony of languages. Different faces, but somehow familiar. A thread of something, like spotting a friend's face in a crowd but looking up into the eyes of a stranger when you tapped them on the shoulder. *Click*.

Fletcher always woke clinging to the thread of two faces: the girl with the tiny lizard and the boy hunched beneath an enormous bird of prey. They reached out toward him, calling his name.

On the third morning, Fletcher twigged. *There are others, aren't there?*

Yes. There is also a walker of the air and the sea. Eva finished his thought. *We must find them.*

Fletcher rolled the words in his mind. *Earth, air and sea.* Robyn sighed in her sleep, nestled into Eva's abdomen. Shaggy curls of caramel fur hung over Robyn's side. Something in him had eased, though he couldn't name it. What happened might be Robyn's fault, but he felt certain she could help them. He didn't have anything to go back to now.

Fletcher nudged her shoulder. "Robyn."

She groaned and brought her knees to her chest. "Robyn," he repeated.

Eva huffed lightly and Robyn sat up, leaning against the bear's warm flank.

"I'm up," she mumbled, running a hand through her hair, looking anything but awake.

"Can your science explain what's happening between Eva and me?" Fletcher asked. He moved to the fire, blowing on the coals to coax them back into life.

Robyn stretched her arms above her head but didn't get up. Eva began to hum, and Fletcher closed his eyes for a moment, enjoying the way the sound relaxed him.

Robyn caught the brunt of it, her shoulders dropping. A vertical shaft of light flickered across her right eye then disappeared. Fletcher blinked, not sure if he'd imagined it or not.

"Maybe." Robyn twisted her hands in her lap. "I don't know, Fletcher. To be honest, I'm still freaking out. When I came to your house, I wasn't expecting to find this." Robyn stroked Eva's belly as her voice softened. "I don't want anything to happen to you or Eva. I don't want you to end up in some laboratory."

Robyn flopped back against Eva.

"There are two more of us."

Robyn's head snapped back up. "More?"

Fletcher nodded. *Air and sea*, he thought.

"I promise I'll do everything I can. It starts with finding Derek, working out who's after you."

Fletcher dropped more twigs on the coals. "Us," he clarified. "The people who are after *us*."

9

Derek

"What about Robyn?"

"No sign of her. We barely cleaned the scene before the local police arrived. The bodies were torn apart by animals, Brock. More than one. This new candidate is much stronger than I envisaged. Can you imagine the power his DNA could give us?"

"I'm still not convinced it's a power we deserve, Miranda."

"Your concern for the girl is misplaced. If the power exists, it deserves to be utilised."

"For every action, there is an equal and opposite reaction."

"Don't quote Newton at me, Brock. Nature's laws are broken and rewritten by every subsequent generation. What we are doing is no different.

Darwin, Margulis. This has existed within us for millennia, shrouded and forgotten as time marched on. You're not a religious man, are you, Brock, I forget this."

"No."

"This transcends all of our limited human perception of spirits, of gods to be worshipped. These children? They hold the key inside them. We are simply taking it. They'll remember us, Brock. It will be the beginning of a new era."

"History is not always kind to its subjects, Miranda."

Derek shoved the keycard into his back pocket as the door slammed shut behind him. Dusk seeped up from the ground, the trees turning a sweet auburn in the growing darkness. Derek barely noticed it; he was too busy replaying the conversation with his supervisor as he strode away from the biology department.

Haven't you finished the target synthesis yet? Surely the genetic mapping, at least?

No.

What do you mean, no?

Not yet. I'm working as hard as I can.

Well, it's clearly not hard enough.

The wall behind Vulcan was plastered in certificates like you see in a doctor's surgery. Shiny frames and calligraphy glared down at Derek, a constant reminder that even if he finished his doctorate, he'd never be a real doctor. Not that he needed it – his father was reminder enough. Derek gritted his teeth. It will never be enough. Scattered data and piecemeal maps of mitochondrial genes aren't enough. Vulcan's close to chucking him off the program, he can feel it. The late night phone calls, the overseas trips. His supervisor was around less and less. Just like his faith in Derek's ability.

Another disappointment.

Derek felt like screaming into the darkness. Instead, he pulled out his phone with shaking hands.

"Maria," he said.

"Derek." Warmth flooded her voice. "Hang on one second, Damian's just finished dinner."

There was a scraping noise in the background. Derek took a deep breath, clenched and unclenched his free fist.

"Okay, he's here."

"Hey, buddy," Derek said.

The response came as a high-pitched shriek.

Derek imagined the grin breaking out across his older brother's face.

"I just wanted to say hi. I'm sorry I haven't been to visit for a while. It's been busy, which isn't really a good excuse."

A disjointed clapping sound followed a strangled gurgle.

"It's hard, actually. Much harder than I thought it would be." Derek sighed. "Anyway, enough about me. What have you been up to?"

The stress fell away as he listened to Damian's burbling, punctuated now and then by loud claps. By the time he neared home, Maria's voice came back over the line.

"Bedtime, sorry, Derek. Say goodbye, Damian."

Another shriek.

"Goodnight, buddy, talk again soon."

The phone fell silent. Derek closed his eyes, breathing in the crisp night air. He'd missed the sunset.

"That's him." Derek whirled around at the voice,

feeling disoriented after talking to Damian. It was another world, where he could divine happiness and anger in a string of moans and hiccups.

"Hello?" he said into the darkness. He could just make out his apartment block on the edge of Duke Forest, well-lit and welcoming. He licked his lips. "Who's there?" Leftover lasagne and a glass of red called his name.

The forest edge rustled and a sapling sheared onto the footpath. Derek took a step backward.

"You go first –"

"Robyn, no –"

Derek stared as two people stumbled out from the trees: a woman and a teenage boy. Derek blinked, seeing Rebecca's face for a moment. He bit his lip as the woman stepped forward, worrying the end of a frayed shoulder strap. She had Rebecca's dark hair, but the likeness ended there. The woman's jeans were splattered with mud and the bridge of her nose was sunburnt. The strip of red made her dark hair stand out like the edge of an eclipse.

The unexpected rush of bitterness hit him in the gut. He hadn't thought about Rebecca in weeks, but maybe the songs were right. Once cheated, twice shy.

"Derek Smith?" The woman stepped into the street light. Now that he could see her properly, the fleeting resemblance evaporated.

"Yes?" he managed. He wondered if he could make it to the sanctuary of the apartment complex if he turned and ran, right now.

"I need to talk to you about your research," not-Rebecca said as she took another step toward him.

Derek paused in his mental calculations. "You're interested in *my* research?" *Yeah, right.* "Look, I don't have any money on me." Derek shifted from one foot to the other. It wasn't that far to his apartment.

A rustling behind the woman made Derek look over not-Rebecca's shoulder. A mass of cinnamon fur lurched out and the boy shuffled backward. Derek choked back a scream as he raised a hand to point at the animal.

A bear.

The boy ran a hand against the bear's golden flank. The animal raised its head and sniffed the air with a twitching wet nose, as if it were a German Shepherd and Derek's accusing finger was entirely uncalled for. Not-Rebecca stood only several yards in front, but she'd barely batted an eyelid.

Derek stared over his quivering finger. He'd seen bears before, but glimpses on the running trails outside the university didn't compare to this. It came up to the boy's shoulder, wide-set shoulders rippling as it shook its fur. Droplets of water flicked onto Derek's clothes, carrying the earthy scent of humus and lichen. Wiping his face with his shirtsleeve, Derek chanced another glance sideways. Over 400 yards to home. He's fast – hundreds of frustrated hours pounding the trails had made him springy. He had no doubt he could outrun not-Rebecca and the boy, but the bear was another story. The beast was calm now, but if he ran he might provoke it.

Maybe it's a rescued animal. Derek's brain whirred through scenarios, each more unlikely than the last. *They've sprung it from a zoo. From a research lab. Russian circus.*

I'm going to live for both of us, buddy. He'd never said it aloud to Damian, but it was true. According to all the gatekeepers in his life, Derek was doing a crappy job so far. Failed to get into medicine, hold onto a girlfriend, and now struggling to stay on the genetics PhD program. Damian was the only one who didn't judge.

"What do you want?" Derek felt that still being on his feet was a good sign. The bear looked up at him with inquisitive green eyes.

Not-Rebecca took another step forward, arms wide as if calming a wild animal. Derek almost laughed. *Like I am the crazy one in this scenario.*

"We're not going to hurt you. Please. Is there somewhere we can talk?"

Derek nodded. "Yeah." *What the hell.* "This way."

The side door buckled as Eva squeezed herself into Derek's apartment. Reversing into the battered screen door, she wailed and hung her head. Fletcher twirled a hand in her fur and she quieted.

Fletcher shrugged at Robyn. "It's not her fault, really."

Robyn glanced toward the kitchen, where Derek stared into the illuminated depths of the refrigerator. She tripped over a box in the hallway as she leaned the twisted metal against the wall. Rubbing her throbbing foot, she catalogued its contents: books, half-full packet of tampons, a dress. *Not Derek's, then.*

Fletcher bounded across to the sofa. "You play?" He held up a singlet with *Smith* emblazoned on the back, above the number 3. Robyn stepped over the box and emerged into the living room, then made a beeline for the kitchen.

Derek yanked a container out of the fridge and dumped it in the microwave. "Yeah." Robyn smelled basil.

"Cool," answered Fletcher. Eva stood motionless in the centre of the living room, sniffing the air. Leather polish and red wine were all Robyn picked up over the strong herby aroma – a far cry from the nursing home fug of her own apartment, furnished exclusively from Vinnies and the Salvos. Robyn wondered how many little old ladies had watched *The Bold and the Beautiful* from her mismatched couches, only to never get up again. She'd shell out for steam cleaning when she got back. Running and cleaning. She could do this.

Derek stared at Eva. Robyn wondered if he was high on something, letting them into his place and reheating dinner, as if this had been on his calendar for weeks. Nobody except Kara came to Robyn's apartment, and even then only to drag Robyn out of it.

The least she could do was to introduce herself properly. "It's Robyn." She held out a hand to Derek.

He eyed her for a second before accepting the offer. Nope, the guy was with it. Just distant, closed off. His grip was firm.

"Derek, although you already seem to know that."

An accusation. The microwave dinged, and Derek turned back to it. Tomatoey steam clouded the kitchen.

"Where are the plates?" Robyn asked, moving behind him. The smell of food clouded every other thought.

"Second drawer, by the sink."

They matched. Robyn had never owned a matching set of anything in her life.

They ate in silence, the lasagne like manna after four days in the forest. Robyn closed her eyes, rolling the flavours around her tongue. Four days. Her eyes widened as she chewed her last mouthful. She needed to call Kara.

She rifled through her backpack and plugged her charger in. The mobile pinged back to life.

"I need to call somebody. I'll be able to explain everything soon." Robyn hoped so, anyway. "Fletcher, can you –"

"Yeah." Fletcher stacked their plates. "I'll give him the run down."

"Kara." Robyn brought her knees to her chest, tethered by the cord.

"Jesus, Robyn, you had us freaking out," said Kara. "Where the hell are you? It's been what, like five days?"

Robyn glanced up at Derek and Fletcher, deep in conversation at the sink.

"We made it to Derek. Look, I've been going crazy trying to figure out what's going on. People have *died*, Kara, and I don't have a clue why."

"Brock. He's not what he seems, Robyn. I know you think the sun shines out of his –" Kate's voice. After a scuffle, Kara's voice sounded on the line again.

"He's part of some organisation tracking mitochondrial research all around the world. Tracking students like you, Robyn. Derek is the same. So are all those other students."

Catherine. Terence. Xiaofang. The names she'd been repeating in her mind like a litany with each step through the woods.

"They're using our research? That makes no sense. I've barely made any progress." Robyn peeked over her shoulder at Derek, took in his hunched shoulders. Defeat, her constant friend. She knew what it felt like.

"Well, you've certainly got their attention now," said Kara. "Be careful, Robyn."

Robyn clicked on the link Kara had sent through. The Mitochondrial Research Institute. Robyn stared at the four faces. Derek is solemn even in his portrait, no teeth visible in his tight-lipped smile. *Catherine, Terence, Xiaofang.* How is it possible she's linked to these people she's never met? Robyn felt like ramming her fist into the plasterboard by her elbow. Instead, she got to her feet and politely asked to be directed to the bathroom.

The shower was heaven. Robyn moaned with pleasure as she worked the dirt and grease from her hair. Derek had laid out tracksuit pants and a clean t-shirt while the washing machine did its best with her soiled clothes. She watched the filthy water shuck and spin as she towelled herself dry with one of those thick bath sheets she'd always lingered over at Kmart. She had to give it to him, he was quiet, serious maybe, but the man had class.

Head clearer, she stopped outside the spare room, pushing the door ajar. Fletcher lay splayed across the bed, Eva curled up on the floor beside him. The door creaked as she closed it, but neither of them moved.

She found Derek sipping wine at the dining table, her chromatograms spread out in front of him.

"I've never seen anything like this," he murmured, pouring her a glass. Too late, Robyn opened her mouth to stop him. She sniffed, took a sip, tried not to cough. "Neither have I." She put the wine glass down. "Did Fletcher –"

"Yes, as well as he was able. It sounds ridiculous, yet …"

"Eva," Robyn said.

Derek tapped the table top, eyes still on the data. "Yes, Eva." Pushing his chair back, Derek straightened. Robyn tried another tentative sip of wine. Spluttering, she tipped the liquid into Derek's glass, hoping he wouldn't notice. She crossed her legs on the chair. The tracksuit pants fit well. Robyn wondered if they'd been missed when the box in the hallway was packed.

"I'm looking for mutations on specific genes, trying to figure out a way to screen for genetic anomalies." Derek brought a laptop back to the table, took a long sip of his wine. "The key word is *trying*. My supervisor isn't happy with my progress."

"Supervisor/monitor, you mean."

"Apparently." Derek swivelled the laptop so they could both see the screen. "I've got partial maps of several mitochondrial gene mutations. Maybe your rogue compounds fit into this somehow."

Robyn took in the 3D string of amino acids. "You've got access to a DNA sequencer?"

Derek nodded, still looking at the model. Robyn resisted the urge to whistle in appreciation. Derek would probably think it juvenile.

"We need to figure this out," said Robyn. "They're willing to kill for whatever it is, Derek." Robyn's headache flared back to life. "Why us? I just don't get it. I haven't found anything until now, and it's not like I understand it."

"Don't worry, you're in good company." Derek closed his laptop and cupped his chin with a sigh.

Robyn noticed the dark circles under his eyes.

"Fletcher and Eva seem to be part of it. I mean, who wouldn't want to figure out what makes such a bond possible? If this group get their hands on them, who knows what they could do with their DNA."

Robyn baulked.

"They could figure out a way to make others like him. Can you imagine having the power to control living creatures? A lot of people would pay for the privilege, not all of them good." Derek sighed. "You concentrate on finding these other students. I'll see what I can do in the lab without drawing suspicion."

"Thank you," Robyn said. Her head spun. This was insane. The safe bubble of her lab routines felt like a distant memory.

Derek shook his head. "I haven't done anything yet, so there's no point thanking me. I might not be any use at all."

"I get this feeling that you're going to help us, though." Robyn toyed with the stem of her empty wineglass. "Why?"

Derek drank some more wine, frowning at the full glass. "My research ... I can't do it on my own. Maybe with all of us, we can work it out. Solve the puzzle."

Robyn yawned. "Okay." She could sense the half-truth despite the tiredness that clouded her mind.

Derek tipped his head toward the hall. "My room is the first one on the left. It's yours."

"No, I couldn't possibly –" Robyn began.

"I insist."

Robyn collapsed into bed and wrapped herself in the down duvet. It smelled of aniseed. Derek, it smelled like Derek.

The aroma of eggs lured Robyn out of her liquorice den. In the daylight, Derek's room was even more minimalist than she'd imagined. Sleek cabinets, monochrome everything. Robyn couldn't help opening the wardrobe and running a hand along the hangers. Organised by colour and season, a spectrum of long shirts to casual tees. Ironed, too. Feeling guilty, she pushed the doors shut. The iron her mother had bought her in first year still lingered in its original packaging at the back of her closet.

When she emerged, Fletcher was demolishing a plate of eggs at the table. Robyn smelled buttered toast.

"Morning," she said. "Nice outfit."

Fletcher lifted the edge of the basketball singlet. "Derek let me borrow some stuff."

Derek carried over two laden plates. He planted one

in front of Robyn and grinned at her expression. "And I thought you'd both appreciate a proper breakfast."

Robyn nodded her agreement as she forked a hunk of herby scrambled egg into her mouth. In the kitchen, Eva eyed a frozen packet of fish with interest. Derek followed Robyn's gaze.

"I'll pick up supplies today," he promised. "I'm not really stocked for bear visitors."

Robyn put down her fork. "Are you sure ... I mean, we could find somewhere else to stay."

"You're more than welcome to stay here." Derek took a bite of toast.

"You don't even know us," Robyn said.

Derek didn't say anything as he sliced his omelette. "Not yet," he said as he brought a wedge to his mouth. "Though apparently we're stuck with the same group, this MRI. That makes us comrades-in-arms, at least."

Eva wailed from the kitchen, pawing the Styrofoam container. The fish slid further down the counter.

"Yeah, I just can't imagine my supervisor being in on this," said Robyn. Fletcher got up from the table and chucked the fish in the microwave. Eva snorted her approval.

"My supervisor can be a pushy moron, but he's smart." Derek pointed his fork at her. "I'm going to have to be careful in the lab. They must know about you now."

"Going rogue? I guess so." Robyn sighed and rubbed her temples. She'd never been the misbehaving type. The Goody-two-shoes Scarecrow. *Rogue researcher* didn't fit the mould.

Derek jerked his head toward the living room. "Your clothes are clean." Robyn tilted in her chair to take in the washing basket of neatly folded clothes. When she turned her attention back to her plate, Derek was hoovering up the last of his breakfast. Had Derek folded her underwear too? The thought made her blush.

"I better get to work." Derek dumped his plate in the sink just as the microwave dinged. Eva lunged forward, snapping at the fish and wolfing it down in two huge bites. She nuzzled the microwave for more, then huffed and turned back to the living room.

"One rule," said Derek, holding up his hand. "No bears on the couch."

Eva moaned and curled up on the carpet.

10

Catherine

Robyn stepped off the bus with a grateful sigh, even though the freezing air took her breath away. The overnight Greyhound bus had been an experience. Her neighbour had flicked peanut shells onto her lap for at least four hours. Robyn dusted her hands through her hair as a guy encased in a hood threw her a weird look. She sighed as she flicked the brown shell onto the pavement. *Figures.*

Pulling out her phone, Robyn checked the address for the sixth time. Snippets of French swirled in the air above the crush of people. If only she'd paid more attention in French class. After the New Caledonia trip had been cancelled, she hadn't really cared about her proficiency. The near-deaf teacher would nod if you could pull off an accent-tinged sentence in English.

Robyn nearly crossed herself at the memory.

A cloud of pot smoke hit her as she passed Mount Royal. It seemed out of place here, Montreal only just emerging from winter. She imagined a knot of kids hunched over a joint, stamping their feet against the cold. Robyn uncreased the map and oriented herself. Her shitty French wouldn't be any use here. She hoped that Catherine could speak English, and that she wasn't a pothead.

Peering at the numbers on the door, Robyn bumped into a blonde-haired girl. *32–38, 40–46.*

"Sorry," Robyn said.

The girl jangled her keys, found the one she was looking for. She tucked a stray strand behind her ear. "That's okay." She looked up. "Who are you after?"

"Catherine Heather."

The girl froze. "Pardon?"

"She's a PhD student at McGill," Robyn continued.

"I know." The girl turned to face Robyn. "I'm Catherine. Who the hell are you?"

Robyn faltered. "It's a lot to explain. Do you mind if I come up?"

Catherine didn't say anything for a long moment. Robyn blushed as Catherine stared at her. She was a good foot taller than Robyn and a mess of bracelets ran up her left arm. Carved wood and jade.

Catherine sighed and turned the key. "Fine."

Robyn swirled her mint tea, admiring the tessellated pattern on the rose-coloured glass. She'd never attempted a pilaf before, never mind one stuffed with pistachios and hunks of grilled eggplant. Every time Robyn bought eggplant from the co-op, it moulded in the fridge before she could figure out what to do with it. A big slimy mess in the vegetable drawer, mocking her.

Catherine sipped her tea, eyes clouded with thought. Robyn's chromatograms were certainly clocking up some miles. A photo of Derek, Fletcher and Eva in Derek's living room had now joined the collection. The carpet was a jagged, ripped mess courtesy of Eva's claws, something Photoshop couldn't superimpose.

Catherine's focus was gene therapy targets, mutations involved in energy metabolism. It was more chemistry than biology, so they spoke a common language – as well as English, thank God. Drug use still to be determined.

The apartment was filled with bright tapestries, and stacks of books covered every surface. It reminded her of a gypsy caravan but stuffed into four walls high above the street.

Catherine shifted in her seat and her knees brushed Robyn's under the tiny table. "Sorry, I don't entertain much up here," she said, gesturing to the kitchen. "Especially strangers claiming my research is being directed by an international group of bad guys." Catherine pushed the photo toward Robyn. "And you say there are more of these children?"

Robyn nodded. She can't say, *Yeah, Fletcher totally had a dream about it*. For some reason, it seemed right. Like she'd always known there would be more. Robyn snuffed out the thought as Catherine's eyes bore into hers. Teal. Not quite green, not quite blue. The colour of the sea as a storm breaks.

"I'll keep my eyes open, but that's really all I can do." Catherine slid her phone across the table. "I'll let you know if anything unusual happens, or if I hear anything that could be helpful." Robyn typed in her number and was about to pass the phone back when it vibrated in her hand. *Sophie, incoming call.*

Catherine took the phone back and grimaced. "I have to take this."

She walked out onto the balcony, sending a draught of cool air curling inside. Robyn yawned and rinsed her mug before turning her attention to the plates. It was the least she could do. She didn't mean to eavesdrop, but the sound carried through the open door and into the kitchen.

She heard Catherine hiss, "Sophie, I'm sorry, but it's *over*."

Robyn scrubbed at the stubborn grains of rice that clung to the bottom of the pot.

"You were the one who left, remember? Goodnight, Sophie. You can't keep calling me like this."

Robyn put the pot next to the sink to drain. The door clicked shut, and Catherine joined her with a tea towel.

"Sorry about that." Catherine ran a finger through her hair.

"No worries," Robyn said. "A friend?"

Catherine snorted, then clapped a hand over her mouth. "Ex-girlfriend."

"Oh," Robyn failed to hide her surprise. *Catherine doesn't look gay*, she thought to herself, then instantly regretted her prejudice. She always edged around the LGBT stall at market day, wavering in the face of so many half-shaved heads and rainbow tie-dye shirts and dresses. She admired their self-assurance but shrank away from it at the same time.

Catherine plucked the pot from the draining board and encased it in the tea towel. "You're welcome to stay here, tonight."

"That would be incredible, thank you. As long as I'm not intruding …" Robyn began.

"You're not intruding on anything. Honestly."

Wrapped in a woollen blanket on the couch, Robyn wondered what Sophie looked like, if Catherine had cooked for her, too. She pushed the thought away.

Three down, two to go.

11

Eli

The room was all white; blinding pale tiles and concrete floor. Eli cradled his left arm at the elbow. The splotched teal galaxy there was beginning to bloom with an algal green. They'd taken so much blood. His head thudded as he strained to feel Una, following the veins that stuck out against his skin with his fingers. Maybe they'd suck him dry, like an insect caught in a spider's web. A slow death.

It had been three weeks. Twenty-one days. Una's mind was a faint thread that sometimes disappeared for hours on end. The longest separation he'd ever endured. Ever. Eli rubbed his temples as the door opened with a thump, the security mechanism grating with a metallic screech. He held his arm out again for the needle. Every morning. He knew the drill.

The hallway was full of people in lab coats. They bustled past him in a blur of faces and starched collars. You didn't linger in the corridor. The thin scientist who'd taken his blood sample pushed him into the crowd, his constant babysitter shadow. Eli shuffled head down to the cafeteria, a long room with splotchy linoleum packed with folding tables. He wondered if it had been a real school at one point. It reminded him of the dining halls of American movies. Legions scattered in a strict hegemony, food fights and mac and cheese, brighter than chamomile flowers. Here, there were no alliances. The other kids didn't speak to him. No-one talked. They ate quickly, eyes down. Minds flitted against his own, disappearing before he could latch on, communicate with them. The place must be full of animals but he never saw them. The absence was painful. No updates on fledglings, wind currents, the feeling of bursting through a cotton-wool cloud, soaked to the skin. Eli's mind felt like an empty cage.

When he finished breakfast, his babysitter came to collect him.

"This way."

Instead of turning back toward his cell, he pushed

Eli down the corridor in the opposite direction. The change in routine sent a jolt of hope through Eli's chest. *Something is happening.*

Heading toward the door, Eli's hand skittered against the crook of his elbow. He'd never been past the end of the long corridor before. The thrum of voices escalated as he stepped into a wide, open atrium. Eli blinked. He saw trees through a huge glass door and a road streaming with traffic. It was much brighter than he remembered. He moved toward the light. He'd never been indoors for this long in his entire life. His skin itched for the sun, for a breeze, anything.

His babysitter turned to talk to a woman at a high desk, leaving Eli unattended for a heartbeat. An insincere laugh rose behind him as the woman reacted to something the scientist said. Eli's legs twitched with the knowledge. He was so close; all he had to do was turn and run, get lost in the crowd. He was fast, he'd be out and away before anyone realised … He stopped, fingertips inches away from the glass. Una.

"Ahem." The lab coat gripped his shoulder, dug in with his fingers. "This way, kid."

He steered Eli away from the glass, past an identical

corridor stretching in the opposite direction. Eli filed the knowledge away as he was pushed through a door, the receptionist staring through him as if he didn't exist.

Maybe he didn't anymore.

Straightaway, anxious cries flooded his brain. The enormous space looked like an aircraft hanger on TV, sans planes. Children filled a line of chairs running through the centre. Some of them he recognised from the cafeteria. Tubes snaked from metal racks into their arms. Some slept, legs twitching. Others stared forward, nails digging into the sides of their chairs. Scientists moved between them, stopping only to scrawl in notepads or adjust the liquid flowing through the tubes.

What are they doing to them? Eli stared in horror at the blank, drugged faces.

Behind the children, cages set into the rear wall housed an orchestra of faint howls. The piteous moans rose through the cavernous space, but nobody seemed to notice. Silent wails filled his mind.

Help us.

Free us.

Kill me.

"Hurry up, kid." His babysitter thrust Eli into an office on the same floor. Eli's breakfast churned in his stomach as he digested the scene. He rubbed his shoulder, watching as the Chinese woman murmuring into her phone dismissed his babysitter. Screwing his eyes shut, Eli concentrated on separating the voices from his mind. It was harder without Una, but he managed to partition them like she'd taught him.

Help. Free. Kill.

"Eli, hello." The woman stood and gestured to the chair opposite her desk. Eli sat, clasping his hands together in his lap. She was younger than the other lab coats. Pretty.

"My name is Xiaofang, but you may call me Fang." Fang sat down again. "It's good to finally meet you."

Eli said nothing. He knew spiders drew in their prey, cooed to them even as they wrapped them in silk, the little embalmed bodies jerking far too late.

Fang leaned forward and placed her elbows on the desk. "I wanted to talk to you about your osprey. What do you call her?"

Eli swallowed. "Her name is Una." He searched the thrum of voices again, but he couldn't feel her.

"She's not out in the main experimental area," Fang confirmed, as if reading his mind. "How old were you when you met her?"

"Twelve." His father carried the osprey fledgling tucked inside his woollen hat, found on a cold spring morning in the remnants of a nest dashed against the rocks. When Una had stepped onto his palm, a shockwave of pain had quivered through his body. Locking eyes on him, her voice had filled his head. *My name is Una, young air walker.* Her absence ached like a phantom limb. His father had described the pain once: how he went to use the leg, the shock fresh each time before he remembered its absence. Losing Una felt the same.

"What is this place?" Eli asked. He imagined Fang spooling silk, suffocating him. He might as well ask while he still had air.

Fang finished writing her notes, continuing as if he hadn't uttered a word. "You're from the Mongolian steppe, is that right?"

Eli nodded into his lap. They knew this. He'd still be herding with his father if these people hadn't taken him away. The scholarship had been a cruel lie.

"Traditional hunting with your father," Fang elaborated.

Eli nodded. "Yes, but mainly for the tourists in the summer." This year they'd saved enough to replace the solar panels on the yurt. Eli wondered if his father had finished installing them yet; if anyone helped in Eli's absence. Maybe the panels are even still wrapped in rugs, the English incomprehensible to his parents. The thought brought angry tears to his eyes. Eli blinked them away as Fang spoke again.

"As I understand it, your routine was quite exceptional." Fang watched him closely.

More than exceptional. Ospreys are unusual compared to the falcons most of the nomads trained. With their connection, Una had been extraordinary in full flight. Word spread. "Ospreys are very intelligent birds," Eli said. "And my father is an excellent trainer."

"I wonder if it's purely training."

"Of course." Eli forced a laugh. The room felt closed in, like a cocoon, too warm. Sweat beaded at his temples.

Then he felt her. Eli grasped the desperate brush of her mind. *Una*, he projected, flooding the thought with all his anguish.

Little one, stay strong. It will hurt.

What will —

The pain seemed to erupt at the same time all over his body, his legs jerking as the muscles contracted and released. Eli fell out of his chair, couldn't stop his head from colliding with the ground. Una was close by; he could feel her. Eli closed his eyes, flitting into Una's mind. The sensation was a momentary relief, almost as if he had stepped back into his family's yurt, his home. The smell of curing pelts and mare's milk reached his nostrils.

The pain didn't stop; long, jarring bursts of it. He saw lab coats holding Una down, the rod singing her flesh, talons rising to rake empty air.

Abruptly, it stopped. The spasms abated. Eli heaved in breath as Una's presence disappeared. The metallic recirculated air made him gag. He swallowed and tasted iron. Wiping his mouth on his sleeve, he left a jagged bloody smear.

"I don't think training can explain a shared pain response," Fang continued at her desk after Eli had pulled himself from the floor onto his hands and knees. His arms wobbled as he strained to hold the position.

"Now, I'm going to ask you some more questions, and you're going to answer them."

Still on the floor, Eli nodded. It was only a matter of time until he was eaten alive. He wondered how much Fang already knew.

When the boy was escorted out, Fang opened the window; the lingering smell of scorched flesh was off-putting. Eli. She couldn't pinpoint the compounds in his distinctive blood work. Fang stared at the chromatogram for the umpteenth time, willing the two peaks to resolve into something, anything.

Eli was special, the Chief had been right, even if Fang was not on board with the Chief's wishy-washy spirit mojo. Fang pushed the chromatogram back into her folder. No, this is hard science. This, she can crack.

Someone knocked on the door. "Fang? The meeting is about to start."

"I'm on my way."

Fang smoothed her jacket as she strode through the experimental area. Heads nodded in her direction and she acknowledged them with a tip of her chin. The children were docile, only mildly drugged but used to the routine. They were being given a new spectrum of compounds this week. Fang paused on the stairs as one of the subjects vomited, yanking her IV with her. The blonde girl kicked out at the scientist who reached down to help her. Leaning on the balustrade, Fang watched as the girl ran a few hesitant steps, tripped and fell to her knees. Dragged back to her seat, the girl didn't protest, head lolling onto her shoulders. A name wafted up the stairs, and Fang tested it on her tongue. Sara. She'd keep an eye on that one too. She liked spirit.

The conference table filled the long boardroom; it was scattered with papers and mugs of coffee. Fang took a seat beside a broad man in a navy sweater.

"Brock," she said.

The MRI agent nodded before returning his attention to the female figure pacing the room. Miranda. The Chief Director could be terrifying. Fang admired that about her. One day, she will command a room like this.

"How is it possible that you failed to capture a young woman, a boy and a juvenile brown bear? Twenty men. You had *twenty men*. The trail has gone completely cold."

Fang cocked her head as the soldier blushed scarlet. He'd grabbed her ass the first time the reactionary team had been on site for transport, and Fang had nearly broken his wrist. He didn't have any snide comments this morning. Fang tried in vain to remember his name; she was pleased that he wasn't memorable enough for her to have retained the information.

"Nobody ever said anything about a bear. It was the bloody bobcats that did it, just came out of nowhere ..."

Murmurs rose around the table. *A bear.* An interesting animal partner. Brock rubbed the bridge of his nose and kept silent. Robyn's chromatograms for the new subject matched Eli's exactly.

"Derek's research time has increased exponentially," said Vulcan. Fang assessed him, a mountain of a man, hard eyes set into a military-grade buzz cut.

"You've been riding him too hard. It's to be expected." Miranda stopped pacing and uncapped a bottle of water. "But we can't afford any more mistakes." She sipped water and jerked her head toward the soldier. "Check it out, discreetly."

The soldier nodded, cheeks still red. "Yes, ma'am."

Miranda addressed the grey-haired woman on

Brock's right. "Weaving? Any developments?"

The woman shook her head. "His mother just passed away and he's gone home to Wales. I expect him to be absent for several weeks."

"Regrettable. Make sure Terence doesn't linger."

The rotund agent wedged next to Weaving cleared his throat. "Catherine is proving amenable to the genes you suggested. No real changes to report," he wheezed.

"Thank you, Deckker." Miranda caught Fang's gaze, nodded.

Fang sat up a little straighter, zinging with pride.

"Fang. Can you provide a report on progress here." A statement, not a question.

Fang swivelled in her chair and faced the other agents. "The scholarship scheme has been extremely effective. The boy, Eli, is our most suitable candidate. We are still working on identifying several elusive compounds and tracing the exact genetic loci on which the mutation lies." She drummed her fingertips on the table. "In the meantime, we are moving forward with our activation trials, applying broad-range mutation targets to the other children."

"Like chemotherapy?" Deckker said.

Fang nodded. "Same principle, yes."

"Is it working?" Brock asked.

"It is too early to tell," Fang replied. "It takes repeat exposure for successful activation to be observable, or –"

"Or death," finished Brock.

Fang nodded. "We'll know more definitively over the next week." Her heart leapt at the impressed expressions on the agents' faces.

"Excellent." Miranda glanced at her watch. "Let's get back to work."

The agents stood and gathered their folders. Fang watched as Miranda sent Brock a faint nod. Frowning, she clutched her papers to her chest. *What was that about?*

Miranda turned to her before she had time to process the strange exchange. "Fang, a moment."

Fang leaned forward in her chair. Miranda sat beside her, taking another sip of water.

"I am surrounded by incompetents," Miranda announced. The Chief hooked her silver hair behind her ears. "I'd be lost without you, Fang."

The first time she met her supervisor, they'd sat in the back of a dark sedan. Miranda had spelled it all out

– the chance to be part of the next genetic revolution with full experimental control, no limitations. The driver had pulled up in front of a gleaming, glass-fronted building. *Beijing International School.* She'd been based here ever since. Eighteen months. She wasn't naive, she knew Miranda had hedged her bets with others. But the others weren't self-aware. Fang made a point of avoiding hubris, but felt flattered nonetheless.

"Eli can speak to animals with the capacity for flight, and it appears this Fletcher is a vessel for those of the land." Miranda drained her water, crushing the empty container. "Judging by the swathe he cut through the reactionary team."

Fang closed her eyes for a moment. *Here we go again.* It weakened Miranda, this dependence on a spiritual domain. Eli possessed unique capabilities, but they were the result of evolutionary advance, rare gene mutations. They were not evidence of spirits.

"That leaves the girl, able to speak with creatures of the sea and lakes." Miranda pushed a folder across to Fang, collecting the little ring of condensation left by the water bottle.

"I know you're sceptical, Fang. But even you have to

admit that the predictions have proved accurate so far." Fang looked at the familiar photograph, a reconstructed series of drawings from some Laotian temple Miranda had scoured years ago. The ring of moisture surrounded three central figures, two boys and a girl. A huge bear dwarfed the first boy, while the second rode astride a great bird of prey. A dragon with long whiskers was entwined around the girl.

"I'm afraid you're going to be disappointed." Fang pushed the photograph away.

"The dragon? It could be a metaphor." Miranda tapped the photo. "Up the experimental dosage. We're close."

Fang opened her mouth to protest, the blonde girl still fresh in her mind. Sara. Miranda lifted a finger to still her.

"We can bear the losses. I need to know if it is possible to trigger the genes. Everything may depend on it."

Fang nodded.

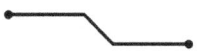

Swing, step. Swing, step. The phone strapped to her arm

buzzed with bright red letters. *15km*. Fang's head torch swept an arc of light in front of her feet. *Swing, step. Swing, step.* The early morning was her favourite time of day, the air quality index usually lowest before dawn. Still, Fang patted the reassuring lump in her pocket. Although she hated her dependence on her puffer, she really did need it.

Around the 20km mark, Fang felt nothing, just floated on the pavement as she dodged vendors opening stalls, the smell of coffee spilling out from alleyways. She'd increased the dosage on each of the IVs in the experimental area. Sara's face rose unbidden. In her dream, the girl's long hair had been streaked with vomit and her eyes were unfocused.

By the time Fang arrived home, her father was awake, doing his stretches in the sunny space by the window. They acknowledged each other with a nod before Fang disappeared into the shower.

There were only two places set at the table. "No Odysseus this morning?" Fang said as she dried her hair. Her brother pretended to hate the nickname, but she knew he secretly loved it. The *Iliad* and *Odyssey* were one of their few shared memories of their mother; they would snuggle in their parent's bed after dinner, bound together by bittersweet mildewy pages and silverfish.

"He's gone down to the orphanage before work." Her father poured the tea, hunched and small in his suit. "He always finds his way home." There was a tweak at the edge of his lips, the closest her father came to a smile.

Fang sighed. They each had their morning rituals, but she wished she saw more of her brother. She filled her father's bowl with congee despite his protest that she take the lion's share. He was getting too thin these days.

She ate watching her father read the paper, pausing now and then to coax his glasses back onto the bridge of his nose. She probably wouldn't see him again until tomorrow morning. The company took so much of his time, even with her brother on board. Fang wondered what it would be like to spend all day with her father; she tried to remember a time when she had. Her chopsticks froze in mid-air. She couldn't recall a single instance, even before her mother fell sick.

Fang carried her bowl to the sink, rinsed it and added it to the dishwasher. She wiped the counter, then set out the chopping board and prepared three lunches. Tofu, rice, steamed vegetables; separate compartments for each ingredient. Her father had been more wedded to his work than he was to his wife. Maybe it was in her genes to crave solitude, self-imposed order.

The chair at the table scraped backward.

"Make sure you make time to eat this." Fang forced the boxes into his hand. "Both of you."

Her father kissed her forehead. "What would I do without you?"

At the door he stopped and turned back to her, eyes filled with warmth. "You're looking more and more like her each day. She'd be proud of you, you know."

Tears sprang to her eyes but she forced them back. They'd made the decision together, she and her father, once her mother became too weak to talk. A frail woman in a hospital bed almost unrecognisable as the woman who'd left new books on her bed and packed her lunch just so. Her mother's face morphed into Sara's, sweaty and shaking.

Fang hoped her mother would understand.

In the experimental area dangling IVs reached empty chairs. Fang quickened her pace, heels clicking against the polished concrete. Miranda stood by the stairwell, talking to the group of monitoring scientists. *Without her.*

"– more successful at winnowing than we would have thought." Miranda paused as Fang reached the knot of people.

"What happened?" Fang clutched her stack of folders to her chest. *Everyone is so damn calm.*

Miranda nodded at the monitoring team and they moved back to the lab benches, dismantling equipment.

"Did we ... did we lose them all?" Could it be that none of the subjects had survived the higher dose of radiation? It just wasn't possible. *Probable*, her brain automatically corrected.

Miranda cocked a finger in Fang's direction. "Follow me." They passed through the experimental area to a set of offices parallel to her own. Miranda pressed a button and the glass panels lightened.

Fang dropped her folders in shock. The blonde girl, Sara, lay in a hospital-grade bed, a jittery heartbeat zigzagging on the monitor. Relieved she'd survived, Fang nearly missed the sinewy cat curled at the girl's feet.

"Is that – the leopard?" Fang's eyes widened in

realisation. "The mutation targets worked." She spun to face Miranda, who smiled.

"We did it."

Fang moved closer, almost pressing her nose to the glass. Sara was pale, with sweat-matted hair plastered to her scalp. The girl's eyes fluttered. Sara had survived.

"The others?"

Miranda walked to the next room, illuminating the interior with a jab at the wall panel. A boy lay in a nest of mussed-up blankets. Fang scanned the room for an animal.

"No pairing, but he survived the night. It's a good sign." Miranda left both rooms bright as she faced Fang.

"Only two." Fang wracked her brain. Maybe she had upped the dosage too high. "None of the other subjects survived?" Or maybe her target compounds had been wrong. Fear gripped her chest and she found it difficult to breathe.

Miranda tapped on Sara's window. The cat angled toward them, tail sliding back and forth across the bed. "We have what we need. We know it's possible to induce the mutation now. We don't need the others. Wheat from the chaff."

Two from thirty test subjects. Fang felt the hairs on her arms rise. A less than seven percent conversion rate.

"I took the liberty of increasing their dosage above your upper limit."

Fang stared at Miranda. "But that would have been an incredible stressor on their systems." Fang hadn't killed them. Relief made her shoulders heavy. She needed to sit down, had to stop herself reaching for her puffer.

"It was necessary." Miranda's clipped voice stopped Fang from saying anything more.

The IV drips and chairs were gone when they moved back to the lab space, all trace of the other subjects removed. Fang didn't want to know where.

12

Flight

Robyn tried to focus on the peaks Derek was showing her; she really did, but Eva wouldn't stop barging around the living room. A 150kg toddler.

"This one, I think, could be some sort of long-chain alkene ..." Derek said. The sofa scraped against the wall as Eva rammed into it, huffing. Robyn rested her head in her hands, counting to three. The screeching continued.

Robyn raised her head. "Fletcher?" He was lying upside down, legs splayed over the object of Eva's wrath.

"Yeah?" Fletcher said.

"Can you ask Eva to keep it down?" The moment the words left her mouth, Robyn knew she'd said the wrong thing. The bear glared at her as Fletcher reoriented himself.

"She's not built for such a small space. She's restless,

129

Robyn." *And it's all your fault*, his eyes said.

"Look, I'm sorry." Robyn closed her eyes again. Tired, she was just so tired, barely back from Montreal and already sifting through Derek's new data. Catherine had cooked her pancakes and she honestly thought it was the only reason she'd survived the return Greyhound bus trip. A maple syrup force field of positivity. Whatever it was, it was long gone now.

Ping. Derek jumped to his feet, knocking several pages off the table. They drifted like snowflakes to the floor.

"What was that?" It sounded like a mobile phone. Robyn reached out to pick up the fallen chromatograms.

Ping.

"It's the doorbell." Derek turned to Fletcher with a shaky hand. "Into the bedroom, now."

Fletcher flipped onto his feet and Eva barged into the wall, chipping a hunk of plaster. Dust rose in her wake as the door clicked shut behind them.

"Any ideas?" Robyn whispered, thinking of the owner of the box. Everyone seemed to have bloody ex-girlfriends.

Derek shook his head. "Nope."

Muffled voices rose from the other side of the door as the knob began to turn.

"Jesus Christ," muttered Derek. Robyn scoured the room for a weapon. She moved to Derek's side as the door burst open, heart thudding. This couldn't be over. They'd barely started.

It took her a good few seconds to comprehend the familiar faces.

"Kate? Kara?" Robyn shrieked, running down the hallway to draw Kara into a hug. Kate rolled her eyes. "What are you doing here?"

"Uh, saving your ass," Kate said. She waved at Derek. "Hi."

Derek froze in the kitchen. "Robyn?" he said, voice wary. "You know them?"

"Yeah. Derek, these are my friends." Robyn stared at Kara. "You guys flew out here?"

"Look, if we could get a cup of tea or something before we play twenty questions, that would be nice." Kate looked defiant, but Robyn noticed the dark shadows under her eyes.

"Of course." Backing up, Robyn clattered mugs onto the table. "Fletcher, it's all right, you can come out now."

The bedroom door creaked and Fletcher stuck his head out. Head cocked to the side, he stared at the newcomers.

"No way." Kate gaped as Eva slunk out of the room. "Can I?" She twitched her hand in Eva's direction. When Fletcher nodded, she bounded over to the bear, rubbing Eva's neck with both hands. Her stiff hair tickled Eva's chin and Eva jerked upward, sending Kate sailing across the living room, landing heavily on the sofa. It warped and clanked apart, finally defeated.

"Oh my gosh, I'm so sorry," Kate said, clasping her hand to her mouth.

Fletcher laughed so hard Robyn worried he might burst a blood vessel. Derek waved her apology away. "Don't sweat it."

A computer arsenal appeared on the dining table confirming Robyn's suspicions. The many group projects, the snippets of code. "So, I take it there's no hacker friend, right?"

Kara sipped her tea. "I didn't mean to lie to you, Robyn, which is why I sort of ... skirted around the truth."

Kate snorted behind her sister, straightening her mohawk. "That's one way of putting it."

Robyn opened and closed her mouth, unsure what to say. An image of the fish in the cave popped into her head and she closed her mouth. Kara didn't expand on what the *truth* entailed.

"You need us," Kara said. "We've both taken the semester off."

Kate nodded. "Snakeskin," she mouthed at Robyn.

"Constant movement is key. We can't stay in any one place too long," Kara continued, oblivious to her sister behind her.

Fletcher raised both hands above his head. "Exactly. This is what I've been saying all week."

"We need lab access." Robyn rubbed her right temple, glancing at Derek for support. They couldn't drop everything and run. Until they worked out why and how Fletcher communicated with Eva, they had nothing. Zip. Nada.

Derek cleared his throat. "She's right. We can't figure any of this out without a lab. We'd be running blind."

Thank you, Robyn felt like screeching, but smiled at Derek instead.

The sleek black helicopter loomed in the darkness above the university, no external lights betraying its presence. The rhythmic whirring of the blades masked the excitement within.

"Sir, we have a heat contact." The thermal imager showed a blue-red blob, too large to be human.

"Could it be the bear?" Vulcan spoke into his earpiece, leaning back into the safety of his padded office chair.

"Possibly, sir." The soldier nodded, still watching the thermal imager.

"Worth a look," Vulcan said. "Stun and capture only. I repeat. Stun and capture only."

"Roger."

Vulcan spun one of the red feathered darts in his hand. He'd calculated the dosage himself. He had thought Derek incapable of concealing anything from him. People were so disappointing.

One of the consoles on Derek's dining table released a string of blips. Robyn stared at the red light.

"Shit." Kara flipped switches. "We've got company."

"In the air?" Kate's hands whizzed on her keyboard.

"Affirmative." Kara shoved computer equipment into

a large duffel bag. "Time to go."

Derek looked as shocked as Robyn felt, frozen in place clutching their chromatograms.

"Move, people," Kate yelled from the hallway. "Everyone in the goddamn van."

"What about Eva?" Fletcher didn't leave the bear's side. Robyn tipped her head as a faint whirring sound reached her. Her eyes widened as the full implications of *in the air* became clear.

Shit.

Derek snapped out of his trance, rummaging in the closet. "Here." He thrust a reflective package into Fletcher's arms. "It's a space blanket. It'll cover her heat signature in the short term."

Kate nodded. "It's worth a shot."

Heat signature? It was like they were speaking another language. Robyn felt herself propelled toward the door. Eva had scampered ahead and hunkered in one corner of the van, crinkling in silver foil. Robyn followed and the van door slid shut behind her, plunging them into darkness. Someone squeezed her hand. Derek.

Kate revved the engine. "Hold on to something back there." The street light caught the pink in her hair, blurring it into a halo. An avenging angel. Robyn gripped Derek's hand right back, her heart hammering in her chest. She could no longer hear the whirring noise. *Maybe it passed over us*, Robyn thought, a kernel of hope slowing her heartbeat.

Kara leapt into the passenger seat and yanked out a laptop, leaving her seatbelt dangling by her side. "What do you think – standard electromagnetic dispersal?"

"If you can get it up and running in time." Kate peeled out onto the road, tyres bouncing. Kara stuck her arm into the duffel bag where it disappeared up to her shoulder.

"Got it." Kara yanked out an aerial, then leaned out the window to slap it against the roof, where it lodged with a dull *thunk* like a heavy magnet on a fridge.

"We need cover. I'm heading for the forest." Kate wrenched the steering wheel to the right and the van lurched. Robyn rammed into Derek, who clutched her shoulder to stop her from falling.

Out of nowhere, the helicopter banked in front of them, hovering above the bitumen with a rush of sound. Robyn heard the static of a radio over the *thwack thwack thwack* of the blades. Her shoulders shook as she fought the urge to duck and hide, anything to get out of the chopper's line of sight. Derek's grip on her shoulder tightened.

"Holy shit," said Kate. "Hurry up, sis."

"This is very complicated." Kara typed a swathe of code. "Plus, they won't shoot. We've got the assets."

The helicopter levelled, and a barrel set into the side rotated.

"Oh, really?" Kate gunned the engine, skidding the rear wheels out just as the pilot fired, screaming "Duck".

Events slowed. Bullets pinged against the runner board as green light engulfed Fletcher, spreading away from his body to envelop them all. As it zipped up Robyn's arms she felt the buzz of energy, like crackling electricity. Bullets raked the side of the van, ricocheting from the orb of green light.

Kate straightened the wheels, shooting the van around the chopper and picking up speed. The green light shot backward toward Fletcher with a rushing sound and disappeared.

Robyn released her breath she'd been holding. Wide-eyed, Fletcher touched his stomach, his legs. He nodded at Robyn, an uncertain jerk of his head.

Somehow, Fletcher had stopped the bullets.

"How about now?" Kate changed gear and the van shuddered.

"Working on it." Kara kept tapping away. By the time the chopper turned around, the van was half a mile away, the road flanked by old-growth trees.

"They won't be pulling that little stunt again," Kate grinned. "Bastards."

Thwack thwack thwack.

"Damn it, sis." Kate stuck her head out the window and swore under her breath.

Robyn pulled away from Derek and crawled toward Fletcher. Wisps of green twined around his arms. Robyn ripped her gaze from the light to the window, shocked to see that the helicopter was so close she could see the implacable mask of the pilot.

"There." Kara's fingers stilled and the aerial on the roof emitted a piercing shriek. Robyn covered her ears, hitting the metal floor with her elbows. Though the noise subsided Eva wailed into Fletcher's shoulder, whose own face was still screwed up in a grimace. Ultra high frequency, Robyn realised, above human range – it must be deafening to Eva and, by extension, Fletcher.

Thwack … thwack … thwack.

The blades slowed. Robyn scrambled to the rear window and watched in horror as the aircraft dropped lower in the sky. It levelled for a moment before tilting forward at an impossible angle, blades rushing to meet the bitumen with a terrible metallic screech. The landing skids crumpled as the body of the chopper disintegrated in a mess of whirling metal.

Flames flickered around the rim of the front window, silhouetting the twins high-fiving in the front of the bouncing van. A loud explosion echoed behind them, filling the van with an eerie orange glow. Robyn didn't look back. Fletcher had stopped the bullets, and her best friend had brought down a helicopter filled with people. Robyn couldn't process it all right now. Instead, she curled up against Eva, who huffed before allowing Robyn to nestle into her shoulder.

Vulcan tore the useless earpiece out. Static poured from it as he rubbed his chin, speechless. Tottering to the cabinet, he pulled out the whisky and swigged it straight from the bottle.

The lab.

Derek's pristine workstation yielded nothing out of the ordinary. Vulcan paused in front of the fridge. Dozens of sample racks stared back at him. Derek *had* been showing more initiative this past week. He wrenched open the door and began pulling out vials.

13

Holding Pattern

Nestled in the space blanket in the back of the van, Robyn woke to silence. "Derek?" she whispered. The blanket scrunched and she winced at the magnitude of the sound. Robyn peeled herself out of the nest and noticed the headlights were still on, illuminating a wooden building directly ahead.

She stepped out into the night, wrapping her arms around her chest as the cool breeze hit her. She hadn't even unpacked from her trip to Montreal. If only she'd had the presence of mind to grab her backpack, just sitting there, propped up against Derek's bed …

"Robyn." Derek stepped out of the shadows as if her thoughts had summoned him. "We've found somewhere to hole up for the night."

A light bounced and Kate's face appeared. "All clear."

Robyn shuffled behind them, her legs stiff from being curled up in the van. The wooden structure was a barn, stove in on one side, moonlight shifting through the vines that had grown up to cover the wound. She smelled rising damp and mildew.

"Mice, but not many." Fletcher stepped into the dappled moonlight with straw in his hair. "There's a loft." He jerked an arm upward.

Kara's voice carried down from above them. "And it's dry."

Robyn hugged the ladder as she slowly climbed, breathing shallowly to avoid inhaling the dust that made her eyes water.

Eva snuffled in the straw on the barn floor with Fletcher, and Robyn felt a pang of jealousy. She missed Eva's comforting heartbeat already. Sighing, she crawled into a corner of the loft. The twins sat against a stack of straw bales murmuring to each other. Too exhausted to talk, Robyn curled onto her side, vaguely registering Derek's body next to hers. Then sleep claimed her.

Her arm itched where she had snuggled into the straw, little red lumps rising where she scratched. Mites, maybe. Gross. Weak light peeked through the old boards, sending dust motes swirling in parallel lines. It was still early. Crawling over to the ladder, she hesitated at the top rung. Kate and Kara lay on their backs, the laptop open by Kara's hip dinging every few seconds. Eva and Fletcher had disappeared. Derek curled on his side next to the nest Robyn had made in her sleep. He looked peaceful, a slack expression on his face that made him look like a stranger; there was no trace of the rigid lines that Robyn had become used to over the last few days. He'd been sleeping on the couch, though Robyn never saw more evidence than a folded blanket with regulation corners. Derek would always be gone, a note on the counter wedged under the still-warm percolator of coffee the only proof of his presence.

Robyn had never really shared a space with a boy. It had never come to that with Levi, or with Travis; couch make-outs at his place barely qualified. A smattering of crushes observed from across the room but never approached in the post-Travis era meant she'd never slept *beside* anyone properly, much less beside someone she cared about. She found spending time with Derek surprisingly easy: someone who knew how frustrating, how belittling and how *humbling* a life in pursuit of discovery could be. How it consumed the waking mind like a vice, sidelining all other instincts.

But now – Derek's fingertips grazed the edge of Robyn's nook, and she wondered what it would feel like if he had rolled over in his sleep, slung an arm across her, pulled her in tight. She pushed the thought away, shocked both at how quickly it had formed and the resultant pool of warmth in her stomach.

"Robyn," Fletcher whispered from below. "Is that you?"

Robyn blinked, realising she'd been staring at Derek the whole time. "Yeah," she murmured. "Coming." She stole a last glance at Derek's tranquil expression, so foreign to her.

Robyn hit the earthen floor and straightened. Fletcher was boning a stack of fish, Eva munching on offcuts by his side.

"Breakfast?"

Fletcher nodded. His movements were slow and methodical despite the rusted knife in his hand.

"Where'd you get the knife?" She was curious, eager to explore now that it was daylight, although half-terrified she might stumble across a farmer in overalls wielding a pitchfork. *Git offa ma land!*

Fletcher pointed to a bench down the rear wall. "Some old tools back there. Even a generator. Maybe your friends can get it up and running."

Kara. Robyn wasn't sure if she really knew her friend at all. Last night came back in a rush: the thrum of the hovering chopper, the pinging sound of the bullets against the van. Robyn shuddered. And Fletcher – the green light almost a force field – he'd stopped the bullets. Without the twins, they wouldn't have made it out of Derek's apartment. Not with her in charge, anyway. Useless. Robyn bit her lip.

Robyn pulled up a cobwebbed milk crate. "Last night. That sort of stuff just doesn't happen in real life."

Fletcher's knife stilled. "I don't want anyone else to get hurt because of me."

"You saved us. With that energy field thing? It was incredible. I don't want anyone getting hurt because of *me*," Robyn said. "This is all because I analysed your blood sample, tracked you down. I'm sorry, Fletcher. I don't know how to make this right."

"We have to find the others." Fletcher glanced at

Eva. "I think that's what I'm supposed to do." He rubbed the worn handle of the knife. "I can't go back, can I?" he murmured.

Robyn knew he didn't need to hear the answer from her. *None of us can,* she thought. Life had inverted in a matter of days, everything she'd taken for granted stripped away. Robyn didn't have a rational explanation for anything.

The remnants of a forgotten vegetable garden stretched along the northern side of the barn. Gnarled pumpkins, beans and drooping corn stalks fought for sunlight. The vines over the breach in the roof were some sort of prickly cucumber.

The generator buzzed into life, jerking Robyn from her reverie. She wiped grubby hands on her jeans and scooped beans into the bottom of her shirt. Soup, maybe a rustic cornbread. Fletcher and Eva could catch some more fish.

When she stepped inside the barn, she saw Kate and Kara enthroned at the workbench, almost yelling at each other over the roar of the generator. Everything smelled like diesel. Robyn ran her eyes over the UHT milk and tinned vegetables. Kate must have just returned from town. Although it was only late morning, Robyn felt like she'd been up for two days straight.

"Guess what?" Kara said. "Toothbrushes." She chucked a plastic packet toward Robyn. Somehow, she managed to catch it.

"Oh, thank God," Robyn said. She yanked the plastic open and Derek appeared at her elbow.

"Let's do this," she said, handing him a purple one.

She could barely brush her teeth for laughing, Derek's exaggerated moans sending foam everywhere.

"Samwise," he spluttered, reaching out toward her. "Take the ring, for I am done for." He convulsed at an imaginary spider bite, eyes wide. White foam trickled down his chin, tributaries merging into one frothy stream.

Robyn snorted, nearly choking on toothpaste. The corn swayed behind them, complicit for several long seconds as Robyn stared at Derek in wonder.

Robyn shook her head to clear it. "You've done that before." Another fleeting glimpse of relaxed Derek, still a stranger to her. Robyn spat out into a clump of chickweed, ignoring the heat in her cheeks.

"Yeah." Derek wiped his mouth on the back of his sleeve. "For my brother, Damian."

"You never mentioned a brother."

Derek's smile contracted. He scuffed a shoe on the ground. "He's three years older than me, but he was born with a rare congenital defect."

Robyn clenched her toothbrush. "I'm sorry," she said. *Don't ask for permission or forgiveness.* She'd read it in a magazine in the doctor's surgery in one of those cringe-worthy self-help columns. Post-Levi, pre-Travis. It had stuck.

Derek peered up at the corn. "It's no-one's fault. These things happen." He sighed. "My parents didn't realise until he didn't try to crawl, never uttered a word. Blind and mute. The specialists were baffled, still are."

Robyn swallowed the next *I'm sorry.*

Derek turned to face her. "I don't bring many people to meet Damian. But I think he'd be happy to meet you."

Robyn twirled her toothbrush. "I'd love to meet him. Thank you." Her voice sounded flat even to her ears.

Derek looked away, nodding at the earth.

"Robyn, what am I doing with this dough? It's bubbling and really starting to freak me out." Kara's voice drifted from the open barn door.

"Crap," Robyn said. The cornbread. Robyn jogged ahead leaving Derek in the warmth of the garden. At the edge of the barn she turned back. He looked out of place among the plants. Robyn wondered if he'd ever planted a seedling, or picked his own dinner. Probably not. Her mother had a word for him – *townie*. But even that didn't encompass Derek, with his imported coffee and thousand thread count sheets.

Kara burst into the sunshine holding a bowl aloft. Relief flooded her face at the sight of Robyn.

"Good. You deal with this, and tell me what to chop."

Robyn carried the bowl inside before heaving the dough onto the rough table they'd fashioned. "The green beans, and some pumpkin." Robyn kneaded as she talked. Sharp pressure with the heel of her hand, stretch the mixture out, then retract, fold over. Bread was one of the few things she could cook.

With Kara clattering away with the knife by her side, they soon had a vat of soup simmering on the gas cooker. It was a long way from ladling alcoholic slurry into college kids. Kara shifted, putting the knife down. Robyn wondered if she sensed it, too.

"Robyn, jeez. I never meant to lie to you. I'm sorry. Our grandparents were very clear that they would only pay tuition for 'proper' degrees. Law and economics were kind of the default ..."

"You didn't need to pretend around me," Robyn said. "You're like my sister. I thought you trusted me."

"Of course I trust you." Kara ran a hand through her hair. "We're not really doing anything illegal, just software development and ..."

"Yo, master chefs, I think I've found something," called Kate from the bench. Kara turned away at the summons. *Software development and what?* Robyn wondered, resentful of the intrusion. The duffel bag spilled strange devices onto the floor. Robyn couldn't help peering in as she passed it, but none of the equipment looked familiar. More like a military arsenal snatched from some futuristic race.

Robyn peered at the screen, a website for some international school based in Beijing.

"Brock. I've been trawling through his email. This Chief Director he keeps up to date on Robyn? I cracked the encryption on her location. It took long enough. This is where she is now. China." Kate pointed at the screen. "Here, to be exact."

"A school? That doesn't make any sense," said Derek. Robyn looked over. She hadn't heard him come in. All trace of fun-loving Frodo had evaporated.

"No newsletter, debate tournaments. Here's the satellite video, the most recent I could get is time-stamped about two weeks ago." Kate clicked on a fuzzy map then zoomed in. "You're going to love this. Screw the cornbread, let's just make popcorn."

Kara glared at her sister and Kate cleared her throat. "Or not, whatever."

The video was pixellated, but the men in dark fatigues standing along the fence line were clear enough. On-screen, soldiers admitted a truck through the gates. Robyn swallowed. She wondered if anyone had survived the fireball; she knew it was unlikely. Some of these men might be dead now. Maybe all of them. The pleasure that ran through her spine surprised and sickened her. They'd killed Fletcher's family, too. This was war, in a way. The knowledge weighed on her shoulders.

More men surrounded the truck as the rear door rolled up. Crates with bars. *Cages*, Robyn realised.

"Is that a –" Derek began. Robyn leaned in closer.

"A leopard? Yeah." Kate paused the video then zoomed in. A window of code flashed up, and she typed a string of commands. The video cleared to reveal the big cat snarling against the bars.

"Oh my God," Robyn breathed.

"That means ... they could be testing already," said Derek, aghast. "If they're collecting animals." He slapped his forehead. "Shit."

Robyn's arm reached for his shoulder before she registered what she was doing. Derek reached up and grasped it, pulling her toward him. A flower of warmth spread through her chest.

Derek squeezed her hand tight. "Robyn, the samples from Fletcher and Eva – they're still in the lab fridge. At least, they *were*."

Robyn swayed and Derek's hand flew to her waist, steadying her. The warmth in her chest turned to ice. She didn't understand. "What ... what are they doing there?" Frankenstein visions flashed across her eyes – horrible animal experiments, shrieks of pain, wide-eyed kids strapped onto beds.

"I'm not sure *what*, but I know *who*." Kate brought up a photo of a serious-looking Chinese woman. "Xiaofang

Fisher. The last researcher."

Robyn straightened, and the pressure on her waist disappeared. She dreaded what Kate would say next.

"She's working with them, Robyn. It took me a while to figure it out, because she calls herself Fang." Kate crossed her legs and jiggled her right foot as she scrolled through code interspersed with foreign characters.

"They've got kids in there, Robyn." Kara's voice was small. "Lots of them."

Fletcher. Robyn closed her eyes for a moment. They would have had Fletcher, too.

"Now they've probably got Fletcher's DNA, and Eva's too," Derek said, deflated. The hairs on the back of Robyn's neck prickled.

"That's not good, right?" said Kate.

"No," murmured Robyn. "It's bad. Really bad."

14

Ariana

The Indian runner ducks waddled toward the pond. Ariana remembered the fête where she'd first seen their costume-wearing cousins: pink frocks, waistcoats and top hats. She was eight, and Terence had bought her a pink orb of fairy floss as big as her head. She'd needed two fillings in the winter. One of the ducks angled his giraffe-like neck toward her. She imagined him in a mini-tux.

Propping herself up on her elbows, she watched them slide into the water. Contented quacks drifted up as they paddled, sifting for bugs with long slurps. The breeze brought whiffs of mown grass, cow manure and fresh zucchini bread. Beyond the pond stretched rows and rows of vegetables, her parents' pride and joy. Spinach, kale, lettuce, bok choy – every conceivable type of edible green. *Bastions of wellness*, her mother called them, the woman with a week's rota of colourful headbands. Val still wore her silver hair in pigtail braids. Well, she used to. Ariana rolled onto her back and tried not to think about the funeral. At least her brother had come back for a while. She wondered who would be the one to go through her mother's drawers, her books and drawings. Ariana hated the idea of anyone else wearing those headbands. She'd stopped braiding her own hair, wearing it loose even though it got tangled when she weeded. Two weeks, her mother had been gone for two weeks. Everything should have stopped, but somehow the world kept turning. Her teachers stepped warily around her, the other girls whispering as if Ariana's loss was somehow contagious.

Ariana ran her fingers through her hair, snagging them in the matted mess at the back. She sat up and worried the knot. Her fingers smelled of soil. Painting her nails was a waste of time, even though the girls at school sniggered at her calloused hands. It was just so dumb, spending time doing something so fiddly when an afternoon crushing white butterfly larvae melted it right off, sizzling like acid.

The brassicas would need attention soon. With her father gone, she'd have to crush hundreds more larvae, or supervise the ducks. Left to their own devices, they'd be less selective and rip the leaves to shreds.

The ducks. Ariana blinked, searching for the mini-harem. They had gone silent, floating in the very middle of the pond in a protective triangle. The reeds rustled and Ariana heard a faint buzz in the air.

A little fire salamander stood on its rear legs in front of her. She recognised it from the book in her father's study.

Hello, walker of the sea.

Ariana stared. She'd imagined it, of course. The buzzing grew louder, more like a cloud of mosquitos now.

My name is Jericho.

The salamander's lips didn't move, yet somehow Ariana knew the words were his. She heard them in her head, like when she read and conjured a character's voice in her mind. Only she had no book. Ariana gazed down at the glistening, bronze-speckled salamander in wonder.

Screwing up her face in concentration, Ariana focused

on making her thought clear. *Hello.* It came out more as a wavering question – *Hello?*

The salamander – Jericho – flicked his tongue onto her palm and stepped aboard. Blue light snaked up her arm. Ariana's skin crawled, like she'd brushed up against one of the low-voltage electric fences around the vegetable garden. Unpleasant, but not painful. She gasped as the voltage abruptly increased, sparking in a huge blue arc onto her chest. Images burst behind her eyelids: a deep watery abyss, an enormous whale orbited by a pod of silver dolphins, then that word again. *Walker.*

Called by the sea spirit, you are furnished with the tongue of my kind.

Your kind? Ariana raised her hand, peering at the salamander. Her skin thrummed with blue light.

Many generations have passed. There is much to do, but first we must find the others. Jericho's smooth voice penetrated all the recesses of her mind.

Others?

Terence jumped when the heavy door clanked open, knocking his muddy gumboots onto the kitchen tiles. His mother would have been horrified. Cringing,

Terence looked up in surprise at the lizard on Ariana's shoulder. It darted across her back before he could get a good look.

"Hey, sis." He wrenched open the oven door, pausing to wipe the condensation from his glasses. The vegetables needed more time, the tofu was still marinating in the fridge. He'd chuck it in the oven for the final twenty minutes. There had always been something reassuring about the larder, stocked with dried beans and his father's home-pressed tofu. The family had weathered plenty of harsh weather before, but no amount of stockpiling would help now.

When he turned around, Ariana had disappeared. Terence propped his gumboots outside and saw her enter the yurt set back in the meadow, the lizard clutching her back. Dusk all but smothered the field. He closed the door, picked up his mug and headed down the hall to his father's study. The glow from his laptop was an alien presence against the gleaming, knotted wood. The study felt cold without his father being there, more like a museum exhibit with its staged array of eccentricities – ammonite fossils, chunks of quartz. Terence sank into the armchair. Bry had been so determined to return his wife's ashes to the Isle of Skye that he'd set off as soon as the last well-wisher departed, disappeared to the windswept rocky outcrops Terence's parents had hiked nearly every summer. A month, maybe two, Terence wasn't sure when Bry would return. Sighing, he pulled his laptop onto his knees. A quick check of his email, he promised himself, then back to the kitchen. His cursor hovered over the sequencing emails from Weaving. His supervisor could wait, but one email caught his eye. Intrigued, he opened it. Sinking into the comforting embrace of the armchair, stunned by what he read, he took a restorative sip of tea. He downloaded the attached files.

"Holy crap," he spluttered, spraying milky liquid over the keyboard. Holding the laptop at arm's length, he wiped it with his shirtsleeve without really processing the damage. His gaze flitted to the window, where Ariana lay on her stomach, watching the lizard gambol on the grass in front of her. Terence felt his brain fog and then darkness washed over him.

Terence woke on the study floor, dust clogging his nostrils, with a concerned aqueous eye in front of his own. He jerked sideways and sneezed, sending the lizard skittering backward. Ariana squeaked, hand rocketing out to collect the reptile. A salamander, Terence realised, smattered with bronze speckles that caught the light.

"Be careful," Ariana remonstrated. "Jericho's tiny."

"Jericho?" Terence managed. Ariana nodded as he brought himself into a sitting position and leaned his head against the armchair. Warm liquid trickled against his shoulder. The mug had sent a stream down the edge, now dammed by his body.

This is crazy, he thought to himself, but he had to ask.

"Ariana, can you – can you talk to Jericho?"

Ariana glanced down at the salamander before turning back to him with new assurance. "Yes. Jericho says you're going to help us."

Terence nodded, eyeing the whisky on the top shelf. Tea wouldn't cut it.

15

Intercept

"Fletcher and Eli. Their DNA is unusual."

"We already knew that. Isn't that the whole point? Like earth-bound coal, deep veins of uranium."

"It's beyond that. It's baffled the staff in Beijing, Brock. They've never seen anything like it."

"So the key is buried nice and deep, I take it."

"You are insufferable, you know that? The others are growing stronger. Sara is ... incredible."

"You can't pump chemicals into everyone, Miranda."

"I know that. Which is why we need Catherine. Losing Derek and Robyn has been a major blow. Fang is brilliant, don't get me wrong, but maybe a fresh set of eyes could make all the difference."

"Derek. Yes, I couldn't have predicted that. He seemed so meek, or maybe that was just Vulcan's influence."

"The man has a presence, I'll say that much. But we will need him."

"Vulcan? The man is unhinged, Miranda. Be careful how much trust you place in him. The others – Weaving, Deckker – are harmless house flies. That man is the march fly that rises with the change of season, intent on only one thing: destruction."

"Very poetic."

"I mean it, Miranda. Once they crack this –"

"So you agree it can be done?"

"Of course. I've shadowed Robyn long enough to know she is more than capable. If the others are anything like her, they will bring you your key. It is only a matter of time."

"Brock. And me?"

"You're the spider, Miranda. But you already knew that."

Catherine's message came at midday as Robyn balanced soup on her lap with a hunk of steaming cornbread.

Fletcher drank straight from his tilted bowl across from her, rusted knife at his feet. He'd been quiet all morning after she'd told him about Beijing. They were all still processing the information. Robyn couldn't believe that someone, *one of them*, could be helping the MRI experiment on kids. She didn't think she could knowingly be part of a group that did that, which made Fang a dangerous wildcard.

The phone vibrating in her jeans pocket jerked her back to the barn. Robyn plonked her food on the bench and jumped to her feet.

Just checking in. En route to a genetics conference in Beijing with my monitor. Should be back in three days. Nothing unusual to report. Hope you're having fun with Winnie and friends.

"Oh, no way." Robyn stared at the message.

Fletcher put his bowl down. "What is it?"

"Catherine. Her supervisor is taking her to Beijing. A conference – yeah, right." Catherine didn't know about the barn, about their close call with the MRI. Robyn had completely forgotten to call her, to warn her. Everything had happened so fast. *Shit.*

"They've got Catherine?" said Derek.

Kara turned around from her laptop. "Not if I can help it." She rolled her shoulders. "Kate?"

The generator stuttered into life. "On it." Kate dusted off her hands and put the jerry can down.

Kara cracked her knuckles as she flipped between screens with alarming speed. "Who have we got in Beijing?" she asked Kate, who scrolled through a long list of names.

"This one's on Bohai. He owes me," replied Kate, singling out a name. Robyn made out a picture of a Chinese man with closely cropped hair and oversized glasses.

Robyn swore under her breath. "How exactly does this man owe you?"

Kate peered over her shoulder. "Later," she promised.

She was getting sick of *later*. She wanted to know what Fang was up to *now*, and she'd had enough of being kept out of the twins' tech loop. The bank of laptops purring under their fingertips looked more at home on an episode of *CSI* than in a dilapidated barn in rural North Carolina. Robyn had never seen such an intense look of concentration on her best friend's face before – a mix of complete focus and abandonment of the world around her, like nothing else mattered except what was going on inside her computer. In a way, maybe nothing did. Robyn sat back down on the straw bale to wait.

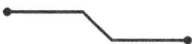

Terence paced along the window, watching the planes manoeuvring onto their respective runways. Tangential journeys. The mysterious Kara had transferred funds and booked their tickets. The passports had arrived by express mail; he had thumbed through them over oats and honey at the kitchen table as he watched Ariana at the gate palming the ducks off to the neighbour. The documents seemed heavy in their illicitness as he weighed them in his palm. Espionage.

Heathrow had been a nerve-wracking jostle of bags and beeping security clearances. Jericho, in a tiny pet box, had sailed through the scanner. Terence hadn't been able to resist peering over the operator's shoulder to get a glance at the miniature skeleton. Part of him had needed to see that the salamander was a real, breathing animal.

Ariana flipped through a magazine on the floor, with Jericho curled up in a corner of the box. The girl reached out a hand without looking up. "Chocolate?"

Terence took the half-eaten bar and turned back to the window. They still had a long way to go before any of this made sense. If it ever would.

Catherine blinked stupidly at the attractive Chinese guy who'd just grabbed her wrist. He held an enormous bouquet of balloons, one of those garish, crinkly concoctions that reeked of overkill. It seemed to shut out the noise of the arrivals hall, cocooning them away from the thrum of people.

"You are in danger and must come with me, please." He pushed his glasses up the bridge of his nose. "Robyn sent me."

Unease settled low in Catherine's stomach. She glanced over her shoulder, but Deckker was stuck behind an elderly couple battling with a mess of fallen knitting. Red yarn had somehow wrapped its way around her supervisor's ankles.

"My name is Bohai." The pressure on her arm increased. The niggling feeling that something was amiss hadn't left her the entire flight; her supervisor had even been humming as they landed. Catherine hadn't heard him hum since his Belgian waffle maker cleared customs in the winter. *Something is wrong.*

"Okay."

Now she wanted to run, put as much distance between her and Deckker as possible. Bohai gripped her arm and shook his head, as if sensing the tension in her body. Catherine settled for the brisk pace Bohai set, heart hammering. Her legs quivered as they reached the security gates. She concentrated on breathing as the line moved forward. *Slow. Too slow.* Her eyes flitted to the gates at each turn of the cordoned area, red ribbon already caging her in. It felt like half an hour by the time they reached the tiny aperture in the window, though Catherine knew it couldn't have been more than minutes. She watched wide-eyed as Bohai slid two passports across. The Canadian one in her pocket burned against her skin.

Bam. Bam.

Two stamps and they were through. Catherine gripped Bohai's hand as he wove between the crush of people. Elbows dug into her back and bags jammed into her ankles. The air was thick with a soupy haze that seemed to thin the air in her lungs. By the time they reached a motorbike propped up against an overflowing dumpster, Catherine heaved for breath. In a daze, she slipped on the neon helmet Bohai handed her. The roar of the bike jolted her back, ethanol rising from something fermenting deep in the bin by her elbow. As Bohai skidded across the pavement onto the road, Catherine clutched his waist, curling her fingers into his belt.

The bike snaked between wheezing trucks and flash cars that careened from lane to lane without so much as a cursory jab of the indicator. Taxis seemed to graze the pedestrians that poured from buildings lining the roadside before disappearing into a haze of smog. It was like landing on another planet.

She must have closed her eyes. When the bike stopped, she squinted into the dark alleyway feeling disoriented. A flaked red door opened and a toddler poked her head out. Motioning toward the doorway, Bohai yanked off his helmet. Catherine followed, her legs tense and stiff. The little girl nudged Catherine's thigh and grasped her hand. Catherine squeezed back.

In the dim room she saw a kid-sized table and chairs occupied by three people – one male, two female. They launched into a flurry of Mandarin; Catherine hung back, wishing she'd learned an Asian language. The old man pointed at her while the woman sent little hand flicks in her direction. Subtle.

Bohai raised both arms and the chatter stopped. The old man shook his head, muttering under his breath.

"Li," said Bohai, jerking his head toward the girl at the table. She was eight, maybe nine, Catherine guessed. A book lay open on the red plastic table. "And Cho." The little girl by Catherine's side released her hand and skittered over to the older girl.

"You can call me Ma, everyone does." The older woman made some sort of sweeping hand gesture that felt like Catherine's grandmother's equivalent of a rushed sign of the cross. Strong fingers pressed into her back, and Catherine folded into one of the chairs. It creaked under her weight and Li giggled behind her hand. Catherine's knees rose high above the table, her height making her a giantess compared to the others. The old lady shuffled back with a pot of tea, wrist shaking as she put it down. Catherine stiffened as wrinkled hands cupped her face, fingertips on her temples, but forced herself to slowly relax under Ma's grip. The woman huffed and straightened, seemingly satisfied. Of what, Catherine had no idea. Ma poured the tea into tiny dollhouse cups. Catherine breathed in the heady jasmine scent as she took a sip.

Bohai waited until she'd put the cup down, then slid over the wine-red passport and a SIM card.

Robyn paced from barn door to workbench. "It's taking too long. Something's gone wrong." Visions of Catherine locked up played before her eyes. *It'd be my fault*, Robyn thought. The MRI knew Derek was on the run with her now; it was only a matter of time before they made a move for Catherine. *Stupid, so stupid.* She should have foreseen this. Robyn clenched her fists by her sides. Kara had assured her that Terence was safe, but for how long?

"Calm down, Robyn. It takes as long as it takes," Kate said from her position on a straw bale, limbs splayed wide. Kara, silent at her laptop, kept vigil with her hands in a prayer position against her lips.

Our father, who art in heaven … Robyn slipped

into her childhood prayers without realising and was halfway to the barn door again when the laptop pinged. She whirled as Kara jerked forward. Kate flipped back onto her feet with more grace than Robyn would have credited her with.

"Bohai got her out," Kara exhaled.

Robyn sank onto the straw bale Kate had vacated. Catherine was safe. Her stomach fluttered, and Robyn tasted soup at the back of her throat. She swallowed with difficulty, and Kate's voice seemed to come from far away.

"Good. And he knows the plan?" Kate was back on her chair.

Kara nodded.

"We've got a plan now?" Fletcher ripped another chunk of cornbread from the stub on the table and dipped it into the pot of soup. Robyn turned away, afraid the smell would trigger the bile at the back of her throat. Her eyes fell on Derek instead, who shrugged.

Kara turned to face them. "Yeah. We're going home."

Robyn frowned. "Home?" Surely she didn't mean …

Kara held both hands up in surrender. "Your place is ideal, Robyn. And with your parents away, it's sitting empty just waiting for us. Come on."

Fletcher spoke over his mouthful. "Where is it?"

"Cobalt Valley." Kara tapped her fingers on the bench.

Robyn stared at her friend. It's not that they grew drugs or anything, but the farm was different. No-one ever came to the farm. Not even her supervisor knew where it was. Robyn started.

"It's perfect."

Kate and Kara shared a glance. "Good. We leave tonight."

16

Convergence

"Deckker lost Catherine. The imbecile."

"Another researcher from the program missing. You think Robyn is involved?"

"It's not just her, that much is clear. First the reactionary team, now this. Someone's helping her. I don't like it, Brock."

"And Terence?"

"Weaving assures me he is still on leave, though she could just be covering her ass. I'll look into it."

"But you've got what you want."

"We're no closer to unlocking Eli or Fletcher's DNA. Sara is promising, I'll admit, but we've had to resort to the implants to maintain control. She's spirited, that one."

"And the other? The boy."

"Jacob still hasn't paired, though he survived the radiation. It's no matter. I've tasked Fang to the gene sequences."

"Do you think she can crack them?"

"Robyn isn't the only one with initiative, Brock. Be patient. You'll see."

Robyn breathed in the stale, turpentine-heavy air, wondering if she'd finally been away long enough to divine the unique smell of home. She paused in the doorway, trying to retain it, but Kate and Kara burst past her and it disappeared, sullied by the intrusion.

"Get some air in here," Kate called to her sister. The twins flooded the kitchen with sound as they wrenched open windows.

Robyn's skin felt clammy and gross after spending most of the day first slumped in a sticky chair in arrivals and then sneezing away in the musty bus seat. Not to mention the preceding flight. Robyn felt like she'd done enough travel to tide her over for a lifetime. Catherine, on the other hand, didn't look rumpled at all. Completely unfairly, she looked like a walking advertisement for a travel company. Robyn glanced at her over her shoulder.

"Come on in." Robyn moved aside. "Home sweet home."

Catherine tucked a strand of hair behind her ear and stepped over the threshold. "It's lovely."

Robyn followed Catherine's gaze as she took in the rough wood, the sloping valleys of the lime-rendered walls, the little alcoves for candles. Robyn had spent two summers stamping dirt into tyres and working render between her toes. This place was a part of her. Light danced from the bottle wall and Catherine moved toward it, entranced. Robyn shifted her weight to the other foot. Catherine hadn't seen the wood burner or the compost toilet. Maybe it would be less lovely then. Robyn sighed at the sight of the spanner and washers stacked by the kitchen sink. There were probably more repairs-in-waiting scattered around the house. Her mother was a fiend with a paintbrush but not remotely confident with wrench and screwdriver.

"Hey, could I borrow some clothes?" Catherine stood in the kitchen, rubbing one arm. Sea-green light foamed in her hair.

"This way." Robyn tipped her head toward the corridor.

It felt strange to have someone she barely knew in her bedroom. Catherine had the wardrobe doors splayed open, and Robyn felt exposed, remembering Catherine's chic apartment. *She must be a traveller*, Robyn mused, thinking of the tapestries, the jewellery. Different continents on her wrist. Robyn perched on the edge of her bed, stifling a yawn as Catherine flicked through the hangers. Camping trips up and down the coast didn't really equate to a cultured childhood.

"Can I borrow these?" Catherine held out a pair of faded jeans, a grey tee and an oversized flannel shirt. It was Robyn's favourite one, a thick blue flannel she'd found at a vintage place in Canberra. She nodded, pleased.

"The bathroom is at the end of the corridor." The bedsprings creaked as Robyn jumped to her feet. "You can leave your bag here," she added as Catherine made to grab her satchel. "I think we'll have to share anyway."

Catherine turned sharply at the wardrobe and Robyn felt her cheeks grow hot.

"The room," Robyn clarified with a limp hand. "I've got a decent camp bed." Her face burned.

"Thanks." Catherine disappeared with a smirk.

There was goat's cheese in the fridge, sealed in oil. Robyn sniffed it tentatively before adding it to the platter of fresh salad and flat bread. The vegetable garden had been a mess, overrun with nasturtiums and fat hen, but it still flourished somehow, lettuce forcing its way through the weedy net.

"Smells good." Catherine came around the corner, head tilted as she combed her long hair. Robyn stared. Catherine looked incredible. A strange tingle ran through Robyn's spine. She looked away, feeling guilty for no real reason. *Get a grip, Robyn.*

Catherine flipped her hair over her shoulder, sending a hint of tea tree and sandalwood wafting in the air. *You smell good, too*, Robyn thought. "Just a few things from the pantry. We'll have to stock up if we're planning on staying here a while." Hating how her voice was slightly too high, she brought the platter over to the table. Kate pounced from out of nowhere, stacking a plate high before bounding off.

"Setting up the tech," Kate mumbled over a mouthful. "Kara's gone to get Terence." She disappeared down the corridor, leaving Robyn very much alone with Catherine. Nice-looking, lovely-smelling Catherine.

Catherine loaded up her plate. She closed her eyes as she took the first mouthful. "God, I'm hungry." Her eyelashes fluttered as she chewed.

Robyn turned to her own plate and focused on chewing in a lady-like manner. She'd had too many nights on her own, slurping noodles with Tarantino for company. Her mother would be appalled to know how low her eating etiquette had slumped.

"They look good on you. The clothes, I mean." *Smooth, Robyn.* She felt her cheeks burn for the second time. No doubt Catherine would think her a freak.

Catherine smiled. "Thanks. You've got good taste." She thumbed the collar of the flannel shirt. "Vintage?"

Robyn flushed. "Yeah, though not in a fancy way."

"Fancy's overrated." Catherine forked up a slice of purple carrot. "Thanks for getting me out of there."

Robyn ducked her head. "Thank the twins."

Catherine reached for more salad, spooning out some diced kohlrabi. "If you hadn't come to Montreal, I wouldn't have had a clue. This one's on you, Robyn. So thanks."

"You're welcome." Robyn squirmed under Catherine's steady gaze.

When they'd finished eating, Catherine stacked their plates and placed them on the bench.

"Can I bake something? If everyone's arriving soon, I thought …"

Robyn steered her to the drawer of home-milled flours and watched Catherine's eyes light up in delight.

"Go crazy." Robyn flopped onto one of the couches. She was just going to close her eyes for a few seconds.

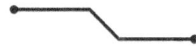

Sydney was bright, with voluminous blue skies that penetrated even the tinted bus windows. Terence wanted to drink it all in. The city gave way to green hills rolling down to the sea, a hint of Wales in the sheer cliffs and pounding surf. So far from home but surrounded by familiar landscapes, he imagined Bry and Val hiking here, Bry no doubt penning another geological guide as they went. Glaciation and mudstone, fossilised history in the rock. Only now his Dad would be solo.

Terence rested his cheek on the warm glass and closed his eyes.

Too soon, Ariana pushed him awake. "We're here."

Terence pushed himself away from the bus window and rubbed his eyes. Ariana stood in the aisle with her backpack already over her shoulders. There was no sign of the pet carrier, but a slick nose peeped out from Ariana's jacket. Glancing at his watch, he was shocked to see he'd slept for hours.

"Cobalt Valley, right?" Ariana had her hands on her hips now. The driver popped a soft drink can open. Terence heard the *clink* and rush of bubbles. At least, he hoped it was soft drink and not beer. He'd read some disturbing papers on casual alcoholism in Australia.

"Yeah." Terence clambered to his feet and snagged his duffel bag. Thirsty, he eyed the can in the driver's stubby fingers with longing. Just lemonade.

The doors snapped at his ankles like a demon as Terence stepped onto the pavement, the bus peeling away with a splutter of exhaust. Terence rolled his shoulders and yawned. They'd been dumped opposite a picturesque mechanic's station with ancient-looking pumps. The main street petered out after sixty or so metres, a cluster of buildings huddled together on each side as if for warmth.

A yellow four-wheel drive slowed toward them,

puttering to a stop. "I think this is our ride," said Ariana. Jericho perched on the crown of her head as she leaned into the gutter.

A woman shielded her eyes against the glare. "Terence and Ariana?" The engine let out a low whine and the woman slapped the dashboard in disgust. "That's enough from you," she growled.

Ariana wrenched open the passenger door. "I'll ride shotgun," she said over her shoulder to Terence. She turned to the driver. "Hey, I'm Ariana."

The woman nodded. "Kara. Thanks for making the trek out here."

Terence scrambled into the back as Kara revved the engine. The whine petered out to a tinny whistle. The mysterious Kara now had a face; in fact she was scrutinising him in the rear-view mirror. Terence wasn't sure what he'd imagined, but she looked far too normal to be procuring fake passports and thwarting international plots.

Books and piles of clothes filled the back seat. Terence clutched his duffel bag to his chest as boxes shifted against his calves.

"Sorry about the mess. I've batched a bunch of errands

with this trip into town. We're a bit out of the way."

Terence blinked and almost missed the main strip as they zoomed out past lush pastures dotted with dairy cows. The fields eventually gave way to dense forest. Out of the way. Right.

"There are only a few permitted residences out here." Kara raised her voice over the rumble of the engine. "And no-one for hundreds of kilometres toward the Great Dividing Range. Nice and isolated."

Terence tried not to think about the psychopaths who would love that description. He'd watched two documentaries on the plane – one on the serial killers speckled across Australia's vast wild spaces, the other on the multitude of animals capable of killing him. He almost wished he'd stuck to the vapid fluff on offer on the main channel.

He studied the back of Kara's head instead, her dark hair bouncing with each new bump in the road. He hadn't noticed the change from bitumen to rough compacted dirt, but the going was tougher now. Kara slowed and turned left into a dusty red driveway, and they jiggled their way down a rutted road, forest creeping in on both sides, vines reaching out like tentacles. Now he understood the need for the four-wheel drive. He could almost feel his teeth moving around. Kara pulled into a clearing in front of a sloped mound lined with solar panels. Terence squinted, unsure why they were stopping but glad that the four years he'd spent shackled with braces wasn't about to be undone. Then he realised – it wasn't a hill, it was a building.

"An earthship," Ariana said in the front, face plastered to the window. Terence smiled. She'd tried to convince Bry to build one last summer, but their father had just laughed. They'd built the yurt instead, from lean stripped saplings and waterproof canvas. Ariana loved it.

"Yeah," Kara replied. "Pretty cool, huh?"

Ariana leapt to the ground, tugging her backpack with her. "Car tyres and earth, right?"

"Yup. All plastered over with lime render. Completely off-grid and nigh untraceable." Kara opened the rear door and grinned at Terence as she grabbed a stack of books. He glanced at their spines. Zoology, mythology, chromatography. Quite the collection.

"Come on, you've got to meet everyone. My sister, Kate, is going to go nuts over your lizard." Kara was already halfway to the earthship. Terence clambered out, pulling his duffel coat to his chest.

A door set into the grassy hill opened and people spilled out. A petite girl with pink hair, holding a keyboard and screwdriver. A dark-haired woman in jeans and a tee.

"Oh my God, is that what I think it is?" The girl with pink hair started forward, the circuitry on the stripped-down keyboard glinting in the sun. Terence's hand flew up to shade his eyes. Just as well. The last person out the door was a tall, blonde woman. A vision. Terence inhaled.

Kate waved the keyboard. "I freaking love amphibians."

Ariana held out her arm and Jericho skittered across onto Kate's hand. Kate stifled a scream of excitement.

The other two women came over. Terence tried to straighten his button-down shirt, realising he hadn't looked in a mirror in over eighteen hours. He was bound to be a disaster, his cowlick living up to its namesake.

Kate pointed. "That's Robyn and Catherine."

Catherine. Such a beautiful name.

It was cool inside the building, and not dark like he'd imagined. Bracelets jingled on Catherine's wrist as she brought over a tray of scones and a crock of butter.

Terence smelled date and ginger, maybe coconut. He wondered if Catherine had made them, found himself hoping she had. A common language.

"So," he said, folding his hands in his lap. "Hi."

Catherine smiled, pulling apart a scone and buttering it before passing the plate to him. "Thanks," he said. The jet lag felt like a physical force, extra gravity pushing him into the couch. The scone melted in his mouth as he sank down further into the worn fabric.

Catherine spoke first. "God, it feels so weird to be here." She placed a scone on Robyn's plate. "And your sister ..."

Terence nodded, eyeing Ariana out on the grass with Kate. Jericho leapt between them, spiralling in the air like a corkscrew. His sister, somehow caught up in all of this.

Robyn jiggled her knee as Terence talked, stifling a yawn. An hour. She'd have slept longer if Catherine hadn't shaken her awake and thrust a mug of tea under her nose. It felt strangely normal, Catherine knowing her way around the kitchen. Robyn studied Terence. Tall like Catherine, with tousled dark hair and thick glasses. He hadn't been freaked out by the house yet, either. Neither the wood burner nor the compost toilet had spooked him. Maybe they were all freaks. Heartened, Robyn closed her eyes. Catherine smelled like coconut and buckwheat flour now, the same wholesome embrace of the food co-op. It was nice.

Robyn stared at the steam rising from the scone on her plate. She blinked, not sure when it had appeared. Unbuttered, the way she liked it. When she looked up, Catherine had tilted her body in her direction and Terence looked at her expectantly. What did they call it? *Imposter syndrome.* Robyn shuddered. *I'm not qualified for this.*

"Sorry, what were you saying?"

"This thing, we have to call it something," Terence said. "The unique bonds ... it's like an extreme symbiosis ..."

"Convergence," Robyn supplied. She'd been thinking about it too. The word popped unbidden into her mind.

Catherine swallowed a mouthful. "Convergence. I like it."

Robyn took a bite of her scone. It melted in her

mouth and a faint moan escaped her lips. Catherine smiled into the lip of her mug.

Derek. Derek would hate the farm, Robyn was sure of it.

Kara leaned in and snagged a scone from the pile. "Robyn, can I talk to you for a minute?"

Robyn nodded. Terence and Catherine started talking about gene loci and the sequencing they'd need to do. So much work. She felt her shoulders sag under the weight of it all.

Kara left a floury trail to the studio. "What do you think?"

The easel was folded up against the wall, her mother's paints stacked in a crate. Two huge monitors sat on the paint-splattered bench, a wicked-looking hard drive connected by a bulky umbilical cord of wires.

"It's different," managed Robyn. Her mother would have a fit if she saw it. "The internet connection –"

"All up and running. Finally." Kate swivelled on the chair to face them. "We're useful again."

Kara finished her scone, leaving white prints on her shirt where she wiped her hands. Kate narrowed her eyes at her sister. "Where's mine?"

Kara froze. "Crap."

Kate rolled her eyes and let out a theatrical sigh. "Gotta do everything yourself around here." She shoved past Kara and headed into the hallway.

Kara dropped into one of the chairs at the bench. "I don't get why you're embarrassed about this place. It's awesome."

Robyn flicked a glance back to the couches down the hall. She heard Catherine's voice as Kate complimented her on the scones, her laugh high and lilting.

"Not embarrassed, exactly. You were right. It's precisely what we need right now."

Kara grinned when Robyn turned back to her.

"What?" Robyn ran her fingers through her hair.

Kara raised her eyebrows. "Nothing. Now scoot. We'll see if we can get a handle on what Fang is doing in Beijing. You go science it up."

Robyn paused in the doorway. "We're good, right?"

Kara rolled her eyes. "Yes, we're good. Don't worry, I'll always have your back."

17

Spirit World

A small boat pulled in to the fishing harbour in the crisp dawn. The trawler sounded a horn and nudged the dock, rope spooling out like wet intestines and landing heavily on the planks. An elderly man peered into the fog from the shore, fishing rod held in mittened hands. The bucket by his side brimmed with fish.

The young lads couldn't be assed to get up before dawn, but that was when the fish were good and ready. He couldn't sleep through anymore. The 2am piss signalled the end of peaceful slumber and he figured he might as well be on the rocks than tossing under his scratchy wool blanket. It was stained now the missus was gone, the bottles under the laundry sink a gaudy, repulsive, floral mess. He simply sloshed a cocktail into the machine these days. Still, the blanket was a comfort on the damp rock platform, tucked over his knees as if he were an invalid.

He yawned, reaching for the thermos of black coffee, already rank from sitting too long, judging by the smell. There was movement on the dock. Heavy crates, muffled voices. The thermos slipped from his grip, sending a deluge of brown liquid onto his lap. For a moment he didn't feel it as his eyes strained for another glimpse. No.

The coffee soaked through, hit his crotch. He jumped up in pain, hips creaking in protest.

It must have been a trick of the light. Not enough sleep. He bent down to retrieve the thermos.

Imagine, a bear striding off the landing plank. Ridiculous. He shook out the blanket, eyeing the seeping diameter of the stain. He'd have to read the labels on those bloody bottles to get rid of this one.

Fletcher liked it here. It was so green, the forest stretching for miles. Different smells, unusual animals. Wombats deep in subterranean tunnels, kangaroos mowing pastures, feral cats stalking unwitting birds.

Thoughts seeped in and out of his mind like the tide. He was getting better at compartmentalising, being able to dip in and snag one thread of consciousness or skim across the whole wavering frequency. He wondered if it was all part of some greater frequency. Maybe he'd ask Robyn about it.

He flopped down onto his back. The thick cushiony grass was a welcome relief after the cramped confines of the ship. He stretched out, feeling his back pop. The air was sweet and clear, punctuated by the gentle burbling progress of the stream. Fletcher swallowed thickly at the memory of the diesel fumes that had seemed to permeate everything on board. Eva had hated it too, her mind thrumming with discontent and leaving him edgy and restless. Too much time to think; it had been a long few days.

It hadn't seemed to bother Derek, who just slept on his bunk or paced the stern. The older boy had stayed quiet, never started a conversation. Maybe he had a lot on his mind. It had royally sucked.

Fletcher wriggled his toes and dug them into the grass. He was far enough from the earthship that no-one could find him to make him wash up or peel potatoes. Robyn's farm was weird – no dishwasher, a cupboard full of jars with benign labels like 'marmalade' and 'preserved apricots' that looked like old museum specimens preserved in formaldehyde.

He closed his eyes and listened to the stream and the rustle of leaves far above him. The lazy push and pull of his mind with Eva's was hypnotic. He cocked an eye when he heard footsteps crunch through the leaves, peering over Eva's shoulder. Ariana.

Fletcher pushed himself upright. He'd only been here a day, while Ariana had already been here nearly three. Fletcher had barely seen her. He'd slept the whole first day and Eva had pulled him out of bed this morning; he'd skittered around the bag of dirt-crusted potatoes with a peeler balanced on top and made a beeline for the outdoors.

"Hi," Fletcher said. "Ariana, right?" His skin felt too hot all of a sudden. He didn't talk to girls at school. He'd always figured that when he made first string in the basketball team they'd come talk to him. Now that was never going to happen. He was going to have to come up with a new plan.

Ariana unzipped the top of her jacket and a lizard

skated out, taking up a position on her shoulder. "Yeah, this is Jericho." She crossed her arms and the jacket crinkled. She wore Kara's boots over tights and a skirt. The Doc Martens, a size too large, gaped at her calves.

Eva rolled over, shaking the leaves from her fur. "This is Eva," Fletcher added. The bear huffed, glancing at Jericho.

Ariana squatted down next to Fletcher and curled her feet underneath her. Her dark hair flopped forward, shielding her face for a moment before she shook it back. Fletcher wanted to ask her a dozen questions about what it was like to hear Jericho's thoughts. If she heard the shifting frequency of other voices around them, if she had the strange dreams too … Instead, he cleared his throat and feigned interest in the trees lining the clearing.

Jericho slid down Ariana's jacket and plopped into the stream with a diver's splash. Ariana shed the jacket and Fletcher caught a glimpse of blue light dancing on her skin. He blinked and it faded.

"Are you having the dreams, too?" Ariana asked. She yanked off the Doc Martens and piled them with her jacket and socks. "Dreams of others?"

She dipped her feet in the water, the blue light snaking up her calves. He hadn't imagined it, then. Fletcher nodded. The dreams had become more vivid.

"I'm still not sure what they mean. It feels like I know all those people somehow, but that would be crazy."

Ariana swirled her feet, sending eddying pools out into the centre of the water. "Me, too. I feel like there's something here" – she tapped her head – "that's just behind a door, like I'd understand if I could just figure out how to open it."

Eva's voice floated through Fletcher's mind, thick like honey.

You bridge our two worlds. Eva's voice, but heavier, laced with what felt like a dozen other minds.

What two worlds? Fletcher was frustrated. The dreams left him anxious and sweaty when he woke up, drained before the day even started.

The spirit world, young walker.

The humming noise began again and Eva's coat bristled with green light. Jericho clambered onto Ariana's leg, surrounded by a blue aura.

"Jericho ... he says it's time we learned." Ariana's eyes looked unfocused as she turned to him. Fletcher wondered if she heard the humming noise as well, or if her skin felt too tight.

"Learned what?" Fletcher said.

Close your eyes. Empty your mind. Focus on me.

Fletcher took a deep breath and exhaled slowly. The stream burbled away on its perpetual flow. Flow. Ariana sat completely still by his side, hands resting on her knees as if meditating. Jericho perched inert on her lap. Fletcher stared at the blue light flickering from the lizard's body to hers, enveloping them in a bright flash of blue. It blazed before disappearing. Fletcher waved a hand in front of Ariana's face, but she didn't respond.

"Ariana?" he said, fear constricting his chest.

She has already crossed over. Come. They are waiting.

Fletcher closed his eyes again, heart thudding in his chest. *Crossed over to where?*

Eva didn't answer his question. *Tap into the infinite. The universe. You feel it there, just beyond your perception of the world around you. Dig deeper, pull aside the facade.* Eva-but-not-Eva's voice.

Fletcher squeezed his eyes shut, resisting the temptation to open them. The natural sounds of the forest began to dim and his heart rate slowed. The delicate boundary between his own mind and Eva's blurred, merging in a heady rush. The ground disappeared beneath him, leaving Fletcher tumbling through empty space. Colours rushed behind his eyelids. He kept his eyes clamped shut.

"Fletcher?" Ariana's voice. Fletcher hesitantly opened his eyes. They were in some sort of grove, surrounded by shimmering trees. The stream was gone. Fletcher blinked, staring at Ariana like he'd never seen her before.

Ariana stood entwined by an enormous, sinuous dragon with long, floating whiskers.

"Jericho?" Fletcher stammered. Ariana nodded, watching the dragon with an entranced expression.

Something heavy moved behind him and Fletcher jumped to his feet, heart pounding again.

"Eva," he breathed. She looked like the drawing of a diprotodon in his science textbook, the one with a man standing to one side as a scale indicator. Fletcher had drawn in little lines of shock around the man's head. Now he understood how tiny the scale man must have felt beside a lumbering dinosaur with claws as big as shopping trolleys. Fletcher had to look up just to see the underside of her jaw. Eva stamped her feet and the ground quaked, clouding her in green light. When it cleared, there was no trace of the jumbo-sized bear. Eva coughed as she emerged, and Fletcher had to clap a hand to his mouth to stifle his laughter. Now she was no bigger than a hamster. Eva lifted a tiny leg to examine it with a *humph* before prancing over to Fletcher's side.

Fletcher scooped her up, shaking his head in disbelief.

How is this possible? He projected to Eva. The little hamster bear glistened with green light.

"Everything is more fluid here in the spirit realm." Wrapped in an orange robe, a boy appeared in their midst. Fletcher jumped. The boy had materialised out of nowhere. "I've been waiting to meet you both for some time. Allow me to introduce myself. My name is Lenti."

It was dinner time and Robyn realised she'd seen neither Fletcher nor Ariana for hours. She'd lost track of time bent over the old gas chromatograph she'd salvaged from uni last year. Robyn shut the operating panel and dumped the screwdriver on the table. Brock had helped her heave it into the service elevator, hidden beneath a tarp. It wasn't stealing, technically, just relocating. She felt the now-familiar pang of betrayal. Kara had shown her the emails. Brock had been spying on her for two years. Bile rose in the back of her throat. She'd made him pop-up birthday cards, and the whole time he'd been looking over her shoulder. Still, a small voice kept whispering in her ear that maybe he didn't realise who it was for, what they were capable of.

Robyn rested an arm against the vibrating machine. Catherine had prepared new samples from both walkers. Ariana's chromatograms lay splayed out on the table, identical to Fletcher's. She couldn't bear to look at them again. Robyn left the ancient loading arm whirring in the background as she pushed into the kitchen. She'd probably find them in there, feasting on chocolate-chip biscuits. Robyn sighed. Always worrying over nothing. Ms Responsible.

Derek pored over the textbooks Kara had lugged back. Robyn caught a glimpse of the Chinese Zodiac circle as she passed his shoulder. Catherine and Terence were curled up on separate couches, looking over the original testing results. No Fletcher or Ariana. Robyn stretched her hands overhead.

"I'm going for a walk to see if I can find those two."

Derek tipped his head back. "I'll come, too. I need a

break from all these myths and legends."

Robyn shrugged, secretly pleased. Catherine and Terence hadn't moved. They'd been working together all day. It put her on edge without really understanding why, though she was more than relieved to give them creative control in the kitchen. Boy, could they cook.

"Sure." Robyn waited as Derek shrugged on a jacket.

They walked in companionable silence for a while, soaking up the twilight. Derek broke it first.

"I, uh, realised I never thanked you properly. For coming to find me, for making me part of this."

Robyn fiddled with the edge of her shirt and Derek's hand grazed her elbow as they walked. He looked different, she realised. He had dark circles under his eyes and his gait was stiffer. She felt guilty for a second before remembering that Derek had volunteered to go with Fletcher.

"Part of what?" Robyn kicked at a loose stone. "I'm not sure how long we can hold our own against the MRI." She rubbed her forehead. "I'm sorry, I'm tired. So many people around is a bit overwhelming."

Derek's hand closed the distance, curling around Robyn's. She flinched at the unexpected contact. Derek didn't seem to notice, and Robyn wondered when he'd become so touchy-feely.

"You're doing a good job, Robyn." She relaxed into his firm grip, closing her eyes for a moment. Duke, the barn in North Carolina, it all felt like months, not days, ago. By herself, she knew how to do a good job. This was much harder. And Fletcher and Ariana …

"It's all happening too fast." Robyn opened her eyes again. They'd rounded a corner and the creek lay dead ahead. She stopped in the middle of the track, staring over Derek's shoulder. Ariana and Fletcher sat motionless by the bank. Too still.

"Something's not right," Robyn breathed. She wriggled out of Derek's grasp and broke into a run, falling to her knees in front of Fletcher. She waved a hand in front of his face. No response. His eyes were glassy, unfocused. "What's happened to them?" Robyn couldn't keep the note of panic from her voice.

"Stay here, I'll get the others." A hand on her shoulder, then nothing. Derek was gone.

"Hurry," she shouted at his retreating form, eyes locked on Fletcher.

Lenti was shorter than Ariana, with a wide forehead. Or maybe that was just because his head was shaved. Ariana instantly felt guilty – she was sure she'd look weird without any hair. She imagined looking into a mirror at the skin stretched taut over her knobbly skull and shivered.

As he sat down, Lenti arranged his robes and brought his fists together in a reflexive way, as if he'd done it hundreds of times before.

Ariana glanced at Fletcher and followed suit, minus the fist bumping. Jericho wound his way around her torso, hovering above her but tethered to her body. His whiskers tickled her chin and made her sneeze.

"This world lies parallel to your own," said Lenti. His head gleamed in the light. Ariana looked around; anything to avoid accidentally blurting out something unkind about Lenti's lack of hair. *Borehead*, that's what they'd call it at school.

It definitely wasn't the clearing by the stream, but it didn't look strange enough to be a parallel anything. It reminded her of photos of the old-world forest in her mother's *National Geographic* collection, with huge trees cloistered together. She squinted as she caught a glimmer of light. The closer she looked, the more the forest seemed to change. Ariana gasped as the trees began glimmering with light, their trunks pulsing with colour like a programmed set of Christmas lights. It was disorienting, like being dumped into an Escher painting mixed with Disney's *Fantasia*. Ariana stared. This definitely wasn't in *National Geographic*.

"What took you so long?" Lenti picked at a thread on his robe.

Ariana blinked, forcing her attention back to the strange boy. "Huh?"

"It's been over two hundred years since the last walker. You couldn't have spread yourselves out a bit better?"

Ariana glanced at Fletcher, who shrugged, eyes wide.

"What are you talking about?" Ariana said.

Lenti stared at her, then rested his head in his hands. "Buddha help me." He cleared his throat, pointing to Eva and Jericho. "You two, you haven't instructed them? They haven't opened the channels?"

Eva humphed, though it came out as a cute squeak. Fletcher stroked her back.

"What are you talking about?" Fletcher's voice mirrored Eva's frustration.

"To your lineages. Earth and water. You are not the first, you realise?"

Ariana felt Jericho's tail contract around her stomach. "The dreams," she breathed. "I dreamed there were others like us."

"Praise be," muttered Lenti. "It's a start."

Robyn squatted beside Fletcher's inert form. Terence checked Ariana's pulse.

"Steady," Terence said. "They're breathing fine. It's like a trance, or something." The veins sticking out on his neck belied his calm tone. Robyn backed away, careful not to bump into Eva. Both the bear and salamander were in identical comatose states. Terence stayed, whispering to his sister.

"Damn it." Derek struggled with two dome tents. From what Robyn could see, the tents were winning. She took a step toward the carnage. She hadn't thanked him for bringing everyone so quickly. She wasn't sure if she could have lasted much longer sitting with the silent walkers.

"Don't." Catherine flicked a glance in Robyn's direction. "I already tried to help him."

Robyn pivoted toward Catherine, taking in a deep breath laced with cardamom and coriander. Catherine scrutinised her as she stirred a pot over an open fire.

"Are you okay? It must have been a hell of a shock, to stumble on them both like this."

Robyn sighed. "Yeah, well, that's an understatement." Her legs felt wobbly, as if she'd cycled too far. She focused on staying upright, wondering if she should stay with Fletcher. She felt an almost parental responsibility for him.

Instead, Robyn peered into the pot, her hunger surfacing in a rush. It was late. Dusk formed a heavy blanket on the trees above. "This smells amazing."

Catherine smiled. "Chicken korma." She tapped the spoon against the rim, then balanced it against one of the handles, looking down at Robyn with concerned eyes.

"Hey, come here," Catherine beckoned with wide arms. Robyn hesitated for a heartbeat before folding into the hug. "The cooking, it's my way of dealing," Catherine murmured into her hair. The ghost of her breath tickled Robyn's ear. Robyn nodded into Catherine's shoulder and her stomach flooded with confusing warmth. Her heart thudded in her chest as her shoulders relaxed and

Catherine seemed to pull her in tighter.

A triumphant sound startled her, and she stepped back from Catherine to see Derek fist pump the air. Two tents stood semi erect on the grass. The hug left Robyn groggy.

Catherine's fingers lingered above her waist for an instant before she ladled curry into bowls. Robyn took a deep breath, trying to clear the light-headedness that had descended on her. *Just the shock*, she scolded herself. She took the bowl of curry from Catherine without really registering it and collapsed in front of the campfire. The others followed. Derek left the second tent swaying with one of the poles bent at an impossible angle.

Terence even dragged himself away from Ariana, though he kept throwing glances in her direction.

Robyn felt Catherine watching her across the flames, but every time she checked, Catherine's gaze slid over her. Terence and Derek focused on demolishing their food. The sound of scraping spoons and the crackle of logs shifting in the fire won out over attempted conversation.

"I'll keep watch," Terence announced as he put down his bowl.

"I'll take second shift," said Catherine, surprising

Robyn. Catherine turned to Terence. "Just wake me up, okay?"

Terence nodded, looking grateful.

Robyn pushed the last few grains of rice around in her bowl. When she looked up, she caught Catherine's eye. Catherine stared at her, eyes thoughtful.

"I'm going to bed," Robyn declared, rising to her feet and avoiding Catherine's gaze. She wasn't quite sure why it made her skin feel prickly. Tired, she must be tired.

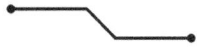

A hubbub of chatter roused Robyn from her sleeping bag, and she was greeted by feeble dawn light. Catherine's sleeping bag lay empty next to her, the tent flaps wide open. The daytime version of somebody differed to the pyjama version; there was something unexpectedly intimate about sharing sleeping space with somebody when you were too old for sleepover parties. The sleeping bag was starting to become synonymous with Catherine. Her silent presence was comforting. Robyn yawned, feeling its absence. She hadn't heard Catherine come in last night. Her stomach contorted when she remembered the hug, the way Catherine had stared at her across the fire. She shrugged the memory away. They'd all been in shock and needing reassurance, that's all. *Catherine's gay*, a little voice in the back of her mind reminded her. Robyn ignored it. Friends hugged all the time, it meant nothing.

The voices came from the creek. Catherine sat next to Ariana and Fletcher. They were awake. Robyn stumbled out of her sleeping bag onto the dewy grass, ran to the creek and engulfed Fletcher in a loud, squealing hug before turning to shake Ariana's shoulders.

"You're all right," she stammered.

Catherine smiled as she wrapped a thick jacket closer around her shoulders. Robyn recognised it as Terence's. A zipping noise preceded the arrival of the two boys. Sleepy and bed-headed, Terence and Derek straightened, squinting in the light, their annoyance replaced by excitement when they found the source of the commotion. Terence bounded over, gathering Ariana in a hug that half-knocked her over. Robyn felt a twinge at the understanding that passed between them. Catherine held up a hand. "Breakfast. Then the walkers will explain."

Terence rummaged around for the clean pot. "Coming right up."

Robyn cradled her porridge bowl in her lap, content to listen. It was a lot to take in.

"Spirit walkers?"

"Jericho's a dragon –"

"– a monk?"

Terence raised an arm, and everyone quietened.

"Yeah, apparently only we can walk between this world and the spirit world." Ariana dolloped more oats into her bowl. Terence passed her the maple syrup and watched wide-eyed as she set the porridge adrift in a sugary sea.

"Lenti says the walkers are part of a reincarnation cycle designed to keep the earth in balance."

Derek snorted into his bowl. "Seriously?" He frowned when he registered the silence around him.

"Why not?" Terence wiped his glasses on the hem of his shirt. "Is it really so crazy, after everything we've seen?"

Derek searched out Robyn for support. She wavered. Science can't explain everything; not yet, anyway.

"This convergent bond is different," Robyn said. She wondered if she'd hurt his feelings, felt a weird urge to defend herself. *Don't ask for forgiveness or permission.*

"So, what, they're going to remember being different people now, too?" Derek said. His bowl clattered to the ground.

Fletcher butted in. "Yeah, though not all at once. Lenti says it'll take time to unlock our past memories." Appealing to Robyn, he said: "You remember my dream, right? When we were … after my house."

"Yes, the three walkers." Robyn propelled Fletcher out of the memory, trying to reconcile the boy who had glowed green and decimated the soldiers with the quiet boy who now sat cross-legged by the fire.

"Mmm. Well, we know where the third walker is now. The air walker." Fletcher tapped his spoon against his bowl.

"Beijing." It was Catherine's voice, flat and level. "They're in Beijing, aren't they?"

Fletcher nodded. "His name is Eli, and we need to get him out of there."

Derek rose to his feet and strode out of the clearing. Robyn started to get up, but Catherine grabbed her arm.

"Let him cool off."

Robyn watched Derek walk back toward the earthship, head down, kicking at loose rocks. She wondered if he expected her to follow him.

"What then? When you're all together?" Robyn returned to the circle. Catherine shuffled closer to her, sealing the gap Derek left.

"Lenti says there are spirits in our world we need to find." Fletcher screwed up his nose. "To guide us."

Robyn shivered. When she was little she used to run and jump into bed to avoid the monster she was convinced lived beneath it. Yet somehow, when Fletcher spoke of *spirits*, she knew he meant the good kind.

Terence poked the coals with a stick. "This is big, guys. Bringing the earth back into balance. Can it really be done?" Robyn wasn't sure if he'd meant to speak out loud. Nobody answered, they just studied the coals flickering to life with new oxygen.

Ariana put her bowl down and lay back on her elbows. "I need to go to the sea. There's someone I need to meet."

"I'll take you," Robyn said. She wasn't sure she was up to a morning hunched over the gas chromatograph.

"Terence?"

"Of course," Terence grinned, stacking the sticky bowls. "Jeez."

Terence and Robyn stood by the shore, soaked to the knees, watching the horizon instead of the foaming waves. Robyn shivered beneath her coat as the wind picked up. In the surf, Ariana showed no signs of discomfort. Terence raised his head for the tenth time to scan the beach, but they were still alone. This was one of the remotest beaches Robyn knew, with only gulls for kilometres of windswept sand. She used to collect sand dollars after storms while her mother added to her basket of ridged shells that had been brought up from the depths, announcing how incredible it was that those delicate Fibonacci whorls survived the crashing journey to the shore.

Ariana bobbed in the midst of a pod of dolphins whose sleek, silver bodies dipped in and out of the water. Behind her, Robyn saw the telltale eruption of a whale. Blue whales could be enormous, hundreds of thousands of kilograms. Steamrollers.

"Do you think she'll be all right?" Robyn clutched the edges of her coat tighter.

Terence stared straight ahead, eyes narrowed against the wind. "She'll be right."

Ariana floated in the swirling, dark abyss, skin prickling with the familiar blue energy. She broadened her mind to the animals around her and began to lose feeling in her extremities. Merging her mind with Jericho's, she hovered on the brink between both worlds. The result was electric – flashes of fishing trawlers, bright coral, dawn penetrating the deep. She whirled along a spectrum of thoughts, all clamouring for her full attention. Abruptly, the voices stopped. Ariana returned to herself as the dolphins backed away, taking up a respectful distance as a much larger presence shifted into focus. The whale hung suspended as if in a dark sky, eyes glittering like stars. Ariana's head filled with a gentle humming that built in pressure as the whale lifted a flipper to graze her forehead. The chorus built to a crescendo as Ariana closed her eyes and embraced the sound that reverberated in her chest. As the whale stroked her temples, a flash of light erupted behind her eyelids, searing her retinas. Ariana inhaled on instinct, the salt water rushing into her throat. Mentally she prepared to splutter, but the reflex didn't come. She reached her hands to her neck, where she felt deep, parallel slits. Gills. Blue light surrounded her body, and Jericho rocketed upward in his dragon form.

When she tore her gaze from Jericho, the whale had left. A name lingered in her mind: *Atlantis.*

She'd just met the water spirit.

Robyn stared at the blinding flash of blue light, her knees buckling as the dragon soared above the water. It had a long, slender body with a whip-like tail. Jericho. He was magnificent.

Terence stood rigid at her side, his gaze not wavering from the small figure at the foaming epicentre of the blast. He didn't relax his shoulders until Ariana breached the surface and waved in delight. The dragon disappeared back into the dark water.

"She's okay," Robyn exhaled.

"I know. I just, wow." Terence hunched further into his jacket that still smelled faintly of Catherine. "I can't protect her like I used to."

"She can handle it," replied Robyn, watching Ariana emerge from the surf, eyes gleaming.

"That's what I'm worried about," Terence said.

"Guys, check this out," yelled Ariana over the rumble of the waves. She turned sideways, watching for their shocked expressions. "I got me some gills!"

Ariana's grin remained plastered on her face the whole bumpy trip back. Wrapped in towels in the back seat, she was almost too blissed out to talk.

"Everything is connected."

Robyn glanced in the rear-view mirror. Ariana traced a pattern on the window, where it clouded under her breath. The gills had retracted into three narrow slits on her neck, fading more and more as they travelled away from the ocean.

"There's so much damage. I saw it. I mean, I know I've seen it on TV before, but this … it's really happening."

Robyn turned onto the familiar red driveway. She knew about the floating islands of debris, whole continental shelves devoid of nutrients, decimated fish populations. But she didn't have to confront it every day. A documentary paled in comparison to Ariana's experience.

Ariana's grin slipped away as they pulled up in front of the earthship. "It's us. Humans are ruining everything. I never knew it was so bad, how many living things it affected."

Terence swivelled in the front passenger seat. Robyn bit her lip.

"You were chosen for this, Ariana. It's time the world was put back in balance," Terence said.

Ariana swatted away her tears. "Damn right." She sighed. "I've got so much to learn, and Lenti says I'm already late."

18

Decisions

"Late. What do you think Lenti means?" Terence said.

A valid question but one with a rather obvious answer. During the night, Robyn had given it some thought, gazing at the cracked ceiling as she listened to Catherine's even breathing, moonlight catching all the divots in the rendered earth and sending shadows twisting across the surface. *Everything is connected.* If the walkers were some form of custodian, they were cutting it fine. In less than two centuries, humans had managed to screw up nearly every natural cycle on the planet.

Robyn examined the huge sheet of butchers paper under her elbow. Ink smeared her forearm as she drew another compound. She added a benzene ring, then rubbed it out. It was too heavy. Nothing fitted the two strange peaks.

"Well, if they're supposed to be keeping the balance, then sure, they're late. Soon there won't be much left to balance." Robyn gnawed on her pencil as she lay on her stomach on the cool tiles. Maybe a carbonyl group instead? She swatted away the mess of eraser shavings.

"Environmentally," said Terence. Robyn kept drawing.

"We're already at the brink for carbon emissions, habitat destruction and marine resource depletion, and plenty more," Catherine added. *Exactly*, thought Robyn.

Catherine's book fell to the floor with a heavy *clunk*. Robyn swivelled under the heat of Catherine and Terence's combined gaze. To them she probably looked about ten years old, scribbling on the floor in an old smock.

"What?" Robyn said.

Catherine gestured to the ceiling. "This whole place. The garden. Your family is really into this stuff."

How could she capture the dichotomy between her green-thumbed mother and her academic father in a sentence? Robyn chewed the inside of her cheek. "Yeah. Self-sufficiency was the dream, though we never even got close."

Terence poured another round of tea. Earl Grey,

she smelled the bergamot. "My parents run a market garden," he said. "I grew up like this, too. Mum's a bit of a hippy. Was, I mean." He sipped his tea. "She died in an accident a few weeks ago."

Catherine rested her head on her arms. The book she'd dropped lay cracked open on the floor, spine contorted under the weight of the pages.

"Terence, I'm sorry, I didn't realise, and we've thrust you straight into this –"

Terence shook his head. "No. I mean, it's good. Being with Ariana – helps."

Robyn's right knee cracked as she got to her feet. Every time, without fail. She scooped up the fallen book – *Unlocking the Secrets of Matter* – and placed it on the coffee table, smoothing out the cover.

Terence gazed into the steam rising from his mug as if it might reveal the secrets of life. Robyn studied her own mug as Catherine stepped around the lounge to look at Robyn's drawings. At the sound of Catherine's voice, tea sloshed over her fingers.

"I grew up in the back of a van." Catherine addressed both Robyn and Terence. "My parents are musicians. Though nowadays the van sits in a driveway outside

Calgary, and my Dad has a *real* job."

Robyn shook her hand to cool the burn. "Well, that explains a lot. No such thing as normal, is there?"

"You said it," Catherine sassed, though her face said otherwise.

"Hey." Robyn turned at the familiar voice, hand dropping to her side. Derek materialised in the doorway, rubbing his face with the edge of his shirt. He hadn't been at the earthship when they'd carted back the camping gear, and Robyn had felt unsettled all morning. Even distracting herself with the problematic peaks hadn't helped.

Derek lifted the shirt higher to swipe at his sweaty forehead and Robyn caught a glimpse of smooth, dark stomach. She jerked her head away in embarrassment. *Christ.* Robyn edged around the paper at her feet and rested an arm on the lounge.

"I'm sorry about this morning." Derek released his shirt. Catherine had a mildly disgusted look on her face, like someone had just farted.

"It's just a lot, you know? I'm not really a spiritual person." Derek pulled a jar of water from the fridge and stared at it for a moment before drinking. She'd be willing to bet Derek had never stored anything in a passata jar. She remembered his terror on realising there was no coffee in the house, an expression Robyn would have reserved for the announcement of a zombie apocalypse.

"But you're right. Fletcher and Ariana – they're different. I guess part of me figured we'd be able to rationalise it genetically. But this spirit world stuff?" Derek drained the jar. "I'm not sure." His arms strained as he leaned back against the counter. Robyn tried not to notice. *Holy biceps.*

"Robyn's right. If we're going to hold our own against the MRI, we need to be looking at Fletcher and Ariana. Figure out where this mitochondrial mutation is. We can figure this out. Why else would they have been watching us all this time? We must be good, right?"

Terence clapped a hand on Derek's shoulder and did that weird man-to-man shoulder shake, like a fleshy earthquake but not quite. "Exactly."

Robyn opened her mouth to point out the various flaws in Derek's plan, first and foremost the shabby condition of their one and only gas chromatograph, but Kate interrupted her.

"Hey, freaks." Kate strolled into the kitchen, unlaced Doc Martens slapping against the tiles. "I know you just returned from your holiday, Catherine, but we have to go back."

Robyn froze midway through rolling up the butchers paper. "You can't be serious." They can't go back to Beijing. Kate must be out of her mind.

Ariana pushed her way inside past an irritated Fletcher. "We have to get Eli. I'm coming, too." Ariana crossed her arms and stared Terence down.

"There's no way –" Terence began.

"Well, obviously." Kate flicked three tickets in the air, fanning herself. "You, me, Catherine. The dream team."

Ariana's eyes lit up with victory and she stalked past her brother, snatching the tickets from Kate's grasp. Terence sank into the lounge with a sigh.

"Hey, what about me?" Fletcher flicked his eyes between Ariana and Kate. "I can help."

How young he looks, Robyn thought, *hopeful eyes crinkled up at Kate in that moment of limbo where anything is possible.* Robyn turned to Eva, who filled the doorway behind him.

"Oh." Fletcher followed her gaze. "Right."

"Pack your bags, ladies, we leave in an hour."

Derek went to say something, but Kate raised a hand. "And you guys are going to stop moping around and start being useful. I found you a lab."

Robyn dropped her roll of paper. "Seriously?" They needed a proper setup. The ancient chromatograph wasn't cutting it. If Derek was stir-crazy after three days, then the rest weren't far behind him. Robyn needed to *do* something other than read old textbooks and continue losing battles with the chromatograph. She was next in line to crack and the machine knew it. Robyn blinked as she realised Kate was still speaking.

"A ballsy startup that failed. Algal biodiesel. The lab is about an hour from here. You three –" Kate pointed at Terence, Derek and Robyn – "head out this afternoon. Kara'll stay here with Fletcher."

Robyn's mind whirred over the possibilities. They needed to make up for lost time. Barging past Ariana, Fletcher muttered something that sounded suspiciously as though it rhymed with "ducking hell".

Lucky they were pretty much the same size. Robyn liked big shirts because they reminded her of her mother's art shirts. They sat just right on Catherine.

Catherine zipped up the backpack and tapped her fingers on her thighs as she leaned against the end of the bed. Even Robyn's jeans looked better on Catherine. Had they no loyalty?

"I guess that's everything," Catherine said. They were alone, properly alone. The door to Robyn's room closed against the world.

"I wish I was coming with you," Robyn blurted out. "I mean, I hate the idea of you guys doing this by yourselves."

Catherine's fingers stilled. "It makes sense to split up. In case something goes wrong, which I'm sure it won't." Catherine plonked down on the bed next to her, and Robyn studied her hands. Had they always been so calloused? Their thighs grazed.

"Kara says they've got kids in there. If that's true, we have to try and free them." Catherine worked at a loose thread on a button. "It's worth the risk."

Robyn nodded. The kids. Who knew what plans the MRI had for them? Who knew what had already happened behind the school facade, without the pressures of ethics committees and free from scientific scrutiny? Her gaze fell on Catherine's hands, curled into hard fists on her knees as if she was sitting in the front row of a school photo. Robyn had always been in the front row, concentrating on squeezing her legs together while battling to maintain a smile. Somehow she could never do both. Catherine would have been on the top tier, free of the fear of knee gap, smile blazing.

"Good luck." The bed shifted as Catherine stood up, hooking the backpack over her shoulders.

By the time Robyn looked up she was gone.

19

Tags

"They don't know what they are meddling with. Two worlds, long separated. If there was a way to reunite them –"

"That's why you're so keen to catch them all in your web. One, two, three. Little energy machines."

"Light has no mass, but the energy has to come from somewhere – what the reactionary team described –"

"– the few survivors, you mean –"

"– they described a sphere of crackling green energy. It's all true. This other world must exist. They can harness its energy. Boundless, high-energy radiation. Can't you see, Brock? We'd hold the future of every technology in the palm of our hands."

"It cannot be that simple. Everything is finite,

Miranda. Everything. We've burned through all the resources this world has to offer. Do we really want to do the same of another? What will run our cities when we drain it dry? What you propose is impossible, especially with only three human generators."

"This is why we have our little chats. This is why we create more. More children, more taps."

"Don't be a fool. I've seen Sara's training. Vulcan will create an army. Energy is nothing to him."

"Vulcan doesn't concur with my views. I'm being pleasant … for now."

"You've already given him too much leeway. He'll suffocate you with your own web."

"I can handle Vulcan."

"I'm not convinced you can. And Fang?"

"Fang has no idea."

"How'd you get this?" Catherine asked as a schematic rendering of the Beijing International School whizzed to life on Kate's laptop.

"In one of the most regulated countries in the world? Please. This was easy pickings." Kate tapped the cursor on the main building. Two identical wings branched from a huge, boxy central area. The heart was choked with blue lines. *Electrics*, Catherine guessed. The wings looked dull in comparison.

"This has to be the lab," Kate said, confirming Catherine's suspicion. "They'd need serious power for running machines and God knows what else." The cursor drifted over to the wings. "Based on the ventilation and heating, this is probably accommodation and living space. A place this size needs staff."

"And somewhere for research subjects," Catherine added. *Innocent kids.* Catherine rubbed her eyes. If all went to plan, she'd be in the MRI compound within the hour. She didn't know what would await her there, and if she dwelled on the uncertainty too long, it turned into a chokehold, strangling her.

Ma tutted under her breath as she carried an enormous pot of tea into the room. Catherine nodded at the shuffling, hunched figure and counted under her breath. *One, two, three.*

"Too many screens, you kids. It is not good for the eyes, or the head." Ma shook hers as she poured small, steaming cups before leaning forward with the copper pot. Catherine reached out to support her hands and Ma smiled up at her as together they guided the pot to the table. It settled with a pleasant *ting* of metal, like a genie's lamp. What would she wish for? That none of this had ever happened? Catherine stared at the screen, unseeing. The tea suffused into a jasmine cloud. No. If she can help these kids, then it's all worth it. Even if the worst happens. Catherine sipped her tea and swallowed. The chokehold disappeared.

Kate waited until Ma shuffled out the door, looking thoughtful. "Our primary objective is to retrieve Eli and his animal guide. We don't hang around. In and out."

"So simple," said Catherine. Kate stuck up her middle finger without turning away from the screen.

"That's for the sarcasm."

Eli faltered in the doorway, but his babysitter dug in between his shoulder blades and propelled him inside. The whole space was different – the chairs and IV drips gone, replaced with a bank of computers and a pair of treadmills. A girl sat on the edge of one, chugging water. Patches of sweat stained her shirt, like she'd been running hard.

A growl sounded from the back of the room. All sinew, the leopard stalked around the machine and dropped at the girl's feet. She stroked its neck, her eyes never leaving Eli's.

He couldn't read her expression. No-one guarded her. Lab coats milled around the computers, talking amongst themselves. *Is she free to come and go? Is she working with them willingly?* Eli didn't understand. He barely had time to gawk at the girl before he was pushed into the familiar office. Fang. Eli pressed his nose to the glass as the door shut behind him. He wondered if the girl heard the thrum of the cat's thoughts, if she was ever swept up in the clamour of voices …

"One of our most promising subjects."

Eli turned at Fang's voice. "Is she …" Eli began. Fang had just said *subjects*. Was he a subject too?

"Like you?" Fang raised an eyebrow. "Yes."

A voice cut through his thoughts, small but firm. *Run. Flee the chip.*

Eli raised his head, scanning for the source of the intrusion. Not Una. He couldn't feel the familiar darting presence of a bird nearby. A bug climbed the other side of the glass window. Eli pressed a finger to the glass and watched its twitching antennae, wondering how it had gotten into the facility. A bee.

The chip is pain.

He closed his eyes, straining to latch on to the voice. It evaded him, floating outside his reach.

Fang opened the door and waved for him to follow. "Come."

The girl on the treadmill rose, shook her hair over her shoulders and scrunched it into a ponytail. Eli drew in a breath at the sight of the metal box at the base of her skull. It blipped with a faint red light.

Flee the chip. The warning echoed in his mind and sweat beaded on Eli's forehead. *Was this the chip? Where did the voice come from?* Eli swiped his sleeve across his temples.

At the sound of footsteps, he looked up. A knot of official-looking people moved down from the upper level. Fang headed toward them and Eli took the chance. It might be the only one he'd get.

"Are you all right? Did they hurt you?"

The girl glanced to the side and nodded faintly. "The treatments, then this." She ran a hand across her neck, her voice firm even in the whisper.

"The others?" There had been so many of them.

Sara shook her head. "Only two of us." She flicked a finger back toward Fang's office, and Eli noticed the other rooms, no – *cells* – like his. A boy sat on the bed, observing them.

"Jacob," Sara whispered. The boy raised a hand and Eli nodded, a shallow tip of his head.

"Directors. Meet Sara and Eli." Eli straightened and let his gaze fall to the floor. Fang had returned with two men and a woman who smelled of mothballs. Another woman stood to one side, silvery-haired but straight-backed.

"Sara, if you please."

Sara stepped back, the leopard moving with her, tail aloft and swaying from side to side like a hypnotist's watch. Fang strode past the treadmills to a long bench covered in electronic equipment – squat boxes among sleek screens, humming in a cacophony. Lights flickered on and off along the bench in a menacing, disorienting dance. Whatever they were supposed to do, Eli knew it wasn't good.

Something whirred beneath his feet and his first thought was *earthquake*. Stupid. He took a hasty step backward as an inlaid panel slid open, revealing a recess in the floor. None of the adults moved; their expressions remained unchanged, as if they'd been expecting the floor to disappear.

Metallic arms grated as they rose from the recess, lengthening to form a long passageway. It was like a tunnel, except there was something strange about the metal rods. Eli peered at the nearest ones and stumbled in shock, his ankle giving way beneath him. Some were tipped with sharp points, others had indented edges like some sort of saw. They jerked to a stop, hovering above the ground. A sawblade kept spinning, catching the harsh fluorescent light. Eli cursed under his breath as he nursed his leg.

It looked like a torture device.

Sara bounced from foot to foot, stretching her neck in front of the labyrinth. The leopard stayed still, a statue by her side. Fang tapped the monitor and lights flashed along the sides of the recess, illuminating it completely. Then arms buzzed to life like an orchestra of chainsaws. Not a torture device, but a strange, deadly obstacle course.

The directors murmured amongst themselves, their

eyes wide. Eli had seen that expression before, when the cockerels slashed and tore at each other in the pits at home, men grasping bills in one hand and egging on their chosen bird with the other, faces filled with the sickening expectation of blood. It only heightened his uneasiness – he didn't know if he could bear to be a spectator here, too. But where else could he go? The lab coats had retreated to the doorway and stood in ranks facing the whirring labyrinth in the centre of the room.

Only Sara seemed unfazed. How could she be so calm? Eli didn't know if he could stare down his own fear like that. He was fast, but he didn't possess the grace this *thing* required. Taking a deep breath, he concentrated on the gauntlet, trying to ignore the writhing mass of deadly edges. The more he stared, the more it seemed to slow down, until he could hear the *whoosh whoosh* of the blades and see the individual teeth of the saw.

He blinked and everything rushed back to full speed.

There was no way Sara could make it through unharmed. There would be blood, and the directors would be satisfied. This wasn't a fair fight. *Maybe it isn't supposed to be.* Eli paled. *Is this what they want? To kill Sara in front of me, set an example?*

"When you're ready." Fang flicked a glance in the direction of the silver-haired woman. Eli felt a surge of anger; he clenched his fists to stop himself charging toward her. So the silver lady was important. Maybe even in charge, running the cockfighting ring.

Eli returned his gaze to Sara, wishing his attention would see her through safely. Sara took a deep breath and stepped forward, centimetres away from the first mechanical arm.

Click click click.

She jumped, bringing her knees high and sailing over the horizontal slashing blade before dropping into a roll under the next. The blades didn't let up, blurring past, obeying the computer algorithm Fang had set in motion. The big cat leapt after Sara as if it had launched itself from a trampoline, then slid forward on its belly. A snarl curled from the leopard's mouth as it cleared the next bar.

Eli let out the breath he'd been holding. The blades sliced against empty air as Sara paused in a narrow strip, evaluating the next section. A set of thick, heavy bars protruded vertically from the sides. To Eli, it seemed to move in a random pattern. One bar sliced outward, then retracted; the next moment a whole wall of metal surged through the space.

Sara ducked and weaved, whizzing around in a figure of eight. The cat at her hip never broke stride, their movements synchronised. Eli stared, afraid to miss anything. He held his breath as she flipped onto her hands as two bars shaved past her. Eli couldn't look away as they dropped, his eyes bugging out of his head. A hunk of blonde hair fell to the ground as Sara flipped upright. Eli began shaking. So close.

Somehow, Sara emerged on the other side, panting but otherwise unharmed. Eli's own legs tensed, the veins on his arms popped out as if he'd been in the terrible labyrinth with her.

The cat wove between Sara's legs, teeth bared in a silent growl toward the applauding group. The silver-haired lady nodded at Fang and the metallic arms jolted to a stop. Eli watched them retract into the floor, his relief at Sara's survival trumping his simmering anger. He flicked his gaze back to the silver lady as she spoke.

"Excellent." The silver-haired woman moved forward, parting the directors. "I've seen enough. I hope you're impressed with our progress."

A huge man in a suit nodded. "The increased agility and stamina is impressive. I'm interested to see what the boy is capable of."

The silver lady nodded toward Eli. "Tag him and we'll begin his training."

Tag him? Hands clamped down on his shoulders and a needle plunged into his arm. His ears filled with a buzzing sound and Eli floated into blackness.

20

Jailbreak

Ariana hopped from one foot to the other as Catherine patted down her jacket. Phone, check. Keys, check. Now Catherine just had to face Bohai's motorbike again. Her bladder constricted at the thought. *One, two, three.*

"Come on," Ariana pleaded. Catherine took a deep breath. Right, she could do this.

The bike seemed to have a presence all of its own, the streetlight on the corner making the edges glow. Technically, she still had her licence, though the forest trails outside Montreal were a whole different ballgame to the super highway that was Beijing. Ariana climbed aboard and pulled on the neon helmet. It transformed her – made the walker look older.

"Catherine, come on. It's now or never."

Lights flashed as Catherine turned the key, and she

narrowed her eyes against the garish blue backlight. She pulled the dark beanie tighter around her ears and studied the gauges. Ariana wrapped her arms around Catherine's waist.

"Hold tight." Catherine revved the engine. The back wheel spun out as they edged off the pavement.

Inside Ma's tiny apartment, Kate turned back to the screen, watching the blue blip of Catherine's phone GPS tracking system as the bike disappeared down the alleyway.

"Let's hope this works," she muttered.

Eli woke on his cot in the blinding white cell with a searing headache. Panicked, he reached for the back of his head. His fingers grazed the small metal box and a shiver ran down his spine. *No.* Eli gripped it firmly and tried to rip it off. His head exploded with pain, spasms ricocheting off his skull. *Okay, dumb idea.* Slowing his breathing, he concentrated on calming his mind as his father had taught him on the hunt.

A faint buzzing echoed from the ceiling. A bee landed on his shoulder and wiggled its abdomen. Eli stared at it.

Catherine crouched outside the west wing, Ariana by her side. Lights flooded the corridor even though it was well past midnight. Didn't this place ever shut down? Catherine frowned, heart still thudding from the bike. She'd probably shaved three years off her life expectancy in only twenty minutes. She focused on the window. No movement, so no more reason to wait. Gritting her teeth, she punched through the glass, thick leather gloves protecting her arm.

"I've always wanted to do that," she whispered to Ariana as she knocked the jagged edges out with her elbow. The fear made her voice sound slightly hysterical, and Ariana gave her a concerned look. *Right, concentrate.*

"Kate?" Catherine cocked her head, listening, but no wailing siren greeted her.

"You call that an alarm system? Please." Kate's voice was loud through the earbud. "You're good to go."

Catherine squeezed through the opening and secured the bud in her ear.

"Go straight ahead. There's activity in the next wing, but you should be able to slip into the lab area," Kate relayed.

Catherine wondered if she'd done this before. She

shrugged the thought away as she jogged down the length of the hallway, hating how exposed they were. If someone opened a door, they'd be impossible to miss. It would only take one nosy scientist … Her heart pounded in her chest as she yanked off her gloves and stashed them in her jacket pocket. Voices rose behind the door when they reached the end of the wing. Catherine pressed herself up against one side; Ariana did the same on the other. They hunkered below the level of the glass. Catherine glanced at her hands and was surprised to find they were shaking.

"He's awake. Fang says to bring him out immediately."

"Can't it wait until morning?"

"You know what she's like. She says now, she means now."

Catherine peered through the glass at the top of the door. Two men in lab coats disappeared into the other wing, doors swinging closed behind them. Catherine clenched her fingers into fists.

"Let's go. Nice and quiet, okay?"

A blossoming sphere of blue light filled the corridor. Ariana rose from the floor surrounded by dazzling blue energy. Catherine stared, awestruck, as a silvery dragon emerged to orbit the body encased by light. She reached out toward Ariana but couldn't penetrate the sphere. It crackled against her fingertips solid as a wall.

"Holy hell," Catherine exhaled as Ariana burst forward, taking the door with her. Hinges ripped from the frame and the glass spider-webbed into millions of cracks. Catherine hit the wall, hard, sliding down in a crumpled heap. She jerked an arm upward to protect her head from the shattering glass. As she shook her shoulders to dislodge the sharp fragments, more pops sounded. Along the next wing, windows blew out in a glittering, deadly rain.

"Ariana?" Rising to her feet, Catherine willed her legs into a shaky jog. The dragon rose up, blue light expanding in volume as a whine split the air. *Shit, that can't be good.* The sound echoed in her ears, had her mind screaming to *duck for cover.* As she dived for the floor, glass digging into her forearms, the surge of energy rushed over her. The two scientists weren't so lucky. Catherine heard a pair of sickening thumps and the sound of twisting metal as the blue wave faded. When she raised her head, she saw a boy clutching his neck and scuttling away from their limp bodies, leaving a bloody smear in his wake. The crushed glass covering the floor could have been snow.

Catherine grimaced as she yanked a dagger of glass from her right arm, feeling light-headed. Ariana's orb began dissipating as Catherine scrambled toward the boy, pressing her injured arm to her side. The dragon swirled above the walker, racing into Ariana's forehead. The force of it drew Ariana to her knees; she was breathing hard. Catherine blinked. Just like that, Ariana was back. Blue light ebbed from her skin, like a child's night light. The whole episode had taken less than thirty seconds.

"Eli." Catherine reached out for the boy, trying not to look at the battered forms with their contorted limbs lying by his side. She swallowed and tasted iron.

Eli nodded, blank eyes staring past her. Catherine looked around, taking in the carnage. Ariana had ripped a hunk of the ceiling away and one wall was open to the air, wires sparking in loose arcs. *Jesus.* Catherine yanked Ariana up by her armpits, adrenaline coursing through her system; she ignored the gashes in her arms, though she knew they were deep. Catherine pushed Ariana toward the open air.

"Time to go."

Eli put a hand on Catherine's arm. "Wait, I have to find Una, my osprey." His voice was thick and sluggish.

Catherine wondered if he'd been drugged – his eyes still had that vacant glaze. Nodding, she wrenched her gaze from the easy escape. "We'd better be quick." She wasn't about to rip the boy away from his partner animal. She knew what Eva and Jericho meant to Fletcher and Ariana. They were a part of each other.

Eli picked his way over the bodies as he ran back down the damaged corridor. Catherine followed through the huge door into an enormous laboratory, Ariana at her elbow. Thuds sounded at a row of windows to their left.

Eli ran toward the sound. "Sara?"

Eli rammed into the door with his shoulder, red light skimming his arm. The door burst open with a crunching sound and a girl stepped out.

Catherine's knees buckled when the big cat wove through the girl's legs. *Holy shit*.

"Una. Do you know where she is?" Eli said to the girl, his voice urgent. *Sara, her name is Sara*.

Sara lifted her gaze to the glass mezzanine of the upper level.

Eli raced to the stairs calling over his shoulder, "Get the other animals out of here. I'll be right back."

Sara jogged over to a bank of computers and yanked a plug from its socket. A monitor on wheels went blank and Sara heaved it toward Catherine, cord trailing.

"I'm not leaving without Jacob," Sara said as she began running alongside it, picking up speed. It collided with the door with a grating metallic squeal, and Sara rolled out of the way of the rebound. The monitor skittered to a stop, revealing a huge, swollen dent in the door. Catherine collected herself enough to add her shoulder when Sara hurled herself at the door in its wake. It hurt, a lot.

A broad-shouldered boy stepped out as Catherine rubbed her side, head pounding.

"About time," Jacob said. Something burrowed into his hair, making its way toward his shoulder. Catherine could see the long, brown hair parting as it moved. Moses and the Red Sea.

"Catherine." Ariana was at the computers, her voice strained. "I can't figure out the locking system."

Sara and Jacob crowded around the monitor. "Only the directors have the electronic key. And Fang," Sara explained.

Ariana slapped the keyboard in frustration. "Great."

"Kate?" Catherine said. "Can you hear me?"

The reply was laced with static, loud bursts of jarring noise. Catherine swore under her breath.

"Stop right there."

Catherine spun toward the voice. Sara bristled at her side, the leopard crouching low.

"Fang," Sara growled. Catherine's heart stuttered in her chest as she took in the figure. Slim, dark hair, the posture of someone used to being in control. *No, it can't be.* Fang stood just inside the laboratory, one hand clutching a slim metal box. She strode forward and the leopard lunged, hissing. Fang didn't falter, just aimed the receiver as if it were a TV remote control and she was merely changing the channel. The cat fell to the ground, writhing in pain. Sara barely made it two steps before she fell to her knees, clutching her skull.

"Stop it," Sara screamed. The cat moaned, a piteous whine that seemed to ring around the echoey space. "Please."

Ariana snarled by Catherine's side, and blue light flared across her limbs. It was enough to stop Fang's advance. The woman stared at Ariana as recognition dawned on her face.

Catherine didn't think, just charged straight at the woman. Anything to stop the screams. They slammed together with more force than Catherine had intended, sprawling to the floor in a tangle of limbs. The receiver flew from Fang's grasp, skimming along the floor like a stone on a river.

The screaming stopped instantly, Sara's choked breathing loud in the silence.

Catherine went for Fang's arms, pinning them by her sides. It took all of her strength to keep them there – the woman was strong. Blood dripped from her wounds onto Fang's face as Catherine leaned over her, light-headed with pain.

"How could you do this?" Catherine hissed, searching Fang's face for something, anything. Fang's eyes flicked to the gashes in Catherine's arms and Catherine swore her gaze softened for a moment. It was short-lived. Fang rushed upward, pushing Catherine back toward the floor. She hit it with a heavy thump, the breath stripped from her lungs as their positions reversed. She gasped for air in vain.

Fang leant over her, crushing her legs. "I'm doing what any one of us would do," she snapped, "given the chance." Catherine winced as Fang dug a hand into the deepest cut on her forearm. It felt like being stabbed all over again. Her synapses screamed at her to get away.

Catherine heaved greedy gulps of air as she got her wind back. "I'd never hurt innocent kids," she spluttered. "Bitch."

Boom.

The floor rattled beneath them. Catherine craned her neck backward, following the strangled cries that rose from the semi-darkness at the back of the laboratory. *The cages*, she realised.

Fang's eyes grew wide, her face filling with fear.

Catherine squeezed her eyes shut as the flash of red light descended, blinding even behind her eyelids, and Fang's weight disappeared.

Shielding her eyes, Catherine brought herself to her knees. Birds swirled in the air around an enormous osprey wreathed in a red orb of light, tendrils flickering outward to rake the cages. Popping noises rippled around the room as cages were thrust open and animals poured out. Big ones. Catherine clung to a wall as a wolf raced past. The grating chorus of animal calls crescendoed.

"We've got to get out of here," Ariana yelled over the rushing wind above them, her hair billowing. "Catherine, come on."

The red light kept spreading. Catherine looked for Fang, but she was gone. Eli stood below the osprey, arms wide as if in a trance.

"Hold on to something," Ariana roared.

Catherine's hand scuttled across the surface of a cage and gripped it. A red pulse of light exploded from Eli and rocketed outward like a nuclear explosion, collecting the walls with it. The cages strained but held as the hurricane of debris rained down. Chunks of concrete smashed onto the floor and sparks flew in the air above her. Catherine narrowed her eyes as Ariana's familiar blue aura fell over her, covering them both in a sphere of light.

"Ariana?" Catherine yelled over the terrible noise of scraping concrete. A huge chunk of the roof dislodged, buckling the steel beam supporting it.

Ariana extended the blue sphere outward, encapsulating Sara and Jacob who were clinging to cages further down the remains of the wall.

The concrete screeched as it broke free of the steel, tumbling down end-over-end. Catherine gritted her teeth, memories flashing before her eyes. Her parents. Sophie. *Robyn.* Robyn?

Thwack. The wedge of concrete connected with the orb of blue light, but the sphere held. Catherine stared as it grated against the energy field, sliding off to pound into the ground. Catherine's whole body shook. *Alive. I'm alive.*

The blue light shimmered and disappeared, leaving Ariana gasping by her side. Dust rose in thick clouds from the crater in the floor where the concrete had settled. *Ariana had stopped the concrete panel.*

The floating red orb in the centre retracted in a rush, and Eli fell to his knees. The spirit-osprey glided full-tilt toward Eli's head. Catherine blinked as the bird transformed back and perched on Eli's shoulder. Blood dribbled from where the bird's talons dug into flesh.

Eli didn't seem to notice. "Sara?" he called.

Jacob crawled out of a cage further down the line, coughing. A pile of metal and dry wall shifted, and Sara wriggled out holding her right arm, her leopard behind her. *They were all alive.*

"Jesus," Sara said. Catherine took it all in. The laboratory had been annihilated. Everything bar the cages had simply been swept up, crushed, and blown aside. Catherine unfurled her fingers one by one from the cold metal of the cage. Every part of her ached.

Ariana clutched Eli's arm as he swayed, the osprey on his shoulder drooping.

"I've got him," Ariana said, taking the brunt of Eli's small frame on her shoulder.

Catherine nodded. *Now* it was time to go.

Fang emerged from the wreckage, shirt ripped and smeared with grease and blood. She wasn't sure what proportion was hers or Catherine's. Nor was she entirely certain how she'd gotten clear. Ignoring the pain in her shoulder, Fang swept her hair back up into its regular efficient ponytail and assessed the damage. She'd never realised the subjects had the capacity for this. And Catherine – she'd been a surprise. Fang wasn't sure what she'd been expecting, but somehow she'd associated Deckker with a flippant, pliable researcher – not the woman who'd nearly gotten the better of her. Damn it.

Maybe Miranda was right. There was more to this

than genetics. Fang shook her head, remembering the blue light shimmering across the girl's skin. The third. The girl from the drawing from that temple. Miranda would know what to do.

The insistent beeping of her radio interrupted her thoughts. It garbled at her when she raised it to her ear. Fang listened to the scientist's stammer for a heartbeat and cut across his hysterics as he paused to draw breath.

"Get Miranda, secure the perimeter." Fang clicked the receiver and shut him off. The building behind her creaked, and another panel of concrete slid to the ground in a thundering crash.

Flames illuminated two scientists picking their way through the debris toward her.

"Fang, we've had some losses. Hawkins, Andrews … the Chief."

"What?"

The scientist faltered. "Fang, she didn't make it. There's no sign of her."

His voice seemed to come from a great distance, fuzzy and weak. Fang blinked. No, Miranda couldn't be gone. Miranda was everything.

Fang closed her eyes. "Solidify the perimeter.

Nobody goes in or out for the next twelve hours." What else would Miranda do? "Get someone on to the press – underground gas explosion, a tragedy. All students killed."

The first scientist nodded and skidded back into the debris field.

Fang turned to the second scientist, a blonde woman with a bad gash in her thigh.

"Salvage what you can. Lab fridge first, then files. We'll move to the secondary location." The woman limped off. Fang called after her, "And make sure you get that leg seen to." The woman stopped and nodded before turning back to the charred concrete. Fang watched her disappear beyond the flames before sinking to the ground and bringing her knees up to her chest.

Catherine swore under her breath. The streets were empty for now, but soon the sun would be up. Her earbud was dead, useless. Catherine dug her phone out of her jacket, relieved to see the screen flash to life.

"Where the hell are you?" Kate screeched.

"Change of plan." Catherine sized up the group behind her. "Two ring-ins, and Eli."

"Jesus."

Catherine heard static as the phone was jostled. She recognised Bohai's voice.

"My father has a warehouse we can use. We'll meet you there in twenty minutes."

Catherine peered at the texted address.

"Okay. Everyone, this way."

The unusual group picked up speed.

Catherine wheeled the bike into the lot of industrial buildings, motioning the others past her into the cavernous warehouse. She cut the engine and brought the roller door down behind them. They were safe, for now. She yanked off her helmet, surprised at how calm she felt, knowing that the moment she stopped, the adrenaline would wear off and panic would catch up with her. *Fight or flight.*

Kate sat hunched over a jacked-up laptop on top of a pile of boxes. Spotting Catherine she jumped down, computer under her arm.

"Holy shit, Catherine, are you okay?"

Catherine brought a hand up to her throbbing temples. Her fingers came away dark and sticky. *Oh.*

"I'm fine for now. We really need to keep moving," she said hoping her voice carried the conviction she didn't quite feel.

Kate nodded, waving the laptop. "I'm on it." She sank down to the floor and plunged straight back into the online world.

"Is everyone okay?" Catherine ignored the pain that was finally creeping up on her. Jacob heaved for breath, hands on his knees. Sara leaned over to rub circles into his back.

"Yeah." Jacob straightened.

Eli and Ariana sat slumped against a wall of boxes. Nodding, Eli listened as Ariana spoke in a breathless rush.

Catherine cast her eyes back to Jacob's hair. She could have sworn she'd seen something move again.

"Jacob, do you have a partner animal?" she said.

Jacob beamed. "Poppy." He held out a hand, and something tiny flew out of his hair and cruised onto his outstretched palm. A bee, Catherine realised, jaw dropping.

As if sensing her next question, Sara added, "We kept her secret from Fang."

Jacob frowned at Eli. "We tried to warn you, didn't you hear her?"

Eli stopped talking to Ariana and looked up at Jacob, at the bee twirling on his hand. His mouth puckered into a little 'o' of understanding.

"Excellent," Kate muttered to herself. "We have to leave now. A ship departs within the hour."

Bohai yanked a dusty white sheet from a panel van speckled with dents.

"Count me in," said Sara, heaving the sliding door open. "Anywhere that isn't that place is fine by me."

Catherine pulled herself into the front and rested her head on the seat. Her skull pounded and she felt woozy. Gritting her teeth, she dug her hands into the seat, willing herself to stay conscious. She was *not* going to pass out.

The streets were already lightening by the time Catherine caught a whiff of briny air. Bohai slowed as they pulled into the harbour, streetlights blurred by the smog.

"Three months," said Sara in the back. "We've been

there for three months, hooked up to their drugs." She shivered in her seat, wrapping her arms around herself.

"We were the only ones who survived the treatments," Jacob added, looking out the window into the dawn haze.

Treatments. "Fang. Fang did this?" Catherine's stomach clenched as she remembered the receiver Fang had used on Sara. She turned in the passenger seat, ignoring the stab of pain in her neck.

"Sara. How did she stop your leopard?"

Sara shifted, exposing her neck. A red gash ran down the base of her skull around a metal box.

"The implant," she said. "Both me and Ming have them."

"Ming?"

Sara stroked her cat. "Yeah, her name's Ming." The cat purred under Sara's hand. "So we did what they wanted us to do."

Jacob shook his head when Catherine's gaze landed on him. "Not me. They thought I was dead weight, not dangerous enough to need a tag."

Eli coughed and cleared his throat. "I've got one."

He was so small, Catherine thought. Caramel-dark

skin, narrow eyes. Catherine flicked her eyes from Eli to Sara again. They were her responsibility now.

"You two, though; wow, that was some light show back there," said Sara. "Do you think me and Jacob could learn how to do that?"

It was false bravado, Catherine thought, but it made her instantly like the girl.

Ariana and Eli shared a glance. "I'm not really sure," Ariana managed.

Catherine willed her eyes to stay open. She had to get this strange little family home.

21

Mutation

Terence flicked the switch by the door and a bank of fluorescent tubes staggered on, revealing the clinical space. Robyn stared. The lab. *Their lab.* A long row of fume hoods and parallel benches ran down one half, and the other side branched into a series of glass-walled rooms. Derek nearly skipped toward the first room.

"Liquid and gas chromatographs, and a DNA sequencer," Derek breathed, sticking his head back around the door. "Brand new, by the looks of them. Holy shit."

Robyn ran her eyes over the contents of the next partition. Gel electrophoresis equipment, centrifuge, mini-autoclave. She opened the fridge and fingered through the stack of reagents, most of them not even opened. This was way beyond the scope of her lab back at the university, and Robyn couldn't hold in a small burst of hope. She itched to be doing something, to be contributing. Kate was right. They had been going a little stir-crazy at the farm, though she still wouldn't go so far as to call it *moping*.

"This is incredible," Derek said, spinning in a lab chair, arms above his head like a little kid. Robyn smiled as she emerged back into the main lab. Dumping the cooler on the bench, Terence pulled out a rack of vials. The blood sloshed with the movement. Four vials: two walkers, two animal partners.

"So, where do we start?" Terence said.

Robyn pulled her notebook from her backpack and clicked her pen open. "I have a few ideas."

They fell into an easy rhythm. Robyn preferred working with the data peaks of the chromatograms; Terence dived straight into the genetic sequencing and Derek shut himself away with the bacterial library he found in the fridge.

Robyn was propelled by the excitement she always felt at the beginning of a new project; everything a possibility, nothing a certainty. It was as intoxicating as a drug. When Terence tapped on the door of the machine room with a sandwich in one hand, she jumped.

"Jeez, you scared me."

Terence pointed to the clock on the wall. It was well after 4pm. *How did it get so late?*

"Lunch?"

Robyn's stomach growled. "Yeah."

Terence pushed through a swinging door at the end of the lab that led into another corridor. Rooms branched off either side.

"There's more?" Robyn peered through the internal windows. Beds on one side, an industrial-looking kitchen on the other. Derek waved from a stainless-steel counter with a sandwich.

"Yeah. I guess we were blindsided by the lab, but there's a whole wing for staff and the kitchen. There's even some outside space." Terence held the door open for her. It was like stepping into the bowels of a restaurant. A huge fridge hummed in the corner where Derek sat at the long counter. He tapped the empty stool next to him. Terence sat on her other side, handing her a paper-wrapped sandwich from a cooler. Robyn eyed it with suspicion.

Terence smiled. "Different cooler, I promise."

The sandwich was good – marinated eggplant, feta and rocket. "Did you make this?" Robyn asked over her mouthful. "It's amazing."

Terence nodded, cheeks tinged pink. "I'm glad you like it."

"I could almost live here," said Derek, finishing his own sandwich.

Robyn chewed thoughtfully. It really did have everything they needed.

"As long as Terence cooks," Robyn said.

"Deal," chuckled Terence.

"Plus we'll get coffee," Robyn promised.

Derek smiled over his mouthful. "Great. When can I move in?"

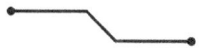

They went to bed late, and even though she was exhausted, Robyn lay awake. The air felt heavy and her mind refused to slow down. She crept out into the corridor, closing the door with a soft click behind her. Derek and Terence were in the room next door; Robyn peered through the internal window at the slumped figures. One like a brother, the other ... Robyn shook her head and followed the lights set into the edges of the floor back to the lab, which purred with machinery. She wasn't sure what Derek was to her.

Robyn flicked her eyes up at the analog clock. Just after midnight. The printer in the machine room spat out paper. Fletcher and Ariana's DNA sequences. Robyn stifled a yawn and spread them out on the table.

Typical human mitochondrial DNA encodes 37 genes on two strands. Brock's voice echoed in her mind as Robyn skimmed over the H– and L– strands in Ariana's sample. All the normal protein-encoding genes were there, as well as the transfer-RNA genes and the two ribosomal subunit RNA genes. Robyn's finger stilled above the page as she recalculated the number of base pairs. That was odd, Ariana's mitochondrial genome coded for 40 genes, not 37. A separate regulatory region separated the normal and abnormal genes, making a whole chunk of the genome different. Really different. This wasn't a generic point mutation.

Robyn reached for Fletcher's output. She traced the genes with her finger, muttering base pairs under her breath. It was the same pattern.

"Why the long face?"

Robyn jumped. Derek leant on the doorjamb holding two steaming mugs; he was wearing track pants and a faded singlet. His presence saturated the air in the machine room, now heavy with aniseed. Robyn wanted to breathe it in, let it cloud her mind.

"My God, you scared me. How long have you been standing there?"

Derek grinned, handing her a chipped blue mug. "Not long. I heard you get up, figured I'd find you here."

Robyn tasted peppermint. "Thanks."

Derek took the chair beside her. "Find anything interesting?"

Putting the mug down, Robyn ran both hands through her hair. "You could say that." She shoved Ariana's sequence toward him and watched his face contort as he scanned the output.

"But this – this isn't possible." Derek held the page closer to his face, as if willing it to give up its secrets.

"I've never seen anything like it either." Robyn closed her eyes. "A whole extra operon." The room was still heavy with Derek's presence.

"So we run the analysis again." Derek turned to the computer and the sequencer stirred to life.

"Duplicate analysis never hurt," Robyn yawned. "Though I don't know how it's going to help."

"Do you think Fang knows about this?" Derek tapped at the keyboard.

Robyn snapped her mouth shut. "I hope they're all okay," she murmured, Catherine's face bright in her mind. "I don't know what they're going to find in Beijing. We know what the MRI is capable of now."

Derek gave a faint nod, still focused on the computer screen.

"All the more reason for us to be here," he said. "I take it that's why you couldn't sleep?" Derek shifted his gaze to her and something clicked in Robyn's mind.

"This morning, at the clearing. When Ariana and Fletcher came back from the spirit world. You were upset because of Damian, weren't you?"

Derek fiddled with his mug. "I just can't believe in anything that would allow my brother's genes to be so malformed. God, spirits, whatever."

They sat together in the machine-lit gloom as the sequencer droned on. Robyn cradled her mug and let the hypnotic sound wash over her as Derek traced a finger along the mutant genes.

Robyn woke to a persistent tapping on the door. She rolled further into her blankets moaning "Leave me alone."

"Robyn. It's seven thirty."

She opened her eyes at the sound of Terence's voice, registering that she was in her bed, though she had no memory of getting there.

"Urgh," she managed, lifting herself to a sitting position. "Okay, I'm up."

"I'm making pancakes in the kitchen when you're ready."

The gene sequence, the midnight cup of tea, Derek. It came back in a rush. The tiredness hung over her like a cloak as she got to her feet.

Feeling more human after a hot shower, Robyn followed the smell of buttermilk to the kitchen where Derek and Terence were attacking a syrup-covered mountain.

Terence looked abashed. "Sorry," he said. "Couldn't

wait." He swallowed his mouthful and pointed to the stack of paper on the counter. "Derek showed me the gene sequences."

Robyn eyed Derek, who smiled at her. "Sleep okay?" he said.

Robyn narrowed her eyes. "Did you –"

Derek cut her off. "Yeah," he snorted. "You fell asleep in your chair." *Great*, thought Robyn, *carted off to bed like a twelve-year-old past their bedtime*. Her ears grew hot at the image of her slumped form in Derek's arms. He must be strong. Robyn blinked and focused on the big red maple leaf on the syrup bottle. Her mind skipped to Catherine. The flash of lying in Catherine's arms instead made her choke on her tea.

Terence stabbed at the paper with his knife. Syrup dribbled onto the mutant operon like golden blood.

"Do you think we can splice this into a vector?"

Derek smirked as Robyn pulled two pancakes onto her own plate. She had hesitated over the stack for a second; it'd be rude not to eat Terence's cooking, though she'd prefer her normal muesli.

"Theoretically, there's no reason why it wouldn't work." Robyn cut the first pancake into neat squares.

Derek pulled out another set of papers. "Yeah, except for one little thing."

Robyn took a tentative bite of pancake. Delicious. She closed her eyes for a second as she chewed. "What little thing?" she asked as she opened them.

Derek splayed the new papers above the original sequence.

"It changes."

22

Sun Song

Ariana leaned against the cool wall of the shipping container and slowed her breathing. Energy skipped across the hand joined with Eli's as the orb of blue light enveloped her. The falling sensation of crossing over to the spirit realm still made her feel nauseous. Ariana wondered if she'd ever get used to it as Jericho uncoiled around her, whiskers tickling her face.

A few long moments passed before Eli materialised next to her, blinking heavily. Red light glazed his skin, and Una shifted into a huge bird of prey at his side.

"Holy mackerel," Eli said, dazed. Una nipped at his shoulder, bringing him to standing. Eli leaned on her back as he heaved in air.

"Before, back in the lab – that was real, wasn't it? Not a dream?" Eli stared at Una in disbelief, tracing his hand across a wing, the fine bones a testament to the wonders of evolution and engineering. "I don't really remember what happened. What I did." His hands dropped from Una's side as he held them up in front of his face. Red light arced between them.

Ariana nodded. She wasn't sure how she'd managed to bring Jericho into his spirit form without crossing over. She'd just reached that in-between place. The same as her encounter with the water spirit.

But Eli had never been here. She glanced up at Jericho, swirling in the air above them. They'd emerged back into the tree-rimmed grove, although there was no sign of Fletcher. Ariana sighed. Maybe it had been foolish to think he'd be waiting for them here.

"This is real, too." Lenti stepped out from behind a tree.

"Jesus, you've got to stop doing that." Ariana clapped her hand to her heart.

"Sorry." Lenti stifled a grin.

"Aren't you supposed to be helping us?" Ariana folded her arms across her chest.

Eli stiffened at her side before bowing. "It is an honour to meet you."

Ariana sent Eli a disgusted look. Lenti cocked an eyebrow, his grin widening.

"Una spoke of a guide." Eli met Ariana's eyes with concern.

"Yes. It is good to see you again, air walker," Lenti said.

Ariana saw his confusion through a shimmering patch of air that appeared in front of her. Fletcher materialised, feet hovering down to the grass. Ariana backed up as Eva arrived. Skidding backward on the grass, Ariana landed on her butt.

"Ow," she said, rubbing her tailbone.

Fletcher pivoted. "Sorry, Ariana." He leaned over and reached out an arm. Lenti chuckled somewhere in the background. Ariana allowed herself to be yanked back up, bristling at the indignity.

"So there are others," interrupted Lenti, moving to sit beneath one of the trees. "Though they are not walkers."

"Yes." Eli crinkled his brow. "You say *again* as if we had met." He waved an arm to indicate the grove. "But I've never been here before."

Lenti closed his eyes. "Great, here we go again."

Catherine gritted her teeth as Kate dug bits of glass from her arm and bandaged the gashes. Filled with furniture and boxes, the shipping container tipped with the pitch of the boat; the feeling was worse than any hangover. Catherine leaned her head against the headboard of an ornate four-poster bed frame. She'd always dreamed of a bed like this, sleeping on her bunk in her parents' battered VW. Now she could barely appreciate it.

"Nearly done." Kate knelt by her stomach, ripping the plastic from a sterile bandage. A cardboard box labelled *Bathroom* lay open at the end of the bed.

"There." Kate rocked back on her heels and scooted up next to Catherine.

"Thanks," Catherine managed, trying not to move her arms. Everything ached. Snores rose from the couches they'd unwrapped. Sara and Jacob slept head to toe on something that belonged in an English manor house. Eli and Ariana lay stiff and unmoving against the side wall, sheathed in red and blue light. It bathed the whole container in an eerie glow. Catherine's eyes grew heavy. Just a little nap. She'd be awake before they got back.

Kate stared at the two walkers. "I think, from what

you described, it was some sort of electromagnetic pulse. Which is incredible in itself, really. Explains why we lost the radio connection." She poked Catherine.

"Are you listening to me?" But Catherine was already asleep.

"So there's never been three walkers at once," Ariana repeated, staring at Lenti. Surely he could have told them this before.

"No, not since ..." Lenti cleared his throat. "No."

Ariana pounced. "Not since when?" Lenti's games annoyed her. He was keeping something from them, she was sure of it.

Lenti scratched his neck, shifting his shoulders. "The legends say that in the before times, the spirit world and the physical world were one. Many humans had spirit-animal partners, but it was only when the worlds diverged that the walkers were called."

"Why didn't you tell us this?" Fletcher said.

Thank you, Ariana thought, sending a glance in his direction.

"I didn't think it was possible for there to be others, but I have felt them." Lenti looked troubled, his cockiness gone. He turned to Ariana. "You have met the water spirit, yes?"

Ariana nodded.

Lenti frowned. "In the before times, spirits and humans lived together in harmony. What do you call it?"

"Convergence," Fletcher supplied.

"Yes. Humans walked alongside animals as equals, as *convergers*. But one spirit rose up and split the two worlds. She called down rocks from the sky and forced the spirits here. She has been called many names throughout history, but we call her Nyx." Lenti gestured to the grove. "But two spirits fought her; they took on corporeal form when the portal closed. They stayed behind."

"Atlantis is one of them," Ariana said, thinking of the enormous, gentle whale.

Lenti nodded. "Both the sea spirit and the air spirit, Notos. They forced Nyx deep into the ground, but they could not reopen the barrier between the worlds." Lenti closed his eyes. "But by sealing the physical and spirit realms, something happened that Nyx did not intend. She created the walkers, the only ones able to pass between realms. The first walkers were born into the same generation, but scattered across the world. They never met as you have."

"What happened?" Ariana asked.

"The walker lineages continued. As one died, another was born; last breath to first breath in a new body. But then the transitions became feeble, skipping generations entirely."

Late. Lenti's words echoed in Ariana's skull. "That's why you said we were late."

"Yes, I feared perhaps you would not come."

"But we're here. What are we supposed to do?"

Lenti stared past them into the forest. "I didn't want to scare you, but we do not have much time."

"What are you talking about?" Ariana's stomach plummeted.

"The sun song." Lenti licked his lips. "It has been building for millennia. The strength of it has called you, but it will also give Nyx the power she needs to break free."

Ariana stared at Lenti. *Sun song?* "Like solar flares or something?"

Fletcher interrupted. "What happens if Nyx escapes?"

Lenti remained silent for a moment, still staring into nothing. "Destruction."

"So, how do we stop her?" Eli said.

Ariana blinked. At her shoulder, Eli stood with fists clenched. Una sat on his shoulder, back to her normal size, though she pulsed with red energy.

"You will grow stronger," said Lenti, pointing to the red glow on Eli's limbs. "You channel the spirit energy, which comes from the sun. But it also weakens the bonds on Nyx, and there is no way to stop the sun. It burns with or without us. But maybe with the others, the new convergers … I do not know if it is possible."

"How long do we have?" said Eli.

"Ten moons," said Lenti, biting his lip.

23

Homecoming

Robyn pushed the new gene sequences to one side of the counter and rested her head in her hands. It had been a long day. The optimism of yesterday had well and truly gone.

"I don't understand," she said. Something garlicky wafted toward her as Terence turned at the stove. "It doesn't make any sense." Normal DNA shouldn't change so quickly. No normal DNA *could*.

Terence tapped the wooden spoon against the edge of the pot, and Robyn couldn't help thinking of Catherine. There was still no word from Kate. Every muscle in her body ached, tensed as if her limbs were about to jerk into some unbidden action. Like bashing her head against the wall or screaming into her pillow. They should never have sent Catherine back to Beijing.

If anything happened to her, Robyn didn't know how she could forgive herself.

"It must have something to do with the whole spirit world thing." Terence leant against the stove, hands crossed over his chest. Robyn felt Derek stiffen beside her. Great, just what they needed, another spirit world debate.

"Maybe some sort of defence mechanism? Or maybe it's beyond what we can feasibly do with science." Terence reached over for the bowl of chopped fennel and mushrooms. Fragrant steam billowed across the room.

"I wouldn't have believed it unless I'd run the sequences myself," said Derek. "It shouldn't be possible."

Robyn sighed with relief. At least Derek hadn't launched into another argument about the existence of spirits. She didn't think she could handle it right now.

"Well, it is," Robyn said into her hands. "Is there anything we can do?" She'd stared at the sequences for hours all afternoon, willing something to jump out at her. Something, anything.

"No," Terence said. "But maybe –" He stirred the vegetables. "Maybe if Ariana comes back with others."

Derek shifted in his seat. "If the MRI has managed to trigger convergent capabilities, their DNA might be more stable." His eyes were bright. "It's a possibility."

"So our only hope is if Fang's testing works," said Robyn. The thought made her feel sick to her stomach; the liquorice smell of the fennel suddenly a choking haze. Robyn coughed and took a sip of water. Who knew what Fang was doing to those kids? If Eli's gene sequence was the same, then it was unlikely that Fang had developed a specific activation vector. She was probably exposing them to chemicals or radiation – anything to stress the cells into gene activation, compromising their entire immune systems and leaving them vulnerable and weak. Robyn doubted if anyone would survive extended exposure to whatever cocktail Fang had devised.

Robyn jerked as her phone vibrated in her pocket.

"It's Kate. They're on their way back. Everyone's coming here." Her heart thudded in her chest. *Catherine is on her way back. They are all safe.* "They've got Eli, and they found two more kids, new convergers."

Robyn stared at her phone. *So there are survivors.*

Terence emptied another packet of fettuccine into the pot of boiling water. "Well, thanks for the advance warning," he said. He whirled around at Robyn's affronted gasp. "Joking." He raised both hands with a forced smile. His grip on the wooden spoon was tight – Robyn could see the whites of his knuckles. Derek's knee jiggled on the stool next to her. For once, he had nothing to add.

Robyn clenched and unclenched her fists by her side as the new convergers poured in. A leopard slunk in under the row of lab benches, knocking a rack of empty vials to the floor. The glass shattered with a popping sound, sending tinkling fragments skittering across the floor. The leopard jumped, startled, and the action was so similar to a normal domestic cat that Robyn managed to unwind her tense shoulders.

"Eli, Sara and Jacob," Kate yawned, pointing.

The leopard wove itself between Sara's legs while a huge bird rested on Eli's shoulder on a padded strap. Terence hurled himself at Ariana, collecting her up in a hug. "I'm okay," she said into his shoulder. "Really."

Robyn looked past them for Catherine. *Where is she?*

Ariana sniffed the air. "Are you making the fennel pasta?"

Terence smiled. "You bet."

Robyn couldn't hide her shock as she watched Catherine shuffle inside the doors, eyes scrunched against the harsh lights. With her blonde hair matted with blood and her arms swathed in bandages, she looked like she'd barely survived a street fight.

"Catherine." Robyn slipped a shoulder underneath Catherine's left armpit and guided her through to the kitchen. She wrapped her other arm around Catherine's waist, trying to ignore the flicker of warmth that curled in her stomach. The leopard stalked silently down the hallway in front of them.

"I'm okay, just sore," Catherine said, easing herself onto a stool. "Terence, I need you to examine them. They have chips implanted at the base of their skulls." Catherine's fingers flew to her own neck in sympathy. "I'm hoping the blast at the facility rendered them ineffectual, but they'll have to be surgically removed."

Terence moved around the counter. "Sara, right?"

The blonde nodded, lifting her hair and revealing a small box, not unlike an SD memory card. Robyn could make out the ugly scar from where she stood with Catherine.

"Ming has one too," Sara said.

Terence cleared his throat. "Wow, okay. Can – can I touch her?" Sara nodded and Terence reached out to the leopard at her feet. The cat whined as Terence prodded the metal box, making him jump backward.

"Tomorrow, after you've recovered a bit, I'll take these out. Catherine's right, they don't seem to be active anymore." His voice was shaky.

"Energy blast?" Derek leant on the counter, watching Catherine. He raised his eyebrows and Robyn took a half-step back from her. Not that she was doing anything wrong.

Catherine nodded. "We only got out thanks to those two." She pointed at Eli and Ariana.

Kate plonked a chunky box onto the counter. "Yep, I've got a theory about that." She raised a wand connected to the box and waved it in the air. Nothing happened. Kate heaved the box with her, still gesticulating with the wand. It started a frantic blipping as she reached Eli and Ariana. Robyn watched the dial ram the maximum end of the scale, then flinched at the high-pitched whine coming from the box. Kate turned the geiger counter off.

"They're emitting some sort of high-frequency electromagnetic radiation that's even higher than gamma rays." Kate crossed her arms, staring past the two walkers. "It's incredible."

Ariana raised her eyes to Kate's. "But what does that mean?"

"It means that you have a lot more power than you realise. Jeez, this is *Captain Planet* meets *Animorphs*. It keeps getting weirder and weirder."

Ariana sighed. "Yeah, apparently."

Fletcher and Kara burst into the kitchen as Terence served up bowls of pasta. Ariana reddened as Fletcher dragged a stool to wedge himself between her and Eli.

"Cute." Catherine brought a shaky forkful to her mouth. Her warm breath danced across Robyn's cheek. Robyn said nothing. She searched the table for Derek, but he'd disappeared. If only you could cocoon yourself away for adolescence and emerge as a confident, functioning adult. If only someone gave you a stamp on your wrist that proclaimed you straight or gay. Maybe life would be easier that way. Robyn choked on her mouthful, unsure where that last thought had come from.

Catherine swayed in her chair and Robyn reached to steady her, leaning into Catherine's shoulder.

"Thanks," rasped Catherine, sending a shiver down Robyn's spine.

The doors clattered open as Derek reappeared. Robyn registered the syringes.

"Derek, what are you doing?"

He held up the packets. "What does it look like?"

Robyn couldn't believe it. They had no idea what Sara and Jacob had been through, what Fang had done to them in Beijing. Surely the gash in Sara's neck was evidence enough that they'd been poked and prodded too much already.

"Hey, what the hell!" Sara said, scrambling down from her chair. Ming hissed, the fur on her back erect. Derek held up the syringe. "The quicker we start analysing your blood, the quicker we'll know more." He moved forward again and Sara mirrored the movement, stepping back into the fridge. Ming growled, advancing toward Derek.

"Derek," Robyn yelled across the counter. It came out with more force than she'd intended and everyone turned in her direction. Robyn cleared her throat, cheeks burning. "This isn't for you to decide. This is up to Sara and Jacob. We can talk about this tomorrow." Robyn angled her head toward Sara. "My apologies. We're all just eager to figure this out, get ahead of Fang."

Sara gave her a stiff nod. "Okay." She stuck out an arm and turned back to the fridge. "Go ahead."

Derek hesitated, sending a wounded glance to Robyn before finding the vein. Sara grimaced as she faced the stainless steel, creating a circle of condensation on the smooth surface.

Jacob hopped down and held out his arm. Derek brought out a new syringe and Robyn cringed at the resigned look on Jacob's face. These were people, not research subjects. *They weren't the MRI.*

Catherine stared daggers into Derek's back as she chewed. Robyn studied her plate as Derek left the kitchen, Catherine's shoulder a reassuring weight against her arm.

Sara rubbed the crook of her elbow as she climbed back onto her stool and resumed her dinner. "Nice guy," she said.

Jacob grunted into his mouthful, shoulders shaking with laughter.

"Look, I'm sorry about that." Terence sighed as he spooned more pasta onto Ariana's plate. "Derek is just kind of driven."

Robyn pushed her plate away, suddenly not hungry. She didn't get Derek – one minute they were chummy, the next he was pulling some stunt like this. Where was the real Derek? Somewhere in between?

Terence let the serving spoon clatter against the pot. "We're just trying to figure this out. We're not the MRI. You don't have to stay here if you don't want to. Once I get those chips out in the morning, we can work out how to get you home."

"I think I'll stick around for a bit," Sara said. Robyn couldn't place the slight lilt to her words. Scandinavian, or Dutch maybe.

Jacob nodded through a slurp of pasta. "Me, too. I want to learn how to send out energy blasts." He moved his arms around his head, making whooshing noises.

Ariana looked up. "Lenti said they might be part of the answer," she said. "I asked them to stay for a while."

24

Oxytocin

"I'm okay, really," yawned Catherine as Robyn helped her to the bottom bunk. "Just tired more than anything."

"Sure," said Robyn. "Not injured after fighting Fang while a building collapsed around you. Ariana filled me in." She knelt by Catherine's feet and started undoing her shoelaces. Catherine gasped as Robyn's hand clasped around her ankle.

"Are you okay?" Robyn looked up, worried she might have hurt her.

Catherine shook her head, voice strained. "No, I'm fine."

Robyn eased off the other boot and Catherine sighed.

"I'm sorry about your jeans," Catherine said, rubbing a dark stain on her thigh.

"Catherine, honestly, it's not the jeans I'm worried

about." Robyn got to her feet. "But speaking of … can you take them off yourself? I've got some old clothes you can sleep in."

Catherine nodded and Robyn turned around. They had the room to themselves; Ariana and Sara were sharing next door, the boys further along the corridor. Robyn felt her cheeks grow hot as she listened to Catherine undress. She'd never felt like this with Kara – her friend was always raiding her closet and peeling shirts off without a second thought, as if she'd grown up in a nudist colony. This was different.

"What was Xiaofang like?" Robyn asked. She heard something drop to the ground, the clang of a belt.

"Intense," said Catherine. "I thought maybe I could talk to her, but she didn't seem interested." She paused. "She tortured Sara without a second thought."

Robyn was silent for a moment. "So she's not like us."

"No," breathed Catherine, her voice momentarily muffled by fabric. "She couldn't be more different. Fang is scary, Robyn."

Robyn shivered. *Fang.* Even the name was scary. Robyn couldn't help imagining a vampire, snarling with exposed sharpened teeth.

"You can turn around now," said Catherine. Robyn managed to execute a stiff pivot, pushing vampire-Fang out of her mind. Catherine was seated on the edge of the bed, wearing a faded pair of Robyn's bike shorts and a baggy shirt. The shorts made her legs look even longer. Robyn averted her gaze, trying in vain to stop the flush from spreading to her neck.

"Robyn?" Catherine shuffled backward and leant against the wall, stifling a grimace. "Could you stay with me?"

Robyn froze, the question echoing in her mind. *Could you stay with me?* She couldn't decide if it was a terrible idea, or a terribly good one. Her heart hammered in her chest as her mind whirled through possibilities. Catherine was injured, she just needed a friend. That made sense. But Catherine was gay, and Robyn's head turned to mush whenever she was around her. What did that mean?

Gay, gay, gay.

Seventh grade. She'd rather have been holding Lyndsay's hand than Sean's. Sean's was clammy and gross, but every girl was tethered by a boy as they navigated their shiny lunch boxes.

In ninth grade, Lyndsay came out. The subsequent witch-hunt ended only when Lyndsay changed schools. Robyn learned that it was a Very Bad Thing to be gay. She'd locked those thoughts away, immersed herself in textbooks and assignments. She'd tried to traverse the dating pool of university, she really had – but after Travis she'd focused all her energies on her research. And those thoughts? They'd stayed away, until she'd met Catherine.

She realised Catherine was staring at her. Robyn ran a hand through her hair and studied her feet. She had no idea how long she'd been standing there like an idiot.

Catherine brought her knees up and pulled the blanket down. Robyn crawled in, drawing the blanket around them both, careful not to bump Catherine's bandaged arms. Her heart pounded; she was sure Catherine could feel it. A physicist on the other side of the planet would surely register it on some machine and be puzzled. How was the bed not collapsing under the weight of the sound?

Robyn tried to stay on the edge but the bed was too small, drawing her into Catherine's side. *Gravity. Physics again.* Catherine shifted onto her hip to face the wall and reached back for Robyn's hand. Robyn held her breath as Catherine drew her into the curve of her spine, focusing on not making a sound as she sank into the contact – all of it. Closing her eyes, Robyn tucked her hand securely under her head as Catherine released it. *Big spoon, little spoon.* So this is what it felt like.

"Goodnight, Robyn," slurred Catherine.

"Goodnight," Robyn whispered into blonde hair. Her skin tingled with warmth. It felt like electricity would jump from her fingers if she skimmed them along Catherine's waist. She clamped them more firmly together on the pillow.

Gay, gay, gay. The schoolyard taunts blurred into one another as Robyn's eyes drooped. *Gaygaygay.*

Bright light prickled against her eyelids. Robyn opened her eyes, startled by the weight against her side. Then she remembered.

Catherine's arm was draped over her hip, their hands grazing. Butterflies erupted in Robyn's stomach. She wasn't supposed to feel this way about a friend. When Derek had held her hand, it had felt nice, *safe* even, but now her skin was on fire. Robyn hardly dared breathe for fear of waking Catherine. She wanted to live in this moment for as long as possible. Catherine shifted in her sleep and Robyn froze as she nuzzled into her neck.

Robyn nearly had a heart attack. *Just an oxytocin high*, she rationalised, *that's all.* Purely chemical.

It didn't stop the faint moan that escaped her lips.

"Robyn?" Catherine stretched and purred into Robyn's back. "You okay?"

The contact was like a drug. Robyn managed a nod, not trusting her voice to stay level, before realising Catherine couldn't see her face.

"Yeah," she squeaked, shimmying out of Catherine's grasp and getting to her feet. "I've got to, um, get to the lab."

Catherine propped herself up against the headboard, a smirk on her face. Her mussed-up hair was like a golden halo.

"You should rest," Robyn finished lamely.

The smirk followed her out the door where she collided with a solid form.

Oomph.

"Robyn?" Derek carried a stack of papers; a few fell to the floor with the impact. Robyn leaned down to help him collect them and they banged heads.

"Ow," said Robyn, laughing. "Sorry."

Derek reached out an arm, guiding her back to her feet. He jerked his head toward the door.

"Was Catherine good?"

Robyn faltered. "What?" *Sure, they'd slept together, but not like that.* Could Derek tell?

Derek frowned at her. "Did she get through the night okay? She looked pretty battered last night."

Right. Robyn managed a nod. "Um, yeah. She's doing all right, I think." *More than all right, judging from that smug look on her face. Had it been some sort of test?*

Robyn's face fell. Maybe Catherine was messing with her. Tears stung her eyes. She felt like a royal idiot. Taking a deep breath, she pointed to the documents in Derek's arms, recalling the late-night sampling. "Sara and Jacob."

Derek shifted his weight to the other foot under her disapproving glare. Robyn had just remembered that she was angry with Derek. Hell, she was angry with everyone right now. Did everyone see her as a naive little pushover?

"Look, Robyn. I know you don't agree, but we needed to move as quickly as possible." He started toward the kitchen. "And I think you'll be as excited as I am with the results."

Robyn didn't think she'd be able to muster up excitement about anything right now. She looked down at her rumpled shirt and track pants, deciding she didn't care as she followed Derek into the kitchen, the tiles cold on her bare feet.

It was feeding time at the zoo. A fort of cereal boxes crowded the counter. The animals snapped at raw meat in a bucket in the far corner. Robyn screwed up her nose as she perched next to Ariana. The terrible lingering smell of chicken necks made her gag.

"Gross," she said, reaching for her muesli.

Derek slapped the gene sequences down on the table, where they soaked up a puddle of milk.

"Crap," he muttered, blotting the paper with his sleeve.

"So, what's the big breakthrough?" Robyn drowned her muesli in soy milk. She was still angry at Derek, and she could feel the egg swelling on her head from where they'd bumped together. Robyn flicked a glance toward the door. She was pissed off with Catherine, too. She couldn't get that stupid smirk out of her head. Robyn stabbed her spoon into her cereal. *Stupid beautiful people. Stupid confusing brain chemistry.*

"Their DNA is stable, doesn't change. We can create a workable vector based on their mitochondrial genes." Derek's voice thrummed with excitement.

Robyn raised her eyes and shared a glance with Terence.

Terence rolled his shoulders. "That is good news," he allowed. Relief settled on Robyn's shoulders. Good. So Terence hadn't completely forgiven Derek either. At least she had someone on her side.

"I'm still not happy with your bullish methods," Robyn said, drowning an almond.

Ariana eased off her stool and tiptoed toward the door. Eva and Ming paused at the bucket, following her progress with their eyes. A gooey string of entrails hung from Eva's jaws. The bear snapped at a haunch of something and followed the walker, trailing blood in her wake. Robyn eyed the splotches with horror – somehow she had to get back to her room without shoes. *The floor is lava.*

"Someone had to do it." Derek pounded a fist on the table. "You know that, Robyn. If these kids mean we can move forward, we have to take the opportunity."

"Sure, but we can treat them better than guinea pigs," Robyn retorted.

"I never said they were guinea pigs."

Robyn snorted. "Well, that's how you treated them last night."

Derek went silent, tapping his fingers on the counter. "I didn't mean – I wasn't thinking."

"No, you weren't." Robyn grabbed her bowl. She wanted some fresh air. She tiptoed over the crimson Jackson Pollock painting on the floor into the corridor.

A door hung open at the end of the hallway, allowing a slant of light inside. Robyn squinted, following the trail of voices onto a paved courtyard. Kara stood next to Sara and Fletcher, holding a walkie-talkie. Eva and Ming bounced with excitement in front of a chalked white line. Robyn skated around the abandoned grisly bone with a shudder.

"We're go at this end," Kara said into her walkie-talkie. Robyn shielded her eyes as she stared past them. A high fence extended from the building and disappeared into thick scrub. She hadn't thought to investigate the rest of the compound, but it was clearly big. Is this what

Terence had meant when he'd said *a bit of outside space*? It was bigger than a football stadium.

A burst of static erupted from the walkie-talkie. "Roger. Let's get this party started." Kate's voice. Robyn sank onto a steel bench, balancing her muesli on her knees. The sun on her shoulders was a welcome caress. The nights were starting to get colder now. Winter was just around the corner.

"All right. On your marks ..." Kara raised a hand. "Get set ..."

Fletcher and Sara tensed, leaning forward.

"Go!"

Sara and Ming flashed past Kara, knocking her to the ground where she spun on her butt.

"Jesus," Kara wheezed. She raised her walkie-talkie. "They're headed your way, sis." She pushed herself to her feet. Eva bounded through the underbrush, Fletcher keeping pace. Robyn watched them until they disappeared from view, her spoon poised centimetres from her mouth, forgotten. A flicker of green light shrouded Fletcher's skin. High-frequency electromagnetic radiation. Catherine had told her what Ariana had done in Beijing, produced a force field like the one Fletcher had created that had encased the van and reflected bullets.

"Moving fast," Kara added over the walkie-talkie, staring at the rustling forest in their wake before turning to Robyn.

"Morning." Kara dropped onto the bench beside her.

"What's all this?" gesticulated Robyn with her spoon. Eli and Jacob walked beside an ornamental flowerbed, Una rocking on the walker's shoulder. All three walkers, right here, together. Eli's aura was red, Catherine had said. Red, green, blue. Robyn frowned at her bowl. After a physics class one afternoon, she'd had an argument with her mother about primary colours. Her mother had insisted they were red, yellow and blue. To an artist, they were. But the primary colours of *light* were red, green and blue. Together they made white light. It felt like there was something there, something buried deep in her mind. Robyn tried to coax it out but was met with a solid wall.

The walkie-talkie crackled and emitted a loud thud. "Jeez, you found me already," Kate moaned. "It's a tie. Stop the clock, sis."

Kara pulled a stopwatch from her pocket. "Four

minutes, twenty-two seconds."

"Nine kilometres in four minutes? I can barely run a kilometre in five." Kate sucked in air. Over the walkie-talkie, it sounded like a vacuum cleaner choking on a small animal.

Kara grinned into the walkie-talkie. "Good work, guys. Take five."

Robyn stared into the forest. "Kate's out there somewhere?"

"Padded suit. She looked like a marshmallow driving out there in the truck."

Sure enough, Robyn heard the thrum of a vehicle, faint but audible.

"Thought we'd keep everyone occupied and away from the shit storm in there." Kara cocked her head toward the open door. "How long before you guys rip each other to shreds?"

Robyn choked on her muesli. "That's not fair," she spluttered. "Though it's tenser than I would have hoped," she allowed.

Kara rolled her eyes. "You're all too similar. Obsessed. Possessed, even." She lifted both hands in mock surrender. "In a good way, don't get me wrong.

We've come this far."

"I just can't read Derek. Or Catherine." Robyn put down her bowl. "I better get back in there." She was terrified to see Catherine again, still furious at Derek. Plus she had nowhere to hide.

"You know, for a smart person, you can be really blind," said Kara.

"What do you mean?"

"The way they both look at you, Robyn. How can you not have noticed? They're both smitten. Jeez. Multiple discovery, or whatever you scientists call it, but you've got them both hooked."

Robyn stared into the milky depths of her muesli. *Derek and Catherine like me?*

"I … uh …" Robyn's mind raced. Derek's touchy-feely hand-holding. Catherine nuzzling into her neck. Is Kara right? Is that why she's so damn angry at both of them?

"So?" prodded Kara. "I never thought about it, but maybe that's why you've been off the dating wagon. You never met the right *girl*."

Robyn didn't trust herself to speak. *Gay gay gay*. She didn't know if her parents would ever speak to her again.

An image of her mother worrying her wooden rosary beads made her stomach clench upward to her ribcage.

"It's okay, you know." Kara shrugged. "If you were. And screw your parents. You're well and truly an adult now, Robyn."

Had she been ignoring a part of herself? Robyn closed her eyes, remembering the feeling of Catherine's weight against her back. She'd never felt that rush of heat with Levi, or Travis. *Or Derek*, she realised in a rush.

Ariana skidded out the door. "Hey, Kara? Would you mind driving me back to the beach?"

Kara got to her feet. "Sure thing, kiddo." She turned to Robyn. "Good luck in there."

Robyn nodded. *I need it.*

Terence washed his hands at the sink and pulled off his scrubs. "That should do it. Lie still while the local anaesthetic wears off." Eli and Sara lay on their stomachs on the stainless-steel counter, Ming sprawled alongside Sara, her head resting on the girl's hip. The dishwasher vibrated as it dealt with the breakfast dishes.

Terence pulled his jacket back on and stuffed the scrubs into a bag. "I'd like to talk to you about your experience in Beijing. Anything you can remember will really help us."

"Whatever we can do to help, short of organ donation." Sara sat up. "Ow, my neck is sore."

"Good," said Terence. "That means the anaesthetic is wearing off."

Sara screwed up her face and ran a tentative hand across her neck. "Thanks for this."

Eli shimmied off the counter onto a stool. Una flapped down from her perch atop the fridge to alight on his shoulder. Terence knew it should still feel weird, but it was strangely normal having the animals hanging around. They just seemed to be extensions of the convergers.

"You guys should take it easy today." He realised as soon as he said it that neither of them would heed his advice. Sara jumped down from the counter with a snort and disappeared into the corridor. Eli trailed after her, taking a final wide-eyed look around the kitchen as the door swung shut behind him. It wasn't until he reached the lab that Terence thought to wonder where Eli was from. He looked at everything as if seeing it for the first time. Somewhere rural, maybe northern China? He'd have to ask Eli about it later.

Derek and Robyn stood side by side, hunched over a broad ream of paper. The gene sequences, Terence realised. He wondered if a truce had been forged. He flicked a glance to Catherine, perched on a stool off to one side. She looked better, he thought. Bruises across her cheek and bandages up to her shoulder, but more vibrant. Catherine gave him a weak wave and Terence brightened.

"Hey, you're looking better."

Catherine smiled. "Thanks, it's good to be back."

Robyn's head thrummed with possibilities. Derek had run the samples three times. The new convergers' DNA didn't change. As much as she was still angry with him, she couldn't dispute the results.

"It's stable," she said, pointing to the sequences. "The operon, it's all there, but it doesn't shift like the walkers' DNA." Terence murmured to Catherine, who smiled as she pushed her hair behind her ears.

Catherine hopped down from her stool and jerked a

stiff arm over the pages.

"We should be able to screen for this," Catherine said. "Sara and Jacob – they were the only survivors of Fang's radiation treatment. Maybe they had these genes all along. Maybe the treatment just triggered transcription."

Robyn nodded, following along, doing her best to bury last night's incident. "So there might be others with the same sequence, who could be potential convergers." She tried to ignore the goosebumps rising along her arm where it brushed Catherine's. She flushed at the memory of Catherine's cheek against her neck. *Focus*.

"And then what?" said Terence. "Could we find them?"

"No. We'd have to do one better. We'd have to figure out how to activate their convergence sequence."

"What?" Robyn turned to Derek. "We have to do what? Even if we could, which I'm not sure we can, how could we force that on people?"

Derek shook his head. "It's the MRI that is forcing our hand, Robyn. Can't you see? If we don't figure it out before them, it'll happen on their terms. You saw the chips. It won't be just a genetic leap. It could be worldwide enslavement."

Robyn hesitated a beat as the reality sank in. She took

a step back from the counter and Catherine filled the space, leaving Derek and Catherine side by side. They were so different – Derek's firm stance, broad shoulders that tensed as he gestured over the sequences. Catherine was taller than him, Robyn realised. Her blonde hair pulled into a loose ponytail revealed an expanse of neck.

"Okay, so we need a vector. Something to transmit an activation signal." Terence's face was screwed up in thought.

Derek tapped the sequences. "Yeah, but first we need to figure out what that signal is. We've got a lot of work to do."

Catherine bundled up the gene sequences. "I'll get started on the screening program."

Robyn's head ached. Catherine looked annoyingly calm and collected as she headed further down the bench. Robyn felt like her brain might implode. Maybe Catherine had forgotten about last night. Maybe Catherine did that to every sexually confused girl she stumbled upon. Robyn rubbed her temples. She had to stop going around in circles before she went insane. Derek was right. They had a lot of work to do.

"You okay?" Terence asked. It was just them in the

big lab space now.

No, not really. She'd seen how Terence's eyes lingered on Catherine. She couldn't talk to him about it, about any of it.

"I guess," Robyn said. "It's a lot. I'm not sure about this."

"Me neither. But we have to try, right? We're not like Fang, Robyn. You can trust us."

Robyn flicked her gaze to Derek, hauling reagents from the fridge in the glass-walled room. "I hope so. I just … at least it couldn't get any more complicated, right?"

"Uh, guys? There's something we need to tell you." Fletcher appeared in the doorway with Eli. "And I'm not sure you're going to like it."

Robyn's stomach plummeted.

Robyn rubbed the bridge of her nose, trying to ignore the dull pounding in her skull. Fletcher had called it *sun song*. It sounded familiar. She kept hitting that block in her mind, as if she had a bank of repressed memories buried deep in there somewhere.

"A solar storm, maybe. An onslaught of electromagnetic radiation. X-rays, charged particles, plasma. A big one hit Earth in 1859. A coronal mass ejection reached the magnetosphere and triggered a geomagnetic storm. That was before computers, electricity networks, the internet. It wiped out the telegram system," said Terence.

"What could it do today?" asked Catherine.

Terence drummed his fingers on the counter. "It could wipe out all our technology. It'd take out the satellites first. Then it would fry the electricity grids. No internet, water, sewage, nothing. It'd be like the Apocalypse. Civilisation would be in chaos and it could take us decades to recover."

Derek shook his head. "See? I knew it would be something quantifiable. Maybe we're just looking at this from the wrong angle."

"Oh, shut up, Derek," Catherine spat. "Can't you see this is bigger than that? You weren't there in Beijing. I saw what Eli and Ariana are capable of. This isn't in a textbook, all nice and neat. It's happening right now, around you, and you refuse to see it."

Derek stared at Catherine in shock. "Did you just tell me to shut up?"

Catherine tipped her head back in exasperation. "Yes, for the love of God, *yes*."

"Stop it, both of you." Robyn stood, pushing the stool under the lab counter as she turned to Fletcher. Derek and Catherine stared at her.

"You think we have just under a year? Ten months?"

Fletcher nodded. "Yeah, that's what Lenti said."

"It's not a lot of time."

Fletcher shook his head. "No, it's not." He scuffed his shoe against the ground. "No pressure, but Lenti thinks we'll need the others. The other convergers."

Robyn closed her eyes. "So we have ten months to come up with an activation dose."

"Yeah, I'm sorry."

"It's not your fault," said Catherine. "It's no-one's fault," she amended, flashing an angry glance at Derek.

"And then what?" said Terence. "We can't stop the sun."

"But maybe we can stop Nyx," said Fletcher, his voice stronger now.

Nyx. Robyn screwed her eyes shut, willing the

memory to surface, but nothing came. When she opened her eyes, Derek and Catherine still stared at her.

"What?" Robyn said, looking between the two of them. Derek stomped out of the lab, slamming the door shut behind him. Robyn felt like punching a wall – it would have about the same effect as trying to get through to Derek. *This is all real*, she wanted to scream at him. It seemed to come from deep inside her, the conviction that everything Fletcher said was correct.

If they only had ten months, they didn't need to squander any more time bickering. Robyn turned away from Catherine's puzzled stare and squeezed her eyes shut. Colours danced behind her eyelids. Red, green, blue.

25

Screening

Fang stood facing the tinted glass, assessing the activity on the lower floor. Scientists scurried around, aware she observed them from above. *Lab rats*, Fang thought. Her brother would groan if she told him, but he never had appreciated her humour. She wondered when she would see him next. The space below was barely more than a hastily converted warehouse, but it was operational. Even if it was in Sofia, Bulgaria.

"Fang?" Vulcan tapped the desk impatiently.

She turned away from the window. Vulcan's office, she reminded herself. Fang sank into one of the armchairs facing the desk; it was made of some rich, dark wood.

"Any progress on the gene sequencing?" Vulcan leaned back in his chair. Fang wondered if Vulcan had made Derek feel quite so insignificant. Her cheeks burned as she studied her fingers.

"Both Eli and Fletcher's DNA is different." Fang wasn't sure how to say it without sounding like a nutcase. "It fluctuates. Each time I analyse the samples, it changes."

Vulcan snorted. "Impossible."

Fang pushed the folder across the desk. Mahogany, she decided, her fingers tracing the smooth whorls. Too good for the interim Chief Director.

Vulcan flipped the folder open with an irritated sigh. He skimmed through the pages as Fang squirmed in her seat. The armchair smelled of stale cigar smoke; it clung to her skin.

"Run them again. You've obviously made a mistake."

Fang's cheeks burned. "That's nine duplicate analyses so far, sir. This is no mistake."

Vulcan waved a hand at her, already turning back to his computer. "Come back with results. I don't have time for this."

The dismissive gesture made her blood boil. Fang coaxed her files back into the folder and strode toward the door. Miranda had never treated her like this. She fumed as she descended the stairs back to the main laboratory. Somehow Sara and Jacob's samples had been lost in the explosion; she hadn't taken long-term samples for cold storage yet. Her fault. Fang dumped the folder on her lab bench. Everything seemed to be her fault.

The clatter of glassware tinkled up and down the row. Fang's neighbour tipped her head in a nod, then froze as she recognised Fang. The blonde scientist with the injured leg. "Fang?" the woman said, almost a whisper. "What are you doing down here?"

Fang's neck prickled with goosebumps. She knew Vulcan watched them from his eyrie.

"Working," Fang managed. "Just like you."

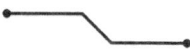

Catherine burst into the lab with wide eyes. "I think I've done it," she announced.

Robyn stared at her, not comprehending. "The screening test?" she exclaimed, jumping to her feet and abandoning Derek's spreadsheets. Robyn's fingers itched to draw Catherine into a hug, but she clenched her fists by her sides instead, remembering the self-satisfied smirk.

Catherine's smile wavered. Robyn felt a small thrill of victory.

"What's up? I heard shrieking." Terence stuck his head out of one of the analysis rooms. Derek poked his out of the machine room. A pair of sentry meerkats.

"Catherine. She may have figured out how to screen for the convergence genes."

Catherine waved the folder above her head.

Robyn perched on the edge of a stool and gave Catherine her full attention, enjoying the way it made her jump. *Take that*, she thought.

Catherine recovered. "Okay. So with Sara and Jacob's gene sequences we know what we're looking for, right?"

Robyn nodded. "But we can't sequence blood samples from everyone. It's not practical. Each analysis takes hours." It would take years to process even a small fraction of the blood bank.

"Yeah. But because it's mitochondrial, it's linked to their energy production."

"Which we can monitor," said Terence, nodding. "Go on."

Catherine sent Terence an annoyed glance. "I was just getting to that. Anyway, yes, we can monitor mitochondrial mass with an assay for citrate synthase activity. I found a spectrophotometer in the back of a cupboard in the machine room."

"Oh, so that's why you pushed me out of the way," Derek snapped. "I thought you just wanted to annoy me."

Catherine closed her eyes for a second and Robyn tensed ready to intervene, but the terse response didn't come. Instead, Catherine pushed a ream of paper across the bench. "Sara and Jacob both have extremely high levels of enzyme activity. Way higher than any elite athlete."

Robyn stared at the numbers. Mitochondrial mass equalled number of mitochondria. More mitochondria, more energy.

"Could it be so simple?" Robyn said. She felt dumb for not thinking of it, especially after seeing Sara and Fletcher sprint into the forest. Too fast. She frowned; she'd been thinking about the light, the colours …

"The assay takes hours, so I'm not sure you could call it simple," Catherine said, hands on hips. "But it means if we can get blood samples, we can assess whether someone is likely to have the convergence gene sequence without going to all the effort of gene sequencing. A shortcut."

It was a brilliant plan. Robyn wished she'd come up with it. Terence looked at Catherine as if she'd just announced a cure for cancer, whereas Derek had the face of a sullen teenager who'd been picked last for the sporting team.

"So we can use the blood bank to get a reading on what percentage of the population is genetically preprogrammed to be convergers. Then we need to figure out how to trigger it." Terence nodded as he spoke.

"Let's test ourselves," Derek said, his gaze challenging.

Catherine's hands fell. "Us?"

Robyn stared at Derek. Her mind felt fuzzy and slow. "It's pretty unlikely any of us will have the gene sequence."

"Statistically, it is possible," said Terence. "We'd be perfect test subjects for the vector, if we manage to create one."

"I … I guess." Catherine ran a hand through her hair, glancing sideways at Robyn.

Robyn slid from her stool. "I'll get the needles."

Derek held up four vials. Blood always made Robyn feel sick — something about how the viscous crimson liquid stuck to the glass. She looked away as Derek racked and passed them to Catherine. Derek was at her elbow the moment he offloaded the samples.

"Robyn, you okay?"

She nodded. His concern made her feel guilty, though she didn't have anything to feel guilty about. Maybe she was coming down with something. That would explain everything, right?

"Just tired," she offered. It sounded lame, even to her.

Derek stepped back. "Okay. Well, I'm going to start on the vector. Terence?"

Terence tipped his head. "Yeah, I'm thinking bacterial plasmid first for petri dish testing, then we fiddle with a viral vector."

The words washed over Robyn like a foreign language. Accident victims could spontaneously forget their native tongue and start speaking another language. She'd read it somewhere. Maybe that was what was happening to her. Derek threw an anxious look in her direction before he and Terence disappeared into the electrophoresis room.

"Right," Robyn muttered to herself. She'd never felt like this in the lab before. At the hardware store, supermarket, doctor's surgery: yes. The environment outside the sterile walls of the lab was alien to her. Doing adult things like booking haircuts and paying bills were nuisances designed to throw her off her game. For the first time Robyn felt overwhelmed within the hallowed halls; the sanctuary of the lab was crushing and dark.

Everything had flipped upside down after one night nestled against Catherine. Catherine had ripped a huge gash into the walls she'd built painstakingly, brick by brick. She'd been safe, content, in that little world. Kara and Kate, her cramped office, her research. Now all that certainty had leaked out, leaving her stranded and unsure of the rules. She craved structure, needed the rules. Without them she didn't know who she was.

Robyn clapped a hand to her right eye in a vain attempt to stop the throbbing pain there. The mini-centrifuge whirred from one of the glassed rooms, sending its high-pitched wail keening through the lab. In her peripheral vision she saw Catherine stalk toward her. Robyn scrambled backward, her butt hitting the bench as Catherine stopped centimetres from her. She wanted to reach out and shove Catherine away. She was still angry at her but couldn't trust her hands not to pull Catherine in closer, to crash their lips together. The thought left her reeling. Her eye pulsated with pain as she brought her hand away.

"Thanks for helping me, yesterday."

Robyn noticed long eyelashes, the sharp angle of her jaw. She replayed the satisfied smirk and gritted her teeth.

"You're welcome," Robyn said stiffly, reaching back to the bench to support her quivering legs. The centrifuge pinged and Catherine turned away.

"Who will be eliminated this week?" said Catherine. She paused in the doorway. "Find out after the break."

Catherine's dazzling smile before she disappeared brought fumbled, staccato laughter tripping from Robyn's lips. *What the hell is happening to me?*

Robyn collapsed onto the lab stool, staring at the pages Catherine had left sprawled on the counter. *Dyke.* It was what they'd called Lyndsay back in grade nine. One syllable, with the power to draw blood. Travis had called her the same thing when he terminated their not-quite-a-relationship: weeks of kissing on his couch that always ended with Robyn peeling away his roaming hands. It had felt like a physical slap. The make-out sessions ended, and if Robyn was truly honest with herself, she'd been relieved.

But now, she was freaking out.

26

Lab Rats

Ariana hovered in the deep, turquoise water; she could see light shimmering far above her head. The pod of dolphins had nudged her offshore, and now she loomed over the edge of the continental shelf – an underwater cliff disappearing into a dark abyss. Ariana shivered, despite her wetsuit. Even the glow from Jericho's scales didn't penetrate more than a few metres into the gloom. The dragon snaked through the water in a figure of eight around her waist. Ariana held out a hand to his flank and emptied her thoughts, staring through the dark water. A shadow moved in the depths, and Ariana jerked backward before she registered the familiar mind.

You know what is coming. It is time for you to learn, walker. You must earn your scales.

The water resonated with the thrum of sound. Ariana

relaxed into it, letting it wash over her. The hypnotic humming noise echoed how she felt when she crossed over to the spirit world. The whale's mind was huge, encompassing her very being and flooding her senses as if she'd dived straight into the murky depths before them. The blue aura enveloped her, and memories began flashing before her eyes – a tropical beach lined with rough-hewn canoes, a jagged spurt of a foreign language, bright luminous coral. Ariana inhaled, a stream of bubbles escaping her mouth. Her gills flared. It all felt familiar.

The enormous whale raised her eye to Ariana's face. Ariana swore she could see the entire universe in the galaxy of her retinas.

I am ready.

Kara hunched underneath a blanket on the sand, looking murderous. "It's been hours," she moaned. "It's freezing out here." Wind whipped along the dune and Ariana shivered as she cleared the water. Kara threw her a thick towel.

"Thanks," Ariana said, cocooning herself in it. She sank down onto the sand and rummaged in the backpack.

Terence had made her favourite – spinach and peanut butter. The spread oozed out the side as she bit into the sandwich. Kara made a face.

"I already ate mine." Kara waved a hand as Ariana made to dig into the bag again. "Just peanut butter, thank God. How can you eat that stuff?"

Ariana shrugged. It'd always been her favourite. "I need to spend some more time in the sea," she said between bites.

"Not this afternoon. I'm heading home before I catch pneumonia," said Kara, rubbing her toes.

Ariana shook her head. "Weeks, maybe months. There's a lot I need to learn."

"Let me get this straight. This sea spirit, embodied in a ginormous blue whale, wants you to take an ocean vacation? To what, learn sea magic?" Kara flopped back on the sand.

"Kind of," said Ariana. "Atlantis chose to live fully in our world and left the spirit realm behind eons ago. She's taught all the sea walkers."

"That's heavy, man," murmured Kara, bringing her arms across her face. "I guess it makes sense, with your spirit energy aura. You must be able to do things we can't."

Ariana folded the empty brown paper bag into a neat square. "There hasn't been a walker in centuries. There's a lot that needs to be done. We've screwed up the seas more in the last few hundred years than ever before. If I'm going to be helpful when it all happens –" Ariana waved a hand weakly in front of her. "Then I've got to get ready."

Kara propped herself up on her elbows. "Yeah, Robyn made me watch a documentary last year. I cried," she admitted. "Though I'll deny it if you tell anyone." Kara sighed. "This end-of-the-world stuff is pretty depressing."

Ariana stared into the surf. It was calming, the predictable rush and suck of the foaming waves. In and out, like breathing. It was hard to imagine everything crashing to a stop. Even harder to imagine she could do anything to change it.

"I don't know if your brother is going to like the idea of you gallivanting around the oceans with a whale for an unspecified amount of time," said Kara.

"That's why you'll help me convince him," said Ariana, getting to her feet and dusting off her hands. "Come on."

Bowls clattered as Catherine ladled soup. Robyn inhaled. Pumpkin wafted from the other end of the counter. Her new strategy was a cunning one: maintaining distance from Catherine *and* Derek. Kara would label it juvenile, which was why Robyn didn't plan on telling her. *Did that make it doubly juvenile?*

Bowls were passed down the chain with hunks of sourdough balanced on their rims. A pot plant sat in the middle of the counter. Bright yellow gerberas. Poppy was having a field day.

Terence feigned a drooling fit as he dunked bread into his bowl. "Divine. Thank you, Catherine." He patted the empty stool by his side. "Sit next to me, master chef." *Yes, stay on the other side of the counter*, Robyn thought.

Catherine grinned as she settled in next to Terence. Robyn turned her attention to her own dinner. The soup was earthy and sweet, spiked with cumin and paprika. She forced herself to eat, even though she wasn't hungry. The thudding behind her temples had raged into a full-blown headache as she'd tried not to get underfoot in the lab. After she dropped the second vial of denatured DNA, Terence had relegated her to the computer where she could do less damage. Catherine had locked herself away with their blood samples. The *Next Top Model* reveal would probably come later. Robyn was too tired to even care about the screening results.

To her left, Eli slurped his soup straight from the bowl, ignoring his spoon altogether. Sara sniggered playfully.

Eli shrugged. "What?" he said. "It's really good."

Robyn rubbed her temples and stared through her soup. The doors swung open with a clang as Kate staggered in under the weight of something that looked like a medieval catapult.

"Trebuchet. Pimped out thanks to yours truly," said Kate as she heaved it into a corner. Robyn realised she'd been staring.

"Wow," Robyn muttered. The smell of untreated pine lingered in the air as Kate dusted off her hands.

Eli put down his bowl and wiped his chin on his sleeve. "It was great. Una loved it."

Robyn tried to imagine the osprey seizing clay discs from the air. She would have loved to have seen it.

Robyn jabbed her soup with her spoon. Nobody would miss her if she disappeared. Terence and Derek had been doing fine without her, and Catherine had somehow managed to cook dinner and simultaneously run the blood samples. Great, functioning adults through and through.

She was about to excuse herself when the doors flew open again. Ariana padded in on bare feet, accompanied by Kara.

"Yes, we made it back in time for dinner," hissed Kara. "I'm starving," she added, flopping theatrically onto a vacant stool. "Just inject it straight into my veins."

Everyone at the table froze.

Kara blinked. "Oh, sorry, that's not what I meant."

Sara paled and pushed her bowl away. Jacob pulled it toward him and swiped a hunk of sourdough around the sides.

"I need to go train with Atlantis," blurted Ariana into the silence.

Kara groaned. "Ariana, we talked about this. It's called *subtlety*."

"This is really happening. If I can become a better walker, I have to try. If there's anything I can do, anything at all – you've got to understand. I have to *try*."

Kara held up a hand. "Ariana will have a radio, so she's always got us on speed dial. Not to mention spirit world hi-fi. She needs to do this, guys."

Terence toyed with his fringe. "I was wondering when this would happen. That first morning, when you got your gills – I knew it would only be a matter of time."

"Is that a yes?"

"We still have a lot of work to do here before we're going to be remotely helpful. You'd be bored out of your brain hanging around here. I know you'd hate me if I stood in your way."

Relief flooded Ariana's face. "Thank you."

"Ariana's right. We have separate tasks in our common goal. I really do think you are destined to bring humanity back from the brink." Terence tipped his head toward Ariana. "Just like we're trying to restore the forgotten links between living creatures. And now we have a deadline."

Robyn raised her head. A terrifying deadline. She wasn't sure how humanity could bounce back from a total loss of technology. If it was even possible.

Derek stood up, pushing his stool away. "You're going

to entrust your sister's safety to a *whale*? You're freaking kidding me."

Anger flared across Ariana's face. "She's not just a whale. She's the water spirit, and she can help us, Derek."

Terence sighed. "I trust Ariana, and by extension, Atlantis."

Derek glowered.

"What about me? And Eli?" said Fletcher.

Sara humphed under her breath.

"Forgetting anyone, chief?" Jacob snorted.

"All of us," amended Fletcher with a guilty look.

"Atlantis is the only spirit we know of," Robyn said. *But there were others.* She frowned, hitting the solid mind-block again. "There's no point in the rest of you splitting up. We need to lay low, at least for a while. Maybe together you can find some answers."

"I don't think Robyn is suggesting we write a bunch of letters to politicians," said Jacob as Fletcher opened his mouth to protest. "She's right. As shitty as Beijing was, maybe this has all happened for a reason. You guys –" he pointed to Fletcher, Eli and Ariana – "are special. I've seen it. You can do things no human should be able to do."

A timer dinged by the stove and Robyn's stomach clenched. Please, no dessert. She didn't think she could manage it right now, not when her stomach felt like it was wrestling her appendix. She just wanted to crawl into bed and sleep. Catherine jumped up and stopped the shrill sound.

In her own bed, wrapped in a fort of blankets, Robyn amended. *Very much alone.*

"Elimination time," Catherine announced. Robyn stared for a long second before it clicked. The screening test. *Next Top Model.*

Catherine twitched an eager hand in front of the printer.

"I mean, the odds are none of us will have the genes, right?" Robyn said. Her headache was being held at bay by ibuprofen and sheer willpower. She suspected the painkillers were doing the lion's share.

Derek leaned against the bench, arms folded. He was wearing one of those gaping singlets that gym junkies wore. He must have changed after dinner. Robyn felt like she would have noticed. *Maybe the distance thing is working.*

"Oh my God," said Catherine, clutching the printed pages to her face. "Two positives."

Catherine locked panicked eyes with Robyn, then her gaze skated over to Terence. Robyn's stomach resumed kick-boxing her appendix.

"Robyn and Terence."

Robyn blinked stupidly up at Catherine. She'd never thought it would be *her.* Sara's pale face flashed before her eyes. If they managed to figure out how to trigger this, she'd be like Sara or Jacob. Robyn had never even had a proper pet before. Racing snails didn't count, even if they'd blitzed the Cobalt Valley Show when she was eleven. God, what if she bonded with a gastropod? It'd be dead within a week, crushed under somebody's shoe.

"Jesus Christ," echoed Terence, as if reading her mind. "I need a drink."

Terence leaned back against the counter, cradling a glass of whisky. Robyn swallowed a gulp of the burning liquid and winced as it hit her stomach. It was probably unlikely she'd bond with a snail, she rationalised. Alternatives kept flashing through her mind. One of those yappy rat-dogs, like a Chihuahua. Or worse, an actual rat.

"Okay, so we've got our lab rats," Robyn said, trying to keep the note of fear from her voice as she gestured to herself and Terence. "I guess all we need now is to perfect a delivery vector." *What if it is marine?* Robyn choked on her next sip of liquor. She had to stop every fifty metres when she did laps, clutching the side of the pool like a life raft. *I'm going to be a terrible converger.*

Derek nodded, draining his own glass. "We've figured out a suitable bacterial plasmid for basic trials. We'll need to do some culturing studies, then it's going to take time to scale it up to a viral vector."

Terence rubbed his glasses on the hem of his shirt. "This sort of stuff takes years to get approved. We only have months."

Derek poured himself another glass of whisky. "Then we need a mass inoculation system. Fake vaccination program, maybe. Or aerosol delivery over cities."

Terence blanched. "We'd be playing God on a massive scale," he whispered.

"We have to," Derek frowned.

"No." Robyn's voice came out louder than she'd

intended. "There has to be another way. If we can find these people, like I found Fletcher, maybe we can just, well, ask them. Tell them everything and let them decide if they want to activate the convergence genes or not."

"We can't take that risk," replied Derek, hands curling into fists by his side. "What if the MRI finds them first?"

Catherine surprised Robyn by stepping in. "We're not Fang. We don't make decisions for other people. We're not going to mess with the biochemistry of innocent people when our treatment is so untested. It doesn't even exist yet."

"But …" interrupted Derek.

Catherine whirled to face him, eyes gleaming. "I said no, Derek."

Robyn's heart pounded as they both turned to her. This distance thing really wasn't working.

"What if I bond with a snail?" she stammered.

27

Action Stations

"You know, when I said I wanted to help, this wasn't exactly what I had in mind." Sara slapped her pen down on the kitchen counter with a sigh.

The doors swung shut behind Robyn as she darted inside. "Sorry," she mouthed at Kara, who leaned against the stove. The kettle panted as it psyched itself up.

"Yeah, I can't believe we still have to study. Aren't there like, exemptions for extenuating circumstances?" added Jacob. Robyn glanced from one to the other, unsurprised to hear Jacob backing Sara up – he shadowed Sara everywhere like a sidekick. She'd never seen them apart during the day. Jacob looked different – slimmer, Robyn realised. Evidence of Derek's afternoon training sessions. What had surprised her was Derek taking the initiative to work with the convergers. She'd watched them run circuits one afternoon, Derek jogging behind the others with Jacob. It was her first glimpse of what he must be like with Damian.

Still, Robyn didn't envy the convergers as they ran laps through the forest in the twilight, though they seemed to thrive on it. They were all getting stronger. Terence and Catherine could never seem to cook enough for them.

The kettle screamed and Robyn turned back to it. It was funny how quickly something could become normal. Ariana had been gone for less than two weeks. Robyn sipped her tea as she picked up the assignment Sara had abandoned. "Algebra?"

"Maths is hard enough with numbers. Why do they have to go and throw letters into the mix?"

Robyn laughed. "Good point."

Kara glared at her. "You guys know the drill. Schoolwork first, then free time." She mumbled something under her breath.

"What was that?" said Sara sweetly.

"Nothing," Kara grumbled.

The doors burst open and Eli and Fletcher raced in. "Blood delivery," Fletcher explained. Eva clambered behind the counter and curled up on the floor with a *humph*.

"That's my cue," Robyn said, skirting around the bear.

Catherine signed the docket, flashing her teeth at the delivery guy who practically quaked at the knees. Robyn ignored him and flipped the Styrofoam lid. Cool air assaulted her. Another five hundred crimson vials from the international blood bank. How many would they have time to analyse before the end of the world as we know it? Nine months away. Robyn closed the lid with a sigh. She'd been reading herself to sleep now that Ariana was training with Atlantis – not a mythical city, but a spirit in the physical form of a whale. Maybe all legends had roots in reality. She'd pored through the books Kate had dug up on animal spirits. Every ancient culture had their own system. Animals were always revered, had always been part of the struggle between light and dark. Maybe the boundaries between humans and animals had always been fluid. She couldn't shrug away the feeling that she was missing something, something big.

"What is it?" Catherine asked.

Robyn shook her head. "Nothing. Let's get back to

work." She couldn't explain it, and Catherine would just think she was crazy.

Catherine frowned and turned back to the cooler. It had been stiff and clunky between them since ... since the incident. Catherine hadn't invited Robyn back to her bed. In fact, she'd been downright icy. Robyn wondered if she'd imagined the whole thing after all. Maybe Kara was wrong about Catherine. And Derek.

Robyn watched Catherine unload the cooler and fill the lab fridge. It was a full-time job running analyses. They all had their niches. Catherine and Terence were the live-in chefs; she and Derek copped laundry duty; and Kate and Kara mixed tutoring with MRI surveillance. A happy little disjointed family.

Robyn grabbed the first rack and headed for the centrifuge. Every minute counted. She'd have time to deal with feelings later.

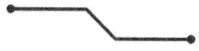

Ariana moved her arms in what felt like a perfect mimic of the form Atlantis had shown her. The complex movements reminded her of a fast series of Tai Chi poses. Below, the abyss seemed to scream as she hovered just beyond the continental shelf.

She brought her arms back to her sides, staring at the floating plastic bottle. Nothing happened. It just bobbed there, taunting her.

The solemn dark whale tipped her head, the barnacles encrusted on her side catching the light.

Close. You need to calm your mind. Try once more.

A flipper grazed her forehead and Ariana felt the familiar jolt of energy as the spirit flashed memories into her mind. Ariana sighed in frustration. She thought she *had* been doing what the whale was showing her.

Again.

The dolphin pod kept a respectful distance, though Ariana knew they were there. She felt blood rush to her neck. This was worse than public speaking. Jericho skimmed across the surface of her mind.

We can do this; I know we've done it before.

Well, apparently it wasn't like riding a bicycle. There didn't seem to be any muscle memory in her limbs. Ariana took another deep breath, sucking oxygen through her gills. Calm, she had to be calm. It was hard to be relaxed when you were very much aware of how poorly you were doing. The ocean was silent around her as Ariana replayed the memory the whale had transferred to her, all shiny and hopeful.

Ariana raised her arms again and focused completely on the rubbish floating in front of her eyes. It was disgusting, one of those ubiquitous cheap plastic water bottles with a sun-bleached label still gummed on. It made her angry imagining whoever had thrown it into a gutter or left it lying on the sand.

I was as if someone had shoved a mirror between her and the bottle. Her mind froze. Disposable stuff in non-disposable containers. It was beyond stupid the bottle even existed at all. *Foolhardy*, her mother would have said. Ariana brought her arms down into the final pose and the bottle disappeared into a froth of bubbles. She blinked in disbelief, staring down at her hands. The dolphins chattered around her and Atlantis bobbed her head in acknowledgment.

Where did it go? Ariana blinked at the empty space where the bottle had been.

Released back to their natural cycles. Freed.

Robyn had called it elemental transformation when Ariana had tried to describe the process over the radio.

Separating carbon from hydrogen and oxygen. "If you could break down complex compounds, you could accelerate recycling everywhere. You could get rid of stuff that takes generations to break down," Robin had said in a rush.

Ariana held her hands up in front of her eyes. Blue light arced between them, snaked up her arms.

Freed.

The sea had its own melody, an interwoven keening song that built from the depths. Sound oscillated in a perpetual eerie soundtrack that seemed to sneak up on you. There were CDs with ocean noises, meant to calm you, but they were nothing like this. They'd played one in the hospital after her mother's accident. Val would have loved this true, ancient sound. Ariana's eyes pricked knowing she'd never hear it. Her mother's absence still caught her by surprise. She wondered if it happened to Terence, too, or if he wore it like a weighted vest all the time. She ran her fingers along the radio sewn into her wetsuit and screwed her eyes shut. The dreams had changed. Suspended in seaweed tethered to the reef, her mind drifted beyond her physical body, memories mingling with the ocean's song. Vivid flashes of a turtle wreathed in blue light, a boy grinning by its side. The boy felt familiar, even though she was sure she'd never met him. Her dreams kept filling with people, different animals, all with her distinctive glow. Spirit energy.

You have lived many lives, walker. You dream of the past walkers, who lived in a world less burdened by humans. Atlantis' voice filled her head.

How can I remember them?

Patience.

It didn't stop the dreams.

28

Revelations

Eli sat cross-legged on the closely cropped grass. The sounds of munching echoed around him as a group of kangaroos continued to graze, no longer frightened by his rigid presence. Fletcher would be able to reach out to them, but their voices were silent to him. A cloud of forager bees swirled in the air above, laden with pollen and nectar, homebound. Emptying his mind of their swirling melody, Eli slipped over into the spirit realm. The kangaroos moved in closer.

Lenti was leaning against a tree in the grove, eyes closed.

"Do you ever leave this place?" Eli asked.

Lenti opened one eye. "I know how to get around when I'm needed." He shut his eye.

The monk didn't look any older than he did. Eli

realised he didn't really know anything about their spirit world guide.

"Lenti." Eli sat down across from the monk, not sure how to frame his question. "The air spirit, Notos, where can I find him?"

Lenti frowned. "I'm not sure."

Eli's stomach plummeted. "What do you mean you're not sure? He's somewhere, like Atlantis. You said so. I need to find him, Lenti. I need to figure out what I'm supposed to do." He was going stir-crazy, despite the best intentions of Robyn and the others. Knowing Ariana was out there, *doing* something, was like a dagger in his ribs.

"How long have you been the guide for the walkers?"

Lenti opened both eyes. "What makes you say that?" He crossed his arms, defensive.

"How can you not *know*?"

"Well, if you must know, it was kind of an accident."

"What do you mean, an accident? You're the guide." Eli stretched his arms overhead in frustration.

"So, the thing is," Lenti began, looking at his feet. "I was never meant to be."

Thousands of red-rimmed vials. Thousands. Robyn was tired at a cellular level but at the same time brimming with energy. It was troubling, but she had no time to assess the strange dichotomy. There was work to do. Lab, eat, sleep. Repeat.

Robyn straightened and her back creaked in protest, posture shot to hell. She could be Quasimodo, except she couldn't sing to save herself and none of this could be resolved in a nice Disney montage. It was a race, and they couldn't stop the clock – against Fang or the sun.

Someone had placed a mug of tea by her shoulder. Robyn took a tentative sip. Cold. She didn't need to look in a mirror to know her eyes were sunken, weighed down with dark shadows. They'd all turned into zombies; no, vampires maybe, with all this blood. She gripped the mug of Earl Grey, staring into the middle distance as Derek shuffled between piles of cultures. A huge Jenga stack of petri dishes. Terence sat behind the tower, shuttling genes into viruses. A shiver ran up her aching spine. Guinea pigs. She and Terence would be the first to feel the sting of the needle.

"One hundred. We've got a hundred positives so far," Terence announced at dinner that night.

It didn't feel like a large number. The vials had all blurred into one another, but she'd handled so many. Delivery after delivery, Catherine's smile contracting as she signed each new docket.

Surely we've found more than that.

Robyn pushed her pasta from one side of the plate to the other, leaving a trail of pesto.

"I've run some simulations to extrapolate numbers in the wider population."

Robyn looked up. Terence had Catherine and Derek's full attention.

"Three hundred people."

"In total?" queried Catherine.

Terence nodded. "From seven billion people on the planet."

Three hundred people capable of converging their consciousnesses with animals. Maybe a hundred positives wasn't so terrible.

"So few," Robyn found herself mumbling.

Terence pushed away from the counter. "And luckily enough, we have two right here." Robyn almost didn't register the two syringes on the stainless-steel surface as Terence rolled up his sleeve. Their tips seem to glint with menace.

"Wait. You've got the vector?" Robyn's voice was steady, but her mind reeled. She wasn't ready; she didn't think she'd ever be ready.

"Just finished it this afternoon," said Terence.

Derek's grip was firm but gentle as he brought the needle to her arm. Robyn looked away. She'd never been able to watch, fainting at the doctor's surgery after six vials on no breakfast. That was before she got better.

"There." Derek stuck a plaster on her arm and rubbed his thumb across it.

"That's it?" Robyn croaked. Derek moved to Terence, and Robyn averted her gaze as the needle slid home.

"That's it," echoed Derek. Terence's eyes were wide. Robyn wondered if she looked just as scared. Probably more so.

Catherine reached out for her plate and sent her a lingering look of disapproval as she saw the crusted pesto trail.

"I'm not hungry now," Robyn said, and it was the truth. The familiar beep of the washing machine rescued her.

Robyn felt woozy as she pulled sheets from the machine straight into the dryer.

"Here, let me." Derek wrestled the heavy twisted mass for her.

"Thanks." Robyn hadn't heard him follow her. Clinks carried down the hallway as Terence loaded the dishwasher. She heard Catherine laugh at something he said.

Spots flickered at the edges of her vision. "Derek?"

"Hey, I'm here." Aniseed engulfed Robyn, rich and earthy. The scent made her head swim. Red, green, blue. The jets of light played under her eyelids when she squeezed them shut. Robyn reached out an arm, meaning just to steady herself until the heady feeling passed, but Derek leaned forward, cupping her neck. A hand curled into her hip bone. Electricity rocketed down her spine and ignited in the pit of her stomach.

"Robyn." She could see his dark eyelashes, his pupils darting from side to side. Her body betrayed her, sinking into the arms that rose to encircle her waist. Everything was spinning.

"Derek, I need to lie down. I feel —"

Derek's lips were soft and exploratory, but Robyn's mind was numb and floating. It was as if she were watching the kiss happen to somebody else. A mild current zipped along her limbs and she rushed back to herself, pulling away from Derek's grip. There was a brightness behind her eyes, a high-pitched whine building in her ears. *How can Derek not hear it?*

The last thing she remembered was Derek's concerned face as the edges of her vision blurred and faded to black.

"What do you mean, you were never meant to be?" Eli stared at Lenti. "You told us you were the guide, that you knew what we had to do." Anger tinged his words. It felt like a betrayal.

"You don't understand." Lenti rocked backward and forward, hands on his knees, a blank expression on his face.

"There's a lot I apparently don't understand," said Eli.

"I was only an acolyte-in-training when Nyx broke free of her earthly bonds. I had only just started learning the lineages. Earth, air, water. Hundreds of you." Lenti looked past Eli into dead air.

"Nyx. She's escaped before?" Eli almost jumped to his feet. "Then how did you trap her last time? We can just do that again!"

Lenti shook his head. "I'm not sure how Liro managed to do it."

"Liro?"

"The true guide." Lenti leaned forward and pressed his hand to Eli's temple.

Eli closed his eyes at the rush of blinding white light. It felt like someone had kicked him in the gut and stripped the air from his lungs. When he opened his eyes, wheezing, he found himself standing in the ruins of a temple. Three walls covered in sparkling mosaics barely supported a thin, crumbling roof. Eli frowned, taking a step closer to the walls. Big scooping lines connected mosaic figures that were surrounded by red, green and blue tiles. *Walkers*, he realised in a rush, *past walkers*. Eli traced a hand along the vein of red. Some of the missing spaces were deliberate, as if awaiting the birth of new walkers that never came. His fingers skimmed the rough edges of the tiles, following the lines that kept dancing across the walls, spiralling toward three figures.

Something about them was so familiar …

"Blessings from the sea, the air and the earth."

Eli whirled around at the voice. A wiry man in orange robes sat in the centre of the temple. Eli blinked. He hadn't been there a second ago.

"We keep the old ways." The man spoke without opening his eyes.

Eli sank to his knees in front of the monk. "Please, how can we stop Nyx?"

The monk opened his eyes, and a vertical shaft of light flared over his right eye. He reached out an arm to Eli, and the familiar wrenching sensation took over. When Eli opened his eyes, he was back in the spirit grove with Lenti.

"What was that?" Eli demanded. *If I'd only had one more minute …*

"Liro. The true guide. My mentor."

"He can … he can use the spirit energy."

Lenti nodded.

"What happened to him? The temple?"

"He died," Lenti said, his voice hoarse. "He stopped Nyx, but he died doing it. I thought, long ago, that the true guide would return. But he hasn't. You're stuck with me." He hung his head. "I hope you can forgive me."

Eli sighed. "Why didn't you just tell us?"

"I've told you everything I know, but it's not enough. You saw the walls of the temple."

Eli nodded. The three figures at the end of the spiralling lines.

Lenti's eyes were wide. "I think … I think you three might be the last. I fear that whatever you do won't make a difference. That Nyx will rise and everything will be destroyed."

29

Transformation

Robyn registered liquid being brought to her lips; she drank, then everything faded back into darkness. Her skin burned. Nightmares skittered across her fevered consciousness as the glacial cycles continued – a metamorphosis. Fragments of memory washed over her, of dark energy mixing with light in an eternal dance. She saw Fletcher, Ariana and Eli hovering in black, empty space, their eyes closed, hands splayed in their laps. But it was like wading through molasses; she couldn't seem to get any closer. Ariana's eyes flickered open. "We've been waiting for you." Her voice was layered, tiered with hundreds of unique inflections. But Robyn was already falling, slipping away.

The room was bright. Robyn cleared her dry throat with a cough and flicked her tongue over chapped lips.

"Robyn?"

Robyn peered down at the blankets. She was in bed, on the bottom bunk. Catherine's bed.

"Catherine, what happened?" Robyn's head felt dull, her limbs lethargic and heavy as if waking up from hibernation.

Catherine's eyes were wide and filled with worry when she knelt by Robyn's bedside.

"You're okay." Catherine twisted her hands together.

Robyn nodded and the room teetered around her. "Catherine?" She loaded all of her questions into the name; a big snowball, rolling downhill, gaining momentum.

"You were out for three days, Robyn. Three days."

Robyn registered the rumpled cardigan on Catherine's shoulders, her red eyes. Had she been crying? Robyn had never seen Catherine look so vulnerable before.

Robyn shuffled to a sitting position. Catherine's hand grasped her own, thumb stroking the back of her hand. It felt nice, some part of Robyn's mind registered, but it was as if it were happening to another person, not Robyn. She still felt like there was something she should be able to remember.

"Terence?" Robyn swallowed the lump in her throat as Catherine raised her eyes to hers. She had definitely been crying. Fresh tears trickled down Catherine's cheeks.

"He … he didn't make it. Robyn, Terence is gone."

They buried Terence at the farm in the clearing by the stream. Derek and Catherine took turns with the shovel while Robyn sat next to the wrapped body. She hadn't cried. Somehow she'd stayed calm on the drive. The trees had flashed by in a blur as Derek had driven them home. No, to her home. Terence would always be part of it now.

It took nearly an hour to dig the grave; the swish of the shovels like a metronome. Catherine paused to throw a look over her shoulder as she wiped sweat from her forehead, but Robyn didn't look up. She'd never seen a dead person before, much less kept one company. Terence's face looked calm, eyes drawn closed under his glasses. The striped button-down shirt clung to exposed collarbones. Robyn leaned down to kiss his forehead.

"I'm sorry, Terence." She didn't know why the vector had claimed him and not her. She only knew that it felt like she'd lost a brother.

The air was heavy and cloying as Derek lifted Terence's body like a baby, slung between outstretched arms. It was exactly how she imagined Derek had carried her to bed that night she fell asleep at the computer, except Terence's body was rigid, hair flopping over his face. He wasn't asleep.

Robyn didn't get up. She stayed with Terence's ghost as Catherine and Derek returned soil to the trench. The thud as dirt hit flesh was unbearable. It was impossible to trick her mind into thinking it was anything other than what it was. Robyn looked upward, imagining Terence's spirit rising into the air, dispersing across the sky. The autumn colours splayed across the trees seemed more vibrant somehow; the air was crisp and laced with scent trails. She was not sure if it was just her body stubbornly clinging to life or something more. She traced the ridged, puckered line across her eyelid that throbbed under her fingers. The blanket on her shoulders felt like a lead weight.

Everything was different now.

"Robyn, you need to eat something."

Catherine's voice seemed to come from far away. Robyn blinked, curling a fist in her blankets. She was back in bed, though she couldn't remember getting there. The bowl of soup on the bedside table sent tantalising steam trails toward her, but she couldn't eat when Terence had gone and it could just as easily have been her. She just couldn't.

"Please, Robyn, for me." Catherine's eyes were raw from crying. She held the spoon like a peace offering on an outstretched palm. Dirt rimmed her fingernails.

They had made a cairn of rocks above the disturbed earth. When Ariana came back, she'd be able to visit him.

"We need to tell Ariana." Robyn choked out each syllable.

The spoon wobbled and Catherine's hand retracted.

"I ... I don't know how." Catherine wrapped her arms around herself, spoon splayed against her chest. "This was never supposed to happen," she whispered.

Robyn closed her eyes. The broth made her mouth water. She pushed herself up into a sitting position and reached out a hand. Her head spun like it used to, and the memory filled her with hatred – a past self locked into a dangerous straddling of hunger and despair. She wasn't that girl anymore.

"I think I'll have some soup."

Catherine nodded and handed her the warm spoon. The food stopped the carousel in her skull; Robyn drained the bowl and pushed it aside.

"Thank you." Robyn fiddled with her sleeve. It didn't seem strange somehow, the words that spilled from her mouth. "Catherine, could you … stay with me?"

Catherine nodded, wiping her eyes with the back of her hand. "Of course." There was no trace of a smirk.

Sleep came easily cradled in Catherine's arms.

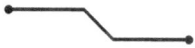

Fletcher sank into the soft grass. Eli sat unmoving on his right, eyes closed, Una rigid on his shoulder. They could have been statues. Part of him wished that he was anywhere but here. That none of this had ever happened; that he was still trying for first string on the basketball team, fishing on the weekends and reading his calculus textbook. Normal stuff. But then he never would have met Ariana.

Fletcher rubbed his eyes. The truck had crunched back up the driveway over an hour ago; Derek had carried Robyn back to bed. Catherine had kept them all away, but even from a distance he could tell Robyn was weak. He couldn't lose her too. How could everything have gone so wrong? He'd never thought Terence … never thought they'd lose someone here. This was supposed to be safe. They were *all* supposed to be safe.

Fletcher watched Eli's chest rise and fall. How could he go in there and talk to Ariana as if nothing had happened? Eli had made him promise. *For now*, he'd said, *just until we know what's happening.*

The vector hadn't worked. It had killed Terence, and Robyn was sick. Tears escaped his clamped eyelids. What was the point? If the adults couldn't make it work, what chance did they have?

Eli was pacing, deep in thought, when Fletcher materialised in the glade. Eva humphed and collapsed onto her haunches.

"Fletcher." Eli stopped. His eyes were clouded, and red light skittered across his torso.

"What is it?" Fletcher asked.

"Everything," Eli sighed. "Lenti doesn't know how we can stop this spirit, and I don't know how to find the air spirit, Notos." Eli grunted and flopped onto his back. "It's all so *insane*. How can we fight something that ripped the two worlds apart in the first place?"

Fletcher opened his mouth to reply, but a blue flash filled the clearing and Ariana materialised. She beamed at them. Fletcher gaped back at her.

"Hey," she said, waving in an exaggerated arc. "Earth to Eli and Fletcher."

The blue light clung to Ariana's skin, not dissipating as it usually did. Fletcher circled her.

"How long have you been in the sea?" Ariana looked so vibrant, so *alive*, it made his chest hurt. He thought his ribcage might explode if he looked at her for too long.

Ariana rolled her eyes. "Maybe I should be asking you how long you've been in the forest, if you know what I mean. Am I right, Eli?"

When Eli didn't reply, Ariana's grin evaporated. "What's up?" she said, dropping to the ground next to Eli. She shook her head, and the light clinging to her faded. She shrugged at Fletcher's stare and tickled Eli in the ribs.

Eli pushed her away and sat up.

"I feel like an idiot," Eli said, crossing his arms. "I'm pretty sure that we weren't all called into the same generation for kicks. There's something we can do that will stop Nyx, I'm sure of it. I'm going out of my *mind* trying to figure it out."

"I'm sure my brother and the others have worked something out by now. Lenti said –"

"Lenti said this, Lenti said that." Eli kicked at the grass. "He doesn't have a clue either."

My brother. Fletcher sat down, not trusting his legs to support him. Ariana deserved to know.

"We miss you," he said.

Ariana turned to face him, eyes full of concern. "Fletch? What's up?"

Fletcher choked back a sob and tore his gaze from her face. "Nothing."

Ariana clicked her fingers in sudden remembrance. "Hey, can you guys tell Robyn and the gang that I'm headed up to the Great Barrier Reef? There's been an oil spill, a big one. I'm going to go see what I can do.

My radio's all gummed up."

"Yeah, sure."

"Fletcher, are you sure everything's all right?"

Fletcher didn't trust his voice enough to reply. He was about to shake his head when Eli pushed himself up and grabbed Fletcher's arm. The ground teetered under his feet as Eli dragged him back to consciousness in the physical world.

"Why'd you do that?" Fletcher snarled, getting to his feet. He slapped Eli's hand away.

"You were going to tell her."

"She deserves to know!" Fletcher almost screamed. Thick, angry tears coated his cheeks. Nothing made sense anymore; the whole world had turned upside down. He'd always had things mapped out for him. School, basketball training, maybe college. All he had to do was turn up and play his part in the script. But now? There was no script. There was only a black gaping hole of uncertainty. Deep down, he didn't know if he could handle it.

"There's nothing she can do about it, and we can't interrupt her training," said Eli. "Can't you see? She's the only one of us making any progress, Fletcher. She

359

might be our only chance now everything's shot to hell. We can't risk it."

Fletcher raked a sleeve across his face and stormed inside.

Derek sat alone at the kitchen counter, staring at a mug of coffee and his phone. Fletcher wrinkled his nose at the bitter smell.

"I wish you had let us come with you." The words tumbled out in an angry rush, but Derek didn't even flinch. Fletcher stared at the back of his head, willing Derek to get up, to *do* something.

Derek shook his head. "It wouldn't have helped anyone. I don't want you to remember Terence like that. None of us do." He sighed. "Have you been in touch with Ariana? Is she okay?"

A murky reflection of a boy watched Fletcher from the stainless-steel counter. He didn't recognise the face.

"Yeah," Fletcher said. "She's going to the Great Barrier Reef for a few days. We didn't tell her," he added. "Though I still think we should have."

Derek took a slurp of coffee, banged the mug down hard. He picked up the phone and squeezed it in his palm. "Catherine wants to destroy the vector." Derek lifted the phone up and down as if he were weighing it against something. His other hand remained clenched on the counter.

Fletcher studied Derek's fist. *Of course they had to destroy it.* Robyn had barely survived – comatose for three days and still delirious. Mumbling about light and dark, her shrill wails echoing down the corridor as Fletcher tried in vain to sleep.

But Fletcher said nothing.

Derek pushed the mug away. "I'm going to go check on Robyn."

30

Betrayal

It took an effort to will her eyes open. Light filled the room and Robyn squinted as her eyes adjusted. She smiled as everything came into focus. She was facing Catherine, their foreheads nearly touching. Catherine's face was slack and calm with sleep, blonde hair mussed up on the pillow. Robyn couldn't help drinking it all in. The familiar urge to reach out and run her fingers along Catherine's side surfaced and she forced it back. Robyn edged away, curling the sheets above her knees, but Catherine's arm shot out and grabbed her hip.

"Nooo," Catherine drawled, eyes fluttering. "You're not going anywhere."

Her voice sent a rush of heat to Robyn's stomach and she shivered. Catherine flailed around with her other hand until the blankets were drawn back up over them.

Robyn chuckled into the pillow. Catherine must have felt the vibrations because she lifted her head.

"What's so funny?"

"Everything." Robyn couldn't stop laughing; maybe it was better than crying.

Catherine laced her fingers through Robyn's hand and clutched it between them.

"I'm glad you're okay. For a moment back there, you had me worried …" Catherine's voice wavered.

Robyn squeezed Catherine's hand. "Thanks. For looking after me."

The air smelled like Catherine, rose geranium and buckwheat flour. The dust motes above them swirled in crisp definition. Robyn felt different. Energy buzzed through her limbs.

A familiar cough at the doorway interrupted her thoughts.

"Robyn?"

Derek. The memory descended like a sheet of ice cleft from an iceberg. Derek's arms around her waist in the laundry room, the colours behind her eyelids. Red, green, blue.

Catherine shifted and Robyn registered the hurt on

Derek's face, like a Greek tragedy mask come to life. "Derek, what are you —"

But Derek had already disappeared down the corridor.

By the time Robyn pulled on shoes and a jumper, Derek had disappeared. "Kitchen?"

"Nothing." Catherine left the doors swinging as she pounded out onto the patio. "Not outside, either."

Fletcher followed them into the hallway, relief plastered all over his face. "Robyn?"

I'm fine, Robyn wanted to shout, but there wasn't time. She pushed past him and raced through the lab, heart skidding in her chest. She felt faster, as if her legs had developed new muscle. Energy surged through her limbs as she burst out into the sunlight.

The truck was gone. A shiny oil spot glistened on the bitumen; Robyn could smell the lingering exhaust fumes. Catherine skidded to a stop by her side.

"Where would he go?" The chain link fence rattled in the wind as Robyn gazed down the deserted bitumen road.

"Robyn." Catherine's voice caught. "The vector — it's gone."

"What do you mean, gone?"

"Derek. He's taken it."

The list was her golden ticket, but combined with Derek, Vulcan would have no choice but to listen to her. Fang sipped her latte and rolled her shoulders. He was handsome, dark skin shifting in the light over muscled shoulders. An unexpected surge of camaraderie washed over her as she appraised him. It couldn't have been easy having Vulcan as a supervisor – she wasn't sure how he'd managed to last this long without ripping his hair out. Overcoming her pride and contacting Derek had been difficult but clearly worth it.

The vial cupped between his thumb and forefinger glistened in the sun. It held the promise of redemption.

"You've made the right choice, Derek. The only choice."

Derek nodded, sliding the vial back into the rack with its cousins. "Here it is."

It took all of her strength to stop herself from surging forward. Instead, she waited until Derek slid the rack over. Fang swept a hand across it, listening to the xylophone-like tinkling of the glass. Harsh sun beat down against the back of her neck. It had been a long time since she'd seen so much clear sky. Brisbane was paradise compared to the choked haze of Beijing.

"The girl, Ariana." The last part of the deal. The girl with the dragon, Fang felt it. The flicker of blue light across her skin could very well mean she was the last one from Miranda's photo. Maybe Fang could still work out what it was Miranda had intended.

The keys rattled in Derek's hand as he pushed his chair back. "Let's go."

31

Changes

It's wrong, all wrong. The black blood coated the reef, choking it. Screams of pain fired through her synapses. Where there should have been grandiose palaces of bright coral and undulating seaweed, there was a thick sheen of oil. Ariana hadn't been able to ignore it, had been pulled here as if by magnetism, riding flush on Atlantis' back.

The Great Barrier Reef needed her.

Her arms ached as the energy coursed through her veins, the lack of oxygen in the water making her dizzy. It was harder, much harder than the floating islands of plastic debris they'd been working on. Even that had left her muscles cramped and weak. The oil seemed to twitch and jerk out of reach like a living thing, and Atlantis was way beyond the edge of the continental shelf, too big to enter the reef. The spirit hummed with her, and Ariana's limbs thrummed with a translucent blue light, but it wasn't enough.

On the second day, Ariana breasted the surface, her wetsuit slick with oil. She struggled to breathe, heaving oxygen into her lungs. Her gills had clogged with the black death; she could feel them receding into her neck. Ariana coughed inky gunk as her breathing levelled. Panic surged through her.

I have to get out. Keeping her head above the water, Ariana breast-stroked toward the beach, empty in the predawn. She crawled out of the ooze and collapsed on the sand, too tired to hear the footsteps crunching out of the forest.

The taser jolted across her wetsuit, and her wobbly legs spasmed. Atlantis' song echoed in her mind as the darkness rolled in.

She woke in an unfamiliar van. A woman sat on a crate, watching her.

"Good, you're awake."

Ariana's head pounded and her throat was dry. "Water," she rasped. She tried to reach forward, but a rope around her wrists held fast. Tied up; that was bad.

"It's not worth struggling." The woman uncapped a canister of water and offered it to Ariana. Ariana lapped greedily at the liquid as the woman tilted the bottle into her mouth.

"What do you want?" Ariana said, yanking at her wrists. The rope must have been tethered to the floor of the van, because she couldn't make any headway. Ariana froze. She recognised that face. "Fang."

"Yes, we've met before. I'm glad you remember me."

A shadow at the door blotted out the light. Ariana squinted in disbelief. "Derek?"

Fang crossed her legs. "You see, we need you." She waved a piece of paper in the air. "We know where to find the others, and how to activate them."

Ariana stared at the paper. "You gave her the list? Why would you do that?"

Derek wouldn't meet her eyes. "Ariana, your brother is gone. Terence is dead."

He seemed to speak in slow motion; Ariana saw the words forming on his lips, the whisper of sound as it curled through the air. No, Terence couldn't be dead. He wouldn't leave her like that.

"You're lying," Ariana said through gritted teeth.

Derek lifted his head, and Ariana choked on a sob. She saw the truth plastered all over his face.

"The vector we made … he didn't survive it." Derek turned to Fang. "We have to co-operate with the MRI if we're going to stand a chance of working this out. It's the only way."

Tears streamed down Ariana's face. Her mother, her brother, both gone.

"It's what Terence would have wanted." Derek's words pierced her mind like a knife.

"You don't know the first thing about what he would have wanted," Ariana spat. "He sure as hell wouldn't have wanted you to team up with *her*. She's a monster."

"It's unfortunate you feel that way." Fang turned and lifted a steel-barred cage.

Jericho.

Ariana couldn't feel him; a flaring wall separated them as she reached out with her mind. It was only then that she registered the lump at the back of her neck. *No.*

"Just a little something to ensure your co-operation," said Fang. Jericho lay motionless on the floor of the cage, but Ariana saw the black chip embedded at the base of his skull. Closing her eyes, she tried to cross over to the spirit realm, but the pain was blinding. She gasped, yanking at her restraints.

Fang toyed with a receiver.

"High-frequency electromagnetic radiation. Your display in Beijing was impressive, but it can be neutralised … with the right equipment."

"You don't understand. There's not much time, we have to –"

Fang pointed the box at her, and Ariana's eyes rolled back in her head.

Fletcher and Catherine stared at Robyn in disbelief. She stretched her neck, feeling stronger than she ever had.

"Are you sure you don't want to sit down?" asked Catherine, hovering near her elbow. "You've been out of action for four days, Robyn. You've barely eaten anything."

"You're okay," Fletcher stammered again. Robyn felt the thrumming aura that surrounded him. It resonated around her like a veil, pulsating in her chest. In the back of her throat, she could taste the humus-rich scent that clung to Eva's shaggy fur.

"I'm fine," Robyn said. They stood on the patio. Her body seemed to have reknitted itself into something new, something stronger. Robyn pivoted as a new wave of scent assailed her; it was as if she could sense the others coming. She turned to the door as Eli, Sara and Jacob burst outside in a rush, shielding their eyes against the glare. Ming and Una looked different to Robyn; shimmering, like a mirage.

Poppy buzzed up from Jacob's hair and erupted into a swirling bronze mass. *A hive.* Jacob stared at her, wide-eyed as if he'd seen a ghost. Robyn blinked and then it was just Poppy again, russet fur catching the sunlight.

Kara and Kate jostled each other through the doorway.

"Robyn?" said Kara, her voice uncertain. She lifted her laptop. "We finally found the MRI. They're in Bulgaria, some big new shiny research facility."

Kate butted in. "They've got the list, Robyn. The hundred people you found. Every last one."

Catherine closed her eyes. "Derek. It was Derek."

"And there's something else." Kara tucked her laptop

under her arm. "We lost contact with Ariana."

Fletcher twitched, and his body slumped to the floor. Kate screamed and jumped backward, but Robyn reached out and grabbed his arm. The scar on her eyelid burned and light clouded her vision. Different resonant frequencies clashed together as the block in her mind disappeared. *Red, green, blue. Three parts of the whole.* A humming noise filled Robyn's ears as her feet left the ground, tugging her into the brightness.

The white light faded, prickling her skin like hundreds of needles. Robyn opened her eyes. Clenching and unclenching her fist, she felt energy zinging through her veins. Rich scents filled the air, frequencies of sound merging into mesmerising melodies. She knew without needing to ask that this was the spirit world.

Fletcher pointed at her, his face pale. "Robyn?"

Robyn blinked, taking in the copse of tall, ancient trees. Light danced along their trunks like stardust.

"This isn't possible," said Fletcher.

A flash of red light filled the glade. Eli tumbled onto the grass, his eyes wide. "It's you, you're the guide," he choked out.

Robyn looked down at her hands, glazed in white.

The guide.

A boy in orange robes appeared in their midst. He hurled himself at Robyn's feet, muttering a string of unintelligible phrases. Robyn caught a name. *Liro.*

"Ariana, are you there?" Fletcher yelled into the trees. "Ariana!"

Eli stepped towards him, but Fletcher pushed him away. "I can't reach her," Fletcher spluttered. "She's gone. Terence is dead, now Ariana is gone. Fang probably has the vector by now. This is all your fault, Robyn! How can *you* be the guide? How can you have let this happen?" Fletcher punched a fist into one of the ancient trees. Light skated upward from the impact site. Green light rocketed out across the sky as if the tree canopy had struck a chord with the atmosphere.

Robyn pulled Lenti to his feet. "Derek has her," she said, her voice strangely calm. "But we're going to get her back." She turned to face all three of them. "Together."

Robyn closed her eyes and felt the white light engulf her. Spinning, she hit solid ground with a *thump*. Fletcher and Eli's slumped bodies stirred by Kate and Kara's feet. Catherine stared at her as if she were a total stranger.

Robyn looked upward, following Sara and Jacob's shocked gaze. Green light filled the sky, the atmosphere flickering in an otherworldly network of flashes.

About the Author

Marita Smith is a freelance editor and gourmet mushroom grower based on the South Coast of NSW. She has a PhB (Hons) in Science from the Australian National University and considers chemistry a language in its own right. She spent several years as a paleo-biogeochemist, splitting her time between Australia and the Netherlands, before travelling through Europe to work on small farms. The first story she can remember writing involved being able to speak to her donkey, Mindy.

© @maritasmithauthor

maritasmithauthor

www.maritasmithauthor.com